A Question of Integrity

Megan Magill

Regal Crest

Nederland, Texas

ISBN 978-1-935053-12-5
1-935053-12-4

First Printing 2009

9 8 7 6 5 4 3 2 1

Cover design by Donna Pawlowski

Published by:

Regal Crest Enterprises, LLC
4700 Highway 365, Suite A, PMB 210
Port Arthur, Texas 77642-8025

Find us on the World Wide Web at
http://www.regalcrest.biz

Printed in the United States of America

Acknowledgements

It is with the help of several people that this book has reached your hands: Jo who has been invaluable, encouraging and supporting me in life and in writing. My family who raised me to appreciate my imagination. Cathy and the team at Regal Crest who saw the potential in my work and assigned me a first class editor. My editor Andi whose talent, professionalism and sensitivity have been the perfect combination for both book and author. L-J Baker, Dejay, and friends who have provided wisdom and companionship on this exciting new journey.

Ultimately, my gratitude goes to all the readers and authors who keep the lesbian fiction community flourishing. I'm proud to be a part of it.

For Molly

Chapter
One

"GOT YOU," JESS muttered with grim satisfaction. Weeks of investigation had led her to this point and it was imperative she didn't give herself away. A combination of darkness and woodland foliage provided a certain amount of cover, but the men she watched clearly had a flippant regard for the law. As she had expected, there were three of them, each with their own vehicle. They reminded her of ants, industriously transferring their cargo from the hire van to their own cars.

Jess shifted position, watching the procession and trying to ignore her desire to go home. She had visited the woods earlier in the day to select her best vantage point. The lay-by on the country road truly was an ideal spot for shady dealings. There were no houses in the vicinity and more efficient routes for drivers to take. The woods seemed a different place now, unnaturally still and quiet. The presence of the intruders had evidently been noted. Jess's viewpoint felt nearer than the twenty metres she had estimated in daylight. She would have preferred to move farther away but knew that she wouldn't be able to see through the undergrowth well enough if she did. *Slow breaths. Focus. Get the job done.*

Cautiously, she lifted her camera and checked, for perhaps the sixth time, that she had disabled the flash. The isolated road had no street lighting but the headlights of the parked vehicles proved sufficient for her purposes. Her pulse pounded in her ears as her body flooded with adrenalin, poised for escape if necessary. Lifting the camera to her face she checked the scene through the lens, and with a nagging sense of foreboding she pressed the button.

An anticlimactic silence ensued. Jess exhaled as she checked the camera's display, satisfied to see the evidence she needed. An unexpected touch on her hand almost made her shout out in fright. Clenching her teeth together, she looked down, relieved to see a large moth, attracted by the light from the camera screen. Come on, just a few more, she thought, trying to resist her growing edginess. Raising the camera to her eye once again she took another series of images, using the zoom function for maximum benefit.

Suddenly, crashing shrubbery seemed to explode just behind her right shoulder. Jess ducked, instinctively seeking deeper cover. One of the men shouted and they all turned to look in her direction. Stay there, she thought, willing the first man to obey her. He didn't. Muttering to his companions, he grabbed a torch and took a step toward her. As Jess desperately debated her options, a reddish creature streaked across the road, illuminated briefly in the harsh glare of the headlights. The men saw it too and evidently reassured, returned their attention to one another. Jess sank down onto her knees, heedless of the soft, dank earth beneath her. *Time to get out of here.* She returned the camera to its pouch on her hip with fumbling fingers. Then, as silently as she could, she made her escape through the woods and back to the safety of her car.

"DID YOU HEAR anything I just said?"

Jess stifled her yawn behind her hand before smiling apologetically at Emma. "Sorry. I was distracted." She didn't want to admit that she had barely been to bed two nights ago or that the ill-effects still lingered. Emma had earned herself the reputation of office gossip and Jess could easily imagine her nighttime reconnaissance being twisted out of context. Still, the hard-won photographs had been worth giving up some sleep for. The camera had worked even better than she had hoped, given the poor light the vehicle headlights had offered. Not only had she been able to identify the three men but she had also been able to obtain a clear record of their illicit activities. As pleased as she was, it was not a subject she wished to share. "Tell me that last bit again?"

"That's okay." Emma smiled condescendingly. "I know you don't go out much so this is probably all a bit busy for you." She waved her hand in a broad sweeping arc, encompassing the crowded bar and the animated customers. The clientele included a high proportion of students, as with most Oxford city pubs in term time. They revelled in Friday freedom, shouting and laughing as they downed choreographed shots. The ritual involved lemon and salt, suggesting tequila slammers.

Jess allowed the implied criticism to roll over her before she responded. "I suppose so. Tell me more about the wedding. Have you chosen your outfit yet?" A spike of guilt prodded her conscience as she asked the question, since she wasn't even vaguely interested in the answer. Emma was an acquaintance from the office, one who currently relished any opportunity to talk about her forthcoming nuptials. *An ideal cover companion for this excursion, however.* Jess smiled at her.

"Well, I was leaning toward cream and claret but that's so—" Emma tapped her fingers on the table as she searched for the appropriate word, "*traditional* for a winter wedding. Then I saw this beautiful plum colour in a quaint little bridal shop in Stow. Of course I must give due consideration to my complexion. When my cousin married, she looked completely washed out. She wore a dark green velvet stole, with freckles like hers, can you imagine—"

Poor cousin. Jess's attention wandered again as a group of women approached the bar. The landlord himself was moving to serve them. Taking a sip of her own drink, Jess watched as he reached for one of the wine bottles that she had been monitoring since the start of the evening. The man chatted easily with his customers as he decanted the wine into glasses. Once they had all been served he returned the bottle to its place and held out his hand for payment. Smiling, he accepted the note given by the lead in the party and moved to the till. Watching him carefully, Jess noted that whilst he took coins from the till, he did not put the payment into it. Jess continued her vigil as he handed the change to the lead and the group moved away to settle at a nearby table. With a surreptitious glance around him, he leant back against the bar and thrust both hands nonchalantly into his pockets. After a few moments he began to collect the dirty glasses on the bar and load them into the washer.

"...One wants the bridesmaids to look nice but it must be in context. The bride is the one that everyone expects to be at her pinnacle so she must not be outdone."

Jess smiled again at Emma. *Note to self. Vet prospective partner's wedding ideas before making any commitment.* Letting her thoughts return to the task at hand, Jess considered the ramifications of what she had just seen. Two nights ago she had collected evidence against the landlord and his accomplices as they transferred significant quantities of this same wine from a hire vehicle to their own cars. Evidently he was selling it but the money wasn't going into the tills. *This is turning into quite a damning investigation.*

"...I always dreamt of an elegant horse-drawn carriage but when your future brother-in-law offers the use of his fleet of stretch limousines, one doesn't turn him down!" Emma giggled happily.

"A fleet *is* very impressive. The whole family can travel in style," Jess agreed solemnly. She noted Emma had yet to mention her fiancé.

"My mother and father won't go in the same car, of course," Emma began again, furrowing her eyebrows and shaking her head dramatically at her own words.

Jess let Emma's voice fade out and leant back in her chair, satisfied with her newfound knowledge. Another fifteen minutes or so of wedding talk and then she could call it a night. All in all, it had been a very profitable evening with remarkably little pain.

Chapter
Two

THE LANDLORD CONSIDERED the intruder idly, thinking that she could be an incredibly stupid customer who had just walked past the closed sign. Given her age and professional attire, he decided it was more likely that she was a salesperson. *They always crawl out on a Monday morning.* Her three-piece business suit fitted her curvaceous body in a testimony to quality personal tailoring. She wore her dark blond hair simply styled, and it hung a few inches above her shoulders. A smattering of freckles gave her intelligent face a cheeky look. She was the sort of woman his mother would have described as a 'hearty lass', not the standard for a sales person. He remained silent as she approached the bar, unwilling to waste energy putting this unwanted intruder at ease.

"Mr. Lockhart? I'm Jess Maddocks." She held out her hand and smiled at him warmly.

"I don't have time to waste on sales reps." He responded curtly, secretly hoping the exchange might end in a satisfying argument.

"Of course," she said, withdrawing her hand. "However, I'm here on behalf of the brewery. I have some research I must conduct but I'm happy to be self-sufficient."

"The brewery?" He couldn't help but question her statement because he hated the intervention of authority, and believed the pub was his to run with full autonomy. "I haven't seen you before and nobody told me you'd be coming."

"It was rather late notice, I'm afraid. Here is my letter of introduction," she held out the document, printed on the familiar headed paper. The signature of Henry Stokes, the tenanted trade director for the brewery, was also clearly legible.

Taking the proffered letter he read it with growing resentment. Whoever this person was, she was obviously important. "Well, Ms. Maddocks, it looks like you're right. The timing is dreadful, as I have too many things to do as it is, but I suppose when the brewery says jump, there's nothing else for it. What do you want me to do?"

Jess smiled sweetly. "Don't worry, Mr. Lockhart. I truly am self-sufficient. I'll need access to your CCTV system, delivery notes and invoice files, and stock reports. Once I have access it would suit me to be left to my own devices."

A growing feeling of unease encouraged him to change his mind. "I can postpone some things till tomorrow, I suppose. After all, there's quite a knack to that CCTV system."

"No need. I'm a dab hand with technology and as you said, you have many more important things to be doing." Once again she smiled. "The office is through this way, I presume?" She gestured to the door behind the bar. The question was evidently rhetorical, as she had already begun walking.

ONCE JESS WAS finally alone, settled in the relative solitude of the office, she allowed some tension to drain out of her body. She had been prepared for confrontation when she walked into the pub this morning, but so far the landlord had not been too difficult. The place seemed surprisingly different considering she had only been here three days earlier. *Perhaps it's because I'm on the wrong side of the bar.* The office was a tiny space, stuffed with haphazard piles of paperwork and lost property. An overflowing ashtray took pride of place by the computer keyboard and sticky patches marked any clear surface. *Beer, I hope.* The door opened, pre-empting any further speculation.

"Here," Al Lockhart placed a tray on the desk. It contained a steaming cup of coffee as well as a small jug of milk, sugar bowl and teaspoon. "The information you want is all in here. Invoices, delivery notes, and stock reports." He patted three piles in sequence. "I'll be in the cellar."

"Thank you." She waited until he had gone before she turned her attention to her work.

Jess did have a knack for technology, a gift she had inherited from her grandfather and one she was often grateful for. The CCTV system was new to her but there were only so many buttons with which she could interact and therefore only a limited number of options. Within ten minutes she was able to navigate around the recordings she had found stored on the internal hard drive. It was a time-consuming process but as her investigation neared completion it became even more imperative to ensure that her facts were indisputable. Unfortunately, no camera monitored the rear door, through which deliveries were accepted. Despite that, her efforts weren't fruitless. After a couple of hours, she had recorded several entries onto a disk she could take with her. These included the late-night arrival of the suspect wine as it was brought through the bar en route to the store room. There were also multiple transactions in which customers were served the wine but their payments did not enter the till. Technically, this alone would be enough to prove her case, but Jess preferred to get as much evidence as she could.

Her efforts with the CCTV system completed, Jess set up her laptop and turned it on. While it went through its boot sequence, she gathered the various documents that she wanted to review.

There were stacks of both delivery notes and invoices from various suppliers as well as the monthly stock take reports. The next section of her evidence gathering was perhaps even more tedious than the CCTV work. She used the hard copy documents and created a spreadsheet that detailed stock movements over the previous three months. After another two hours and several intrusions from the increasingly anxious landlord, Jess began to pack up her equipment. As she did, she printed out a report from the computer program that controlled the till system. It would make more work for her back at the office, but it would be invaluable to see how the money that went through the tills compared to the stock movement for the period.

"Is that it?" Mr. Lockhart asked, as he watched her gather the last of her papers.

"Yes," Jess responded politely. "Thank you for your help and hospitality." She walked back through to the main bar and turned to face him. "Good bye."

The landlord gave a stiff nod before hurrying back toward the office.

Jess smiled as she left the building, knowing that the cheating landlord would probably spend the rest of the day trying to figure out what she had found.

JESS RETURNED THE various greetings as she walked through the corridors of her workplace toward the desk she used when she was working from the office. "Afternoon," she said with genuine warmth to one of the women from the administration department.

"Jess!" The hail came from behind.

She turned, recognising Jeff Lewknor, her boss, moving rapidly to catch her. "Good afternoon," Jess answered politely.

"Good afternoon," he responded in his gruff, businesslike tones. "How are you coming along with your current assignment?"

"Very well," Jess replied confidently as they continued to the executive area of the building. "I have made some significant progress over the last few days and I hope to have the matter wrapped up by the end of the week."

"Excellent." Mr. Lewknor nodded his approval. "I was playing golf with an old buddy of mine. He retired from his company some time ago but has kept his hand in—he started the thing from scratch, after all. Anyway, there seems to be a spot of bother on the business front. I said I would assign my best analyst to the case should he wish to get us involved."

A flush of pride heated her cheeks. Her boss was not one to

administer compliments, even though her hard work and successful record were undeniable. Curious, she looked at him. "What's the case?"

"An odd one." His brow furrowed. "I'll let you hear it from the horse's mouth. I suspect we'll be gainfully employed on this before the week is out."

"I understand," Jess confirmed simply, pausing at the door of her office.

Jeff continued along the corridor without slowing his pace. "Get the brewery case put to bed," he called back over his shoulder. "I want you available for this."

Settling herself at her desk, Jess slotted her laptop into place and retrieved the disks and documents that related to the brewery case. She was nearing the conclusion of the investigation but she now felt the pressure of Mr. Lewknor's expectations pressing down on her. While the computer progressed through its starting sequence Jess thought about this new opportunity. "Best analyst." She recalled the unexpected compliment. *Now I just have to live up to my own reputation.*

The chime of her laptop brought her attention back to the task at hand. Calling up the spreadsheet she had prepared earlier at the pub, she began the laborious task of comparing the stock movement information to that gleaned from the till activity report. *First things first. Al Lockhart, it's time to learn it's wrong to swindle.*

Chapter Three

"MORNING HENRY," JESS smiled at her client. As usual, he had met her in the reception area of his offices. She appreciated the personal touch.

"Hello, Jess. Do I take it you have some answers for me?" He raised his shaggy eyebrows at her hopefully.

"I do indeed," she said with satisfaction. This was possibly her favourite part of the job, the time when she explained the inexplicable, and threw light on confusion. It could also be one of the most difficult times, especially when her news was disappointing or angered the people she spoke with. From what she knew of him, she expected Henry to be hurt more than anything else. When she had first met him he had talked about the landlords in his care as though he valued each of them. If it were her, she would find the betrayal hardest to accept.

"Great. Follow me." Henry led them down a short corridor into a small meeting room. "Take a seat, I'll get some drinks. Coffee?"

"Water please."

He nodded and disappeared back into the corridor.

Temporarily alone in the room, Jess busied herself with her laptop. Pulling it out of its case, she plugged in the power cable and turned it on. As she waited for it to boot, she looked at the large framed photographs hanging on the walls. There were three pictures, all showing scenes of the brewery in different periods. Her favourite was the one with two sturdy shire horses hitched up to a dray.

"Those were the days, eh?" Henry paused to glance at the picture as he returned.

Jess nodded and keyed her password into the waiting laptop. "I suppose it's all lorries now?"

"I'm afraid so, though we still have the dray and sometimes hire horses for promotional events. It always goes down well."

P.R. is such a calculated business, Jess thought, not for the first time. She settled in the chair opposite Henry and shifted from niceties to business. "I have various points to report," she began, "but I think it's important to start with the key issue. The three landlords you asked me to investigate are working together in activities that are both illegal and against the contracts the pubs have with the brewery. I have evidence that proves they hire a vehicle then travel to the continent and purchase enough alcohol to fill it—about eighty per cent wine, but I believe there's also champagne and some spirits." Jess paused to take a sip of water, giving Henry time to think about what she'd said.

"HM Customs and Excise might have something to say about that," Henry responded grimly.

"Quite. Here are some photographs I took of them meeting up and sharing out the bootlegged goods. The lighting's not ideal, but it's still possible to see clearly who's involved and what's happening."

Henry took the enlarged colour photograph she passed across the table to him. "What time was this?" he asked.

"About half past two in the morning. They obviously wanted the cover of night but with the unsociable opening hours of the pubs, it needed to be really late."

"So you were wandering around the woods in the dark at half past two in the morning?" Henry looked at her, his eyes wide with surprise.

"All part of the service." Jess smiled self-deprecatingly. "I'm sorry to have to confirm that the goods are entering the pubs which, as you will know, puts the brewery in a difficult position with regard to the authorities." She paused, then continued, serious. "The three landlords disperse the goods between them and store them at their respective premises. The landlords themselves sell the products to customers, and as far as I can tell, no junior staff are involved. When the customers pay for their drinks, the landlords pocket the money and avoid ringing the transaction through the till."

"Why pocket the money? They could take it from the tills at the end of the night."

"I wondered that for a while, too. My theory is that it's because other staff sometimes do the cashing up. They have a responsibility to check for and attempt to correct errors. If the transaction bypasses the till completely, there will be no such errors to make anyone suspicious." She retrieved a disk from her laptop case and passed it across the table to him. "Here's CCTV footage of Mr. Lockhart stocking his bar with the illegal goods at about half past three in the morning. A rather odd time for stocking the shelves." She smiled wryly, trying to keep the mood of the meeting as light as possible given the unpleasant news. "There's also footage of him serving wine and champagne to customers without entering the transactions through the tills. He does access the tills to provide change at times, but he seems to do balancing transfers of cash at quiet moments throughout the evening. Of course, if he kept removing change it would also draw unwanted attention to his scam so it's something he tries to minimise."

Henry accepted the disk. "Clever sods. Why couldn't they put that much ingenuity into running their businesses legally?"

Jess smiled sympathetically. She didn't envy him the job of sorting this mess out. "These till reports demonstrate that the 'no sale' key is pressed an implausible number of times on a shift where these activities are taking place. As you know, this is the key that opens the till drawer. You don't need a preceding transaction to occur. You will see that this action spans the various clerk numbers but if you compare the time index to the CCTV footage, you'll see it's all done by Mr. Lockhart shortly after serving wine." Jess paused again, this time to pass some more documents across the desk. "I have been through the till activity reports and compared them with the stock reports. There is genuine wine being sold which in turn is put through the till systems properly."

Henry shook his head. "That's probably an effort to cover their tracks. After all, if these pubs didn't sell any wine at all, we would have been able to pinpoint their little game a lot sooner."

"I agree. I've spent many evenings monitoring the sales of wine in these pubs. Certainly for Mr. Lockhart, for whom I have comparable till reports, I can confirm that approximately three-quarters of the wine sales are bypassing the till system. That's the main reason the pubs are underperforming." She paused and looked at him sympathetically. "I'm sorry to have to be the bearer of bad news."

Henry sat back in his chair and sighed. "I'm sorry, as well. It all makes sense when you explain it like that. I just don't have the time to watch what they're selling and even if I did, they wouldn't put a foot wrong with me on the premises. I suppose if I go to the other two pubs I'll be able to get the same information as you have for Al Lockhart?"

She nodded. "I believe so. It's probably a good idea to do so sooner rather than later, though," Jess advised. "Mr. Lockhart was suitably perturbed by my recent visit."

Henry smiled, though it looked forced. "This is exactly what I needed, as disappointed as I am to hear it. Thank you for all your help. I'm interested to see what else you've found, but we have enough to go on with this alone."

Jess smiled back, appreciative of his praise. "I'm glad I could help," she replied simply, chalking up another success. The feeling was pleasant but familiarly empty. She wondered when her efforts would ever be enough for her. Pushing the unwelcome thoughts away, she returned her attention to Henry and the remainder of her report.

Chapter
Four

JESS ENTERED THE outer office and smiled nervously at Sue, her boss's personal assistant. "Hi. Mr. Lewknor wanted me to come and meet a new client?"

"Take a seat. He said he'd buzz when he's ready for you."

"Thanks." She sat down in one of the two chairs and proceeded to wait. *I feel like I'm back at school.* She positioned her hands palms down on her thighs, spreading her fingers deliberately. Shaking hands with a sweaty-palmed stranger was one of her pet peeves.

"I'm glad it's Friday," Sue commented. "It's been a long week."

Jess smiled cordially, despite the fact that she hated small talk. "Yes." Yesterday's meeting with Henry had marked the conclusion to her brewery assignment. Jeff had wasted no time in getting her started on this new investigation.

"Jess Maddocks, please." The brusque voice crackled through the intercom a few minutes later.

At an encouraging nod from Sue, Jess vacated her chair and approached the inner office. Squaring her shoulders, she rapped confidently on the imposing wooden doors.

"Enter," Jess's manager responded with his usually brevity.

After closing the door quietly behind her, Jess crossed the plush burgundy carpet toward the two men. The office had not changed in the three years since her interview. The matching desk, bureaux, and meeting table were finished in a highly polished dark wood. Each time she was in there, Jess imagined the horror of scratching those smooth surfaces. This time she was distracted by the presence of a stranger. His eyebrows were raised but she kept her face passive. It was not the first time her gender had surprised a client.

Both men stood in recognition of the entrance of a lady and Jeff spoke. "Theodore, I would like to introduce Jess Maddocks, one of my most talented business analysts." He smiled at her, encouraging. "Jess, this is Theodore Willis, an old friend of mine. He has approached us with regard to an investigation he would like us to conduct."

Jess shook the proffered hand firmly in greeting then took her place at the table as the men resumed their seats. As always, knowing someone was forming a first impression of her made her feel uncomfortable. *Girl. Fat. Gay.* Her mind unhelpfully paraded out her familiar insecurities. Knowing how important her boss considered the assignment only made matters worse.

"Now," Jeff addressed his new client, "perhaps you would provide us with some background information?"

Theodore nodded. "I'm the founder of Image Conscious, a highly successful public relations company. I began the business in my early twenties and spent my entire working life building it up. Now it's one of the premier organisations of its kind." He glanced at Jeff then Jess to see if they were following before he continued.

"Two years ago I retired, and passed leadership to my son-in-law, Marcus Gibson. I had hoped that I might stay involved in some capacity, but Marcus is ambitious and, as he put it, he refused to work in my shadow any longer. He must have pleaded his case very successfully to my daughter because she approached me and asked me to take a step back. He is key to why I'm here today."

Jess scribbled a note on her pad, using a combination of shorthand and tight handwriting so that her companions couldn't read it. "Had he already approached you directly?"

"Not really. Our relationship started to deteriorate as soon as he took over as CEO. Presumably, he decided using Catherine was the most effective way to get what he wanted." His voice was bitter.

She looked up at him. "What was your relationship like before the change in leadership? Did he work for the company then, too?"

"Yes, he joined five years ago. He worked as a client manager for most of that time although he did spend some months moving around the whole organisation prior to his promotion. His performance was always excellent. He's a sharp businessman and charismatic. I thought we had a good working relationship but given how quickly it changed, I have since decided it was probably just an act to further his career. I had thought a family member would be a good choice for successor but it has proven to be one of my most heartfelt regrets."

The family dynamic is going to make this investigation ten times harder, Jess thought. "So what has brought you to us today?"

"Since my retirement, Marcus seems to have become a lot more arrogant and I don't trust his ambition. I suspect he's working more for himself than for the company." Willis sighed and adjusted his tie, smoothing down the material then lining it up with his shirt buttons.

"Why do you think that?" she asked, keeping her expression noncommittal.

"Unfortunately, I can't give you specifics and that's why I need you to get involved. At first it was just a gut feeling. Then, the other day I ran into an old employee of mine—a damn fine photographer with real artistic flair. He told me he had retired early, and implied that it was because of changes that Marcus had made. Not all good. He suggested I distance myself from the business, as he didn't want to see my personal reputation damaged alongside that of the company's. He didn't say much more, just that people still thought of it as my company but that things were run very differently these days." Willis shrugged, more to himself than anyone else. "Perhaps it's nothing, but since I spoke to him I've been able to think about little else." He paused to take a sip of water.

"Have you tried to find out what is going on yourself? It would be the most subtle way to address the problem." As usual, Jess opted for honesty. These initial meetings were the time to iron out any doubts.

Willis looked at her, his downcast expression making him appear rather pathetic. "I did try but it only made matters worse. He sidestepped direct questions and seems to have fostered a culture of evasiveness amongst the staff. When I tried to press the issue he threatened to tell Catherine I was forcing him out. My presence is a contradiction for the employees. Whether I like

Marcus or not, if they think I have no confidence in him to run the business then all hell will break loose."

Jess wrote notes quickly as he spoke. "I see. In what guise would you like us to get involved? Have you thought about our level of visibility?"

"Yes. At first I was going to ask you to be as inconspicuous as possible. Under cover, if you will. Then I realised that if Catherine were to find out I had employed such tactics, she would be very upset. All in all, I think it is better if you work in the open. I had hoped the cover of an 'efficiency analysis' would be enough to answer the employees. Marcus may see through it straight away but he can accuse me of little worse than caring for the company. I hope that by employing an external, impartial business consultant, I can circumvent the worst of the family fallout. I'd like you to go in there as soon as possible and look at all aspects of the business. If you can't find anything then I at least get peace of mind. If you do, then I'll have some ammunition with which to tackle the problem."

Jess studied Willis's face, deciding that either he was a good actor or he believed the situation to be as he reported. "It sounds as though Marcus will not like an 'efficiency analysis'. What authority will I have?"

"I am the majority shareholder for the company, therefore what I say goes. As you will be acting under my instruction you will have ultimate authority. You're right, Marcus won't like it but he will have no option other than to comply. He could delay matters by calling an Extraordinary General Meeting but he would still be out voted and he'll know it."

"Are the shareholdings arranged that he can't forge an alliance, either?"

"Yes. I retain seventy-five per cent so even if he united all the minor shareholders he would still be unable to affect my decision." Theodore leant forward and studied her earnestly. "Dealing with Marcus will be challenging but it is imperative you do so with tact and sensitivity. My relationship with my daughter is at stake."

"I understand. I have worked on many investigations where discretion is paramount." She smiled in an attempt to reassure her new client. "What timescale do you have for this project?"

"The quicker the better," he replied readily. "I would like to minimise disruption and get a prompt resolution. Having said that, you must be thorough because I will not get a second chance to do this. Can we work using a weekly update format and judge the progress that way?" This time he looked at Jeff for confirmation.

"Of course." He smiled reassuringly.

Jess made a last addition to her notes. "Right. I'll book an appointment to see Marcus first thing on Monday morning. It would smooth matters if you were to give him advance notice," she suggested, looking at Theodore expectantly.

"I'll call him straight after this meeting."

"Great." Jess allowed a note of conclusion to enter her voice and she checked for her manager's approval. When he nodded, she gathered her notepad and stood. "Thank you for your time, Mr Willis. I'll be in touch." With a quick smile she turned and left the room.

BACK AT HER desk, Jess tapped her pencil against her top lip, thinking. The assignment had two major problems. First, the family dynamic was likely to make everything ten times harder. Traversing unknown family politics was not her idea of fun. Second, although she could understand Willis's concerns, he had given her very little to work with. Vague threats to his reputation and a troublesome son-in-law were hardly major problems.

Retrieving her pad she jotted some action points. She would need to speak to Willis again, preferably on his home turf. Before that, though, she needed to meet Marcus and form her own opinion. Some research on the company and market would be valuable too, because she needed to put the whole thing in context. Until she had done these things, she wouldn't know the reality of what she was dealing with. There was no point wasting a month looking for something that only existed in Willis's imagination.

She opened her web browser and keyed in the Image Conscious Web site address. She continued to ponder her new case as the flashy site loaded. Most assignments she had worked on had far more solid foundations, such as profit levels that were inconsistent with turnover or a declining market share. The symptom of suspected damage to reputation was going to be quite difficult to prove either way. *Still, it'd be no fun if they were all easy.* She grinned at the anticipated challenge.

No assignment in Jess's experiences to date had been purely about what was initially reported to her. If they were, the client would probably be able to solve them without paying for an external analyst. Assignments often appeared to be one thing on the surface, but they almost always had a more complex basis. She might begin an investigation expecting it to be accountancy-focussed but instead it turned out to be a matter of human resources or a strategic issue masquerading as a problem in production. The job certainly suited her. Problem solving, variety, and autonomy. She didn't know how anyone could enjoy a job without them.

Turning her attention to the Web site, she started to make basic notes about Image Conscious. It was a marketing consultancy, one that had carved out a niche for itself working with large, often multinational companies that needed to revamp their image. One such example was a hotel chain that wanted to change the segment of the market to which it appealed. Jess suspected there were probably some less flattering reasons for businesses to want to refresh their image but understandably, they were not given in the case studies. Image Conscious undertook both brand portfolio analysis — recommending which brands would benefit from further investment and which would not — as well as the organisational image itself. Based on the evidence of the website, Image Conscious had been instrumental in several high-profile, successful cases. The growing global awareness of the environmental and sociological impacts of large organisations had left Image Conscious ideally placed to market itself as *the* public relations solution.

Jess already knew that the image makeovers had been successful, since she kept up-to-date with the global business news as part of her job. Still, she had enough experience not to trust the word of the marketers alone. She reviewed the publicly published accounts for some of the organisations Image Conscious had worked with. The growth and profit figures were impressive. Image Conscious's services were certainly worth their doubtless large fees. Jess could also understand the importance of reputation to such a company. A public relations company with integrity provided clients with considerably more credibility than one without.

The growth and success of Image Conscious backed up Theodore Willis's claims of a lifetime of dedication. Jess could see he probably felt about the company the way others would about a child. If his concerns were justified, she could certainly understand his bitterness toward Marcus Gibson.

Jess widened her Internet work to look for comments relating to Image Conscious. One thing that struck her as odd was the lack of critical comments about the company. Given what Willis had heard with regard to the reputation of the business, it would be logical to assume that at least one person might have had a bad experience. If that were the case, where were the complaints? There was always the possibility this whole thing stemmed from the combination of a disgruntled ex-employee and a paranoid founder who was having trouble letting go. Either way, Jess mused, it was going to be an interesting few weeks.

Chapter Five

JESS MANOEUVERED HER Lexus into a space and switched off the engine. She checked the clock. *Ten to eleven. Perfect.* Angling the interior mirror toward her, she took a moment to check her appearance. Satisfied, she slid out of the car and smoothed her suit back into place after the drive. A quick scan of her surroundings showed the Image Conscious building just ahead. The landscaped car parking area seemed to be shared with the other offices on the same site. Content she knew where she was going, she retrieved her laptop case, secured the car, and headed for the sign that said "Reception". She paused to admire the stunning Aston Martin parked in a spot marked "reserved". Gorgeous, she thought, although she'd never know how anyone could justify spending that much on a car. *I'll stick to my hybrid any day.* As she walked the last few steps to the entrance, she made a bet with herself that Marcus Gibson was the Aston's owner.

She passed through revolving glass doors into a cavernous atrium that formed Image Conscious's imposing reception area. Approaching the equally imposing sculpted oak reception desk, Jess smiled at the woman behind it. "Good morning. Jess Maddocks to see Marcus Gibson. I'm a little early," she finished apologetically.

"Good morning, Ms. Maddocks." The receptionist smiled formally. "Please take a seat in the waiting area and I'll inform Mr. Gibson that you're here."

With a nod of thanks, Jess moved toward the cluster of leather sofas and seated herself with her back to the wall. One of her reasons for arriving early was to spend a few moments getting a feel for her surroundings. In past investigations, her attention to detail had proved invaluable because it gave her a wealth of background information. She glanced around, assessing the decorations and overall look of the place.

Clearly, the company was making a statement with the daunting reception area doused in large prints of modern art. Jess decided this was to be expected for a public relations company to whom image was everything.

A steady stream of people traversed the reception area clutching papers or talking animatedly to colleagues. Sitting unobtrusively, Jess took the opportunity to indulge in some people-watching. Two young women crossed her vision first. *Slim, toned, gorgeous. Lucky genes or self-deprivation?* Next was a man carrying a large art portfolio case. *Nice suit. Designer, I should think. I must check the competitiveness of the remuneration packages.* A man who looked in his forties walked briskly past, gesticulating with his hands as he spoke to his female companion. *The first one over thirty. Still one of the beautiful people, though.* A single woman came next, deeply involved in her mobile phone call. Jess reminded herself not to ogle. The procession continued with surprisingly little variety. *I feel like I've been stranded on a movie set,* she thought mournfully.

She checked her watch, not surprised to see she had been waiting for half an hour. Although she had been early, Marcus Gibson was now twenty minutes late. Reflecting on the uncomplimentary character report she had heard about the chief executive officer of Image Conscious, Jess considered her options. It was tempting to take the lift to the top floor, find a vacant meeting room, and set up camp. It would get his immediate attention, too. She suspected that he was making a point but recalling Willis's request for sensitivity, she decided to give him the benefit of the doubt and wait him out.

After five more minutes, a short, willowy young woman emerged from the lift and headed unwaveringly toward her.

"Ms. Maddocks? Mr. Gibson can see you now."

"Thank you." Jess smiled, ensuring her manners were intact. Following her guide into the lift, they travelled the journey to the top floor in silence. The woman avoided eye contact and kept her body huddled in a defensive stance. Jess wasn't sure if she was shy or whether negativity around Jess's visit preceded her. Either way, Jess was far too distracted by feeling bulbous and ungainly by comparison to strike up conversation with the willowy beauty.

"This way, please." The woman led the way out of the lift and toward a nearby office door. She knocked twice and roused a "Come in," from inside. Pushing the door open a little, she leant her head and shoulders through the gap. "Ms. Maddocks for you, sir."

"Send her in."

The woman pushed the door fully open and stepped back to let Jess pass through. She then retreated and closed the door behind her.

Jess took a moment to study the grand room with its polished walnut desk, minibar, and flat-screen television. It reminded her more of a hotel room than an office. A plethora of framed certificates littered the walls. Gibson apparently wanted to commemorate everything he ever did. She wondered if a 'cycling proficiency' or 'junior swim champion' award were among them. Maybe 'class prefect' during his childhood years.

She looked over at Marcus Gibson, who sat imperiously behind his desk, eyeing her with a disturbingly fake smile pasted on his face. He was handsome in a distinguished, immaculately groomed way. His suit looked tailored and expensive and he wore a burgundy handkerchief arranged artistically in the breast pocket. She noted he did not stand to greet her.

"Ms. Maddocks." Marcus smiled smugly, gesturing at the visitor's chair in front of his desk. "Please take a seat. I'm so sorry to have kept you waiting. It's been such a busy morning. But then, aren't they always!" His laugh sounded forced.

Jess considered responding with a comment about time management skills but opted against it. "No problem," she said, seating herself in the inappropriately decadent recliner her host had indicated.

"I gather my father-in-law thinks we need an efficiency test." Again he laughed humourlessly. "I will be candid. This is a distraction the business can do without, but what the old man wants, the old man gets."

Jess did not return his smile, aware that if she did it would set the tone for a union between them. Instead she maintained eye contact and silence, letting the comment fall uncomfortably in the air.

The smile pasted to Marcus's face faltered momentarily and he revised his strategy. "Of course, whatever my personal feelings on the matter, you will receive the full cooperation of myself and my staff. What do you need?"

False professionalism was certainly preferable to fake camaraderie. Jess nodded once. "Thank you, Mr. Gibson. I'll need a private working area at my disposal for the duration of my investigation," she began, mentally reciting her checklist. "And a phone and network point. I'll also need a user account with full access rights to your network. I will certainly want copies of your management accounts, payroll reports, strategic planning documents, and a standard customer and employment contract." She ticked the items off on her fingers as she spoke. "There will, of course, be much more in the way of documentation, but those are sufficient for the time being. Finally, I will need a point of contact, whether you or someone else." She smiled at him in exaggerated sweetness. "After all, if your workload is already stretched perhaps you could suggest a more suitable alternative?"

Marcus eyed Jess with momentary wariness before the smug smile returned. "A prudent suggestion, Ms. Maddocks," he said before turning to his intercom. "Hilary, please ask Rosalind to join us."

The knock on the door came so quickly Jess wondered if this had been a contingency plan all along.

"Come in," Marcus called. As the door opened, Jess turned and nearly lost her composure at the sight of Rosalind. The newcomer glided into the room with an air of self-confidence Jess knew she would never achieve. Rosalind's auburn hair fell around her shoulders, the perfect contrast to her classically tailored black dress suit. High cheekbones, penetrating blue eyes, and tall, lithe body blended together to create a vision that seemed utterly incongruous in this office environment.

"Thank you for joining us." Marcus smiled. "Ms. Maddocks, let me introduce Ms. Rosalind Brannigan, my most invaluable client manager."

Oh, crap. Jess tried to hide her panicked reaction. *Okay, I can do this.* She coached herself, her preferred technique for dealing with stressful situations. *Yes, she's stunning but that's fine. I don't need to compare myself to her. This is a business situation. I'm good at my job.* She risked another look at Rosalind. *Oh lovely. I'm attracted to her, too.* Jess let her own sarcasm calm her. There wouldn't be many people on the planet who weren't. *You're fine, nothing to see here. Back to business.* "Ms. Brannigan," she said, smiling, "it's a pleasure to meet you."

Rosalind retuned the smile. "And you, Ms. Maddocks. Please call me Rosalind."

"Jess," she replied succinctly. She turned to Marcus as Rosalind seated herself in the other visitor's chair. His eyes were narrowed and he looked at her with a predatory expression. Cool professionalism, she reminded herself, nobody can see inside your head. "I'm not sure if either of you will have been involved in an efficiency analysis before, but I wanted to let you know it's a positive exercise." Jess began, ignoring Marcus's derisive snort. "There does tend to be resistance at first but the whole point is to help you do your jobs. This translates to less stress and happier staff." Marcus's sneer left little doubt as to his opinion. Jess chose to ignore it. He was doing little to ingratiate himself but that was no reason for her to cut corners. Keen to get this initial meeting complete, she patiently continued explaining the merits of an efficiency analysis.

Chapter
Six

THE REMAINDER OF the meeting with Marcus and Rosalind was mercifully brief. Both Image Conscious employees had looked sceptical as she talked about what she was there to do. Jess tried not to let it colour her opinions of either of them. After all, she was an outsider and mistrust went with the job. Marcus had reported Jess's requests to Rosalind and reiterated his full support, though both Jess and Marcus knew he had no option but to comply. Doing so graciously allowed him to maintain an illusion of choice.

Upon leaving the meeting, Rosalind had led Jess through the open plan working area to another office on the east side of the building. It was a decent-sized room that, judging by its impersonal furnishings, looked as though it was rarely occupied. What furniture there was suggested it was used flexibly for meetings or as an office, depending upon need.

Rosalind stood aside so Jess could enter the room. "It may not be the most elegant," Rosalind said, "but this room should be adequate for your needs. Plus, it's close to my office." She pointed to a doorway on the opposite side of the corridor. "My assistant, Lucy—" again she gestured, this time to a young woman working at her computer at a nearby workstation, "will be able to assist you should I be unavailable."

"Thank you. I appreciate your time." Jess managed a smile, somewhat dismayed that one of the amenities her new desk boasted was an unrivalled view of her highly distracting company mentor. *It could've been worse*, she consoled herself. *At least I don't have to stare at Marcus for the next month.*

"I have other matters I must deal with," Rosalind said, checking her watch. "I'll make sure Lucy brings the documents you requested and I'll ask her to contact the IT department and arrange for the network account."

"Excellent." Jess searched for something intelligent to say. Unfortunately, nothing was forthcoming. Instead, she smiled again but the smile faded as Rosalind departed, leaving the room disproportionately drab without her presence. Sighing, Jess closed the door behind her, conscious that it didn't afford much privacy. There were blinds against the internal windows but she resisted closing them. It would give too negative a statement so early on.

She stood assessing the space for a bit. The furniture was functional but limited. There was a meeting table with four chairs, a desk with telephone and computer chair, and a small filing cabinet. Pulling the two drawers out it turn, she noted they were empty. A small external window behind the desk was covered with a standard slatted blind. Jess stuck her fingers in at one edge and peered out. An uninspiring vista of the car park greeted her. She let the blinds fall closed again and began setting up her laptop, reassured by the familiarity of the task.

Settling into the chair, Jess waited for her computer to go

through its warm-up. It was always hard starting a new assignment, not knowing whom you could trust or what the politics of the organisation were. She was trying to remain impartial about Marcus, as she had barely met the man. Past experience had taught her never to take someone else's opinions as her own. There were plenty of possible reasons for the strained relationship between Willis and Marcus that had nothing to do with the latter's work ethic. However, Marcus's sneers and suspected power games did little to endear him. Whatever he was, she would find out soon enough. It was her reaction to Rosalind that caused her the greatest worry.

It's just another puzzle. Take it in pieces. Deal with it logically. First, she had a bad case of an inferiority complex and around women like Rosalind, that complex was always exacerbated. Rosalind didn't know about Jess's issues, so the best thing Jess could do was to just keep cool and remain professional. The second issue was also pretty simple. Jess was already attracted to Rosalind but any form of romantic interaction would be completely inappropriate and unprofessional. Besides, even in the statistically unlikely scenario that Rosalind was gay, she was so far out of Jess's league it was laughable.

A knock on the door interrupted Jess's self-analysis. "Ms. Maddocks?"

"Come in," Jess called, rising to her feet. The door opened and Lucy, Rosalind's assistant, entered.

"Sorry to disturb you," she began, "but I have these documents for you." She timidly placed the pile of paper on the surface of the desk. "I also thought I could show you where the restrooms and coffee facilities are, if you'd like."

Jess smiled her gratitude. "Lead on." She followed Lucy back the way she had come with Rosalind earlier, and took the opportunity to study her environment more closely. The theme of young, trendy professionals she had observed in reception continued on this floor as well. The working area was mainly open plan, divided into groups through the use of strategically placed shoulder-height partitions. To her right a few offices with doors dotted the back wall, presumably for the team managers. To her left a chrome and glass balustrade marked the divide between the office space and the atrium of the reception area. Looking across the gap it appeared that the building was roughly horseshoe shaped, the atrium forming the middle void.

"Those are the restrooms," Lucy motioned toward nearby doors but continued into a small kitchenette area. "This is the coffee machine," she stated, somewhat redundantly. "It's on free vend so you just have to press the buttons for what you want.

Pretty standard, really." She looked around the space before continuing. "That's the fridge. You can store your lunch in there but be warned, things can get pretty heated if someone takes the wrong sandwich."

Jess grinned. Some things were the same wherever she went. "Great. Thanks, Lucy. And I'll be sure to only take my own sandwiches." The tour complete, she followed her guide back into the corridor. "Thanks again. I'm going to make a stop here," she said, gesturing at the restroom. "See you back at the office," she added lightly.

"Of course." Lucy smiled and headed down the corridor while Jess veered off and entered the sanctuary of the ladies' restroom. Commensurate with the rest of the building, the room was furnished to a high standard, boasting granite bowl basins and contemporary chrome tap fittings. Glad to see she was alone, Jess entered the farthest cubicle, closed the toilet lid, and sat down to enjoy the closest thing she could get to privacy. She glanced at her watch and groaned inwardly. It was barely afternoon but she already felt drained. She held back her sigh as she heard the door open.

"...Acts as though he's a real stud that one," a youthful, feminine voice proclaimed. "Pity he doesn't know what the girls really think of him!"

Judging by the twittering of laughter, Jess estimated there were probably three of them, near the mirrors. They were probably touching up their makeup and seizing the opportunity for a quick gossip.

"Hey," a second voice said, "did you see the new suit with you-know-who? I wonder who she is."

"Yeah, I saw her. Whoever she is she must be pretty important to get *her* attention, especially since Pete walked out."

"Maybe she's a tax inspector or something and the big cheese is playing matchmaker to try and soften her up." The third voice was lower, speaking in hushed tones that heightened the sense of intrigue. "Who knows? Perhaps she wouldn't mind a bit of action." Her companions giggled.

"I'll bet she's just you-know-who's type. Business suit and tits. That about covers it." The first voice continued theorising, much to the amusement of her companions. Further speculation was aborted by the sound of the door opening again.

"Morning, Dorothy," one of the gossips greeted the newcomer soberly. The door sounded a third time, and Jess figured the three gossips had left, since things quieted noticeably. Dorothy also soon left, leaving Jess alone once again.

Her heart was hammering in her chest, her mind a muddle of

thoughts. Rosalind was gay? That is, if the gossips were correct. Not only that, but it sounded like Rosalind didn't keep her personal life away from the office. Jess was the first to acknowledge that chatter in a restroom didn't necessarily mean much, but she also knew that there was rarely smoke without fire. From what she had just heard, at some point in the past, Rosalind had pursued a romantic interaction with a woman under the critical scrutiny of the office.

Jess took a deep breath and focused on the job she was sent here to do. Whatever the situation with Rosalind, Jess was a capable professional who was good at what she did. She had already let this distraction affect her more than it should, and it was time to take control and stop thinking of herself as powerless as a schoolgirl suffering her first crush. With renewed determination, she let herself out of the cubicle and returned to her office.

A small note rested on the table next to her laptop on which was written her network username and password. Settling back into her chair, Jess keyed the characters into the machine, satisfied when the login sequence completed successfully. She pushed distracting thoughts from her mind and started reading the documents that Lucy had left earlier.

Chapter
Seven

JESS PRESSED THE doorbell then took a step back to wait. She resisted the urge to fidget and kept her expression pleasant, conscious that she might be under observation through the spyhole. The Tuesday afternoon appointment with Willis had suited her well. Although she had wanted to meet Marcus before talking to Willis again, she didn't want to leave it too long before the follow-up interview.

The door opened and a silver-haired woman greeted her with a questioning glance. "May I help you?"

"My name is Jess Maddocks. I have an appointment to see Mr. Willis." Jess wasn't sure if she was addressing Mrs. Willis or the housekeeper. From the moment she had driven through the electric gates, everything she had seen testified to her client's wealth. The period home was brick built with elegant features and grand windows. It stood in large, landscaped gardens complete with a pond and fountain opposite the front door.

The woman eyed her carefully before opening the door fully. "Come through."

"Thank you." She resisted the urge to assure the woman that she wouldn't run off with the family silver. Instead, she looked around with interest as she followed the woman through the house. High ceilings and strategically placed mirrors made the space seem even bigger. Traditional art in both painting and sculpture form dressed the rooms.

"Please wait in here." The woman ushered her into an unoccupied room. Heavy curtains draped the windows and shelves of books lined the walls. The room was dominated by a large fireplace complete with dried flower arrangement of epic proportions. I'm in my first real, working drawing room, Jess thought, smiling at her own awe.

After a few moments, the double doors opened again, this time admitting the familiar form of Theodore Willis. "Ms. Maddocks, how good of you to come." He strode toward her then shook her hand vigorously.

"Good afternoon, Mr. Willis." Jess replied, pleasantly surprised by his friendly manner.

"Please, take a seat. I've asked for tea to be brought in." When Jess was settled, he continued. "I hope you found us all right. Sometimes the country roads can be a little confusing."

Jess nodded. "Yes, I did. Thank you. You have a lovely spot here." She looked out the large windows and admired the view. The landscape stretched for miles with no sign of humanity spoiling its surface. The peace and isolation might scare some, but it greatly appealed to her.

"We're very fond of it. It's been a good place for the children to grow up." He paused. "Do you have any children?"

Jess shook her head. "I made the choice to focus on my career. Maybe one day, though." It was her stock answer and usually proved successful in fending off further questions.

"Well, don't leave it too long," Willis advised. "Parenting's a hard job but very rewarding."

A knock at the door saved her from having to respond. She waited in silence as the woman who had answered the front door laid out the tea things. Pity I don't like tea, she thought, knowing it would be one of those occasions where she'd have to drink it anyway. Willis struck her as a traditional man and she didn't want to offend his sensibilities over something so trivial. The woman left and he poured tea into two cups, indicating that Jess flavour hers to her liking. She dropped two sugar cubes in then followed them with a generous amount of milk. The additions didn't mask the flowery taste but she sipped it with good grace.

"So, how can I help you today?" Willis asked, the niceties now concluded.

Jess considered her response. She needed to get a better idea of where he was coming from. Was he sending her on some wild goose chase? Was this really about business or was he holding a grudge against Marcus for other reasons? Ultimately, she just needed more of an understanding of the sort of man he was. "I usually have at least two meetings with new clients at the start of an assignment," she answered honestly. "There is often useful information that it's easy to overlook in the first conversation."

"I see." Theodore nodded before taking a sip of tea. His expression suggested he was amenable to questions.

Jess retrieved her notepad and pen from her briefcase to foster a more professional atmosphere. "May I start by asking how Marcus and your daughter met?"

"At a polo match," he answered readily. "It's an event the company sponsors every year."

"And how long ago was that?"

"Just over four years."

Jess surreptitiously checked her notes from her first meeting with Theodore. She was unsurprised to note the couple had met since Marcus joined the firm. "How did you feel about her dating one of the company employees?"

Theodore frowned slightly at the question. "As long as she was happy, that was all that mattered."

"Quite," she agreed, deciding it was too sensitive a subject to push. "Tell me about when you were considering making Marcus your successor. Did you go through some kind of grooming process?"

He relaxed visibly at the change in subject. "Yes. He spent several months moving around the company to understand how each of the different sections work. He also spent a couple of months shadowing me directly for a greater understanding of the CEO role."

"How did you get on during that time?"

"Adequately. It is an intrusive arrangement for both people, spending that much time together. However, I believed it was necessary for a successful handover."

Jess jotted a note on her pad, nodding as she did so. "At what point did you begin to doubt Marcus's approach to the role?"

"Straight away. The first thing he did was to replace my old secretary. It was a foolish decision. She was an excellent worker and would have proved very useful in the transitional period." Willis pursed his lips.

"Did he opt for a secretary he had been using before?" Jess questioned, giving Marcus the benefit of the doubt again.

Theodore shook his head. "No, he recruited from outside the company. To be honest, I had little to do with her but I was never able to see the virtues he reported."

"Was it Hilary?" She asked, recalling the name of the willowy woman who had collected her from reception the day before.

"No. She's a new one, I think. None of them seem to last long."

Jess avoided commenting but made a note to check this fact in the employee records. "Marcus has appointed Rosalind Brannigan as my point of contact. I gather she has worked for Image Conscious for several years. Would you consider her a suitable point of contact?"

Willis smiled for the first time since they had started discussing the assignment. "Yes. Rosalind knows her stuff. Charming woman. There were some evil rumours about her a while ago, I suspect borne from jealousy. I don't know if it's still doing the rounds or not but you shouldn't give it credence. Office gossip is a nasty thing."

Jess nodded reassuringly, suspecting she had already heard the rumours in question. His word choice simultaneously interested and concerned her. Deciding she had the information she needed, Jess asked a few more general questions then politely concluded the conversation. Within fifteen minutes she was heading home, her mind mulling the discoveries she had made.

Chapter
Eight

THEODORE HAD BEEN right about Marcus's secretaries, Jess decided as she studied the employment records. Checking his statement had been the first thing she did when she arrived at the Image Conscious office the following day. Hilary was secretary number eight since Marcus had become CEO just over a year ago. The obligatory exit interviews provided no meaningful information. Either the women did not want to volunteer information or anything incriminating had been edited out of the reports. The reasons they gave for resigning were predictable. Three wanted to seek fresh challenges. Another had been offered a better package by her old employer. A third wanted to start a family. The last two had simply said they hadn't settled. Jess was tempted to try and get in touch with some of them. Unfortunately, she knew she would contravene the Data Protection Act if she did.

A light knock caught Jess's attention. She looked up in time to see Lucy's head appear around the office door.

"Hi. Would you like a coffee? I'm just going to grab one."

Jess smiled gratefully. "That would be fantastic, thank you." She watched Lucy go then returned her attention to the employee files. When she heard the door open again she looked up, expecting to see Lucy. Instead, Rosalind stood smiling at her from the doorway. Jess's stomach lurched in acknowledgement.

"Hi, Jess. I hope I'm not disturbing you?"

"No, not at all. Come in."

Rosalind crossed the small office and settled herself into the visitor's chair opposite Jess. "I just wanted to check in on you. Do you have everything you need?"

Jess found herself mesmerised by Rosalind's elegant calves as she walked and then sat. She wondered how anyone could make walking in high heels look graceful. "I, uh, yes. Thank you." *Come on, pull it together.* "There's a lot of information to go through but so far everything I need has been here." She patted the pile of documents placed squarely in the corner of the otherwise empty desk.

"You keep a very tidy desk," Rosalind observed, reaching out to the same pile of documents. A shadow of a smile crossed her face when Jess quickly removed her hand.

"I like things to be ordered." Jess leant back in her chair, subtly trying to give herself more space.

"There is a lot to be said for order." Rosalind shrugged. "But sometimes I like a little unpredictability myself."

Jess didn't know her well enough to deduce whether her flirtatious expression was real or not. "Variety is the spice of life, they say." *No, not the dodgy clichés, please.* "How is your workload shaping up?" Jess forced herself back to safe, professional topics. "It would be really helpful if I could have some time with you to get a better understanding of how the company operates."

"That's a good idea. How about tomorrow afternoon?"

"Suits me." Jess wrote a quick note to remind herself.

"I'd welcome the opportunity to get to know you a little better." Rosalind smiled and leant forward as she spoke, creating an air of intimacy.

Jess felt the warmth of a flush creep from her chest up her neck. She hoped it wasn't visible.

"Here you are, Ms. Maddocks," Lucy said as she entered the room, carrying a steaming plastic cup. "Oh, I'm sorry." She glanced at her boss nervously.

Megan Magill

"That's all right. We've finished, anyway." Rosalind flashed a last charming smile at Jess then left.

"Thanks, Lucy." Jess smiled as she accepted the coffee. As soon as the door closed, she flopped back into her chair and exhaled. Suddenly remembering the windows, she looked up. Rosalind was grinning at her with a knowing expression. *Oh, crap.*

JESS SAT IN the restroom cubicle, contemplating her sanity. She had been there for twenty minutes and she was bored. Nobody could argue the logic of her thinking, though. Employees went for cigarette breaks at regular intervals, why not toilet gossip sessions? She had deliberately picked the same time as the first day. She heard the door open and sat quietly. The visitor was on her own and soon left. Jess checked her watch. It was only an hour before her meeting with Rosalind. She should probably leave and review her notes. She was just about to stand when the door opened again.

"...It's a whole different atmosphere when he's not around."

"I know. Pity it can't be like this all the time. Even the managers are more approachable. Did you see Kirsty? She caught Lisa on the Internet and just told her to get on with her work. No dragging her off to the office or anything."

Jess listened intently, fairly certain these were the same women who had inadvertently outed Rosalind to her.

"Hilary even smiled at me today," the first voice said soberly, suggesting it was a rare occurrence.

"Poor woman, who'd want her job?" The third voice sounded sympathetic.

"Nobody, evidently. I doubt she'll stick it out much longer."

Tell me why, Jess silently urged them. *Why do they all leave?*

"I'm not sure I can stick *my* job much longer," the first woman said dramatically, sighing for additional effect.

"Oh, no, you can't leave." The other two voices spoke in unison.

"I've had my fill of being unappreciated. The salaries here used to be good but my sister-in-law earns more in telesales. The management better buck their ideas up if you ask me." The woman mumbled the last part, her voice sounding odd. She was probably contorting her mouth to reapply lipstick.

A brief pause in the conversation ensued. Clicks and scuffs echoed in the small room, suggested the other women had followed suit and were reapplying or checking their makeup.

"Well," the first voice started, evidently the leader of the posse, "I suppose we'd better get back to it. I don't want any more lectures on time keeping."

Jess listened to the murmurs of agreement then the silence as they left the room. She stood and stretched, giving the women a minute to return to their desks. When she thought she was safe, she returned to her office.

She had just sat down when Rosalind appeared at the door.

"Jess, I'm really sorry," she said quickly, remaining in the doorway in evident haste. "Something has come up and I can't do this afternoon."

Jess was both disappointed and relieved. She pushed the feelings away as unprofessional. "That's all right. I can do any time tomorrow."

Rosalind shook her head. "I'm stuck in meetings all day. How about Saturday? We could grab some food at the same time or something?"

Jess imagined the two of them out together and a rising panic roiled in her stomach. "I'll have to work, I'm afraid," she replied, relying on her standard excuse.

"Not another workaholic," Rosalind said with a laugh. "It's bad for your health, you know. I'll pick you up at seven, that way you can work the whole day if you feel you must. What's your address?"

Jess reeled at the idea of her carefully constructed boundaries being under threat. "It's all right. I'll meet you there." Too late, she realised her attempt to avoid giving her address had committed her to the meeting.

"Great. Shall we say Giovanni's at seven? You know where it is?" Rosalind fidgeted and looked at her watch again.

Jess nodded. She did know where it was.

"Fantastic. See you then." Rosalind beamed at her. "Have a good day tomorrow."

Jess shook her head as Rosalind walked away, cursing herself for getting so flustered. It's just a business meeting, she reminded herself. *Yeah, one that sounds like a date.* She huffed out loud. *Put your hormones away, the poor woman's just being friendly.*

Chapter
Nine

WHEN SATURDAY CAME, Jess had no inclination to spend it working. Instead, she treated herself to a leisurely shower then moved into the garden to read while basking in the sunshine. As the minutes slipped past, the book remained unopened on her lap. Instead, Jess watched puffy white clouds cross the sky. With a gentle sigh of contentment, she reflected on how lucky she was.

It may not be on par with Willis's mansion, but her cottage in the Cotswolds was something she had dreamt of since childhood. When she was about eight, she had seen a television series set in the area. With a child's determination, she had decided she would one day live there. A combination of her healthy salary, performance bonuses, and private investments had allowed her to purchase the two-bedroom, detached cottage when she was twenty-four. It had been a little run-down at the time, because the elderly lady who had owned it previously had been physically unable to maintain it. Jess considered that an odd benefit, though, and by the time she had lavished some care and attention on the property, it had felt much more like home.

The garden was disproportionately large for the size of the cottage, with a collection of gnarled old apple trees at its end. It backed onto open farmland and the slight gradient afforded a beautiful view of the rolling countryside. Although she did not have as much time for it as she would like, Jess had made some headway in tending the flowerbeds. In the early summer, as it currently was, the floral display was at its best.

She realised she had been staring at the same lupin for several minutes. She sighed. The prospect of dinner with Rosalind loomed over her like a menacing shadow. It didn't help that she was swamped with her own insecurities. Her imagination furnished her with a vision of Rosalind in eveningwear, elegant and beautiful, soured by the image of Jess standing next to her. In the scene, she pictured an obese caricature of herself. Rosalind would speak intelligently, entertaining her captive audience. By comparison, Jess would fumble with the inarticulateness that plagued her whenever Rosalind was around. The vision had shamed her into fasting, in the vain hope she might lose some weight beforehand. It had only been two days, though, so she knew it would do little good.

The melodic ring of the telephone distracted her from her self-critical thoughts. She picked up the cordless handset that rested on the ground by her chair. "Hello?"

"Hey Jessie, whatcha up to?" The cheery voice of Jess's younger brother was always a welcome intrusion.

"Hi, Nick. I'm just sitting in the garden, admiring the view."

"How did your first week on the new assignment go? Any exciting gossip?"

"You are so nosy. And you know I shouldn't tell you even if there was." Jess chastised him but couldn't keep the humour from her voice.

"Maybe not, but you know I'll get it out of you sooner or later," he teased. "Fancy an impromptu practice this afternoon? This cute girl has started coming to the club nights, and I thought I could impress her at the re-enactment fair next month. There's a hand combat demonstration but I haven't practiced for a while. How about it? Help me get back in shape?"

"Why is it that whenever you want something from me, there's always a cute girl involved?"

"What other reason is so worthwhile?" Nick parried the question with one of his own. "Besides, I know you're with me on this one."

Jess laughed. "Fair enough," she acquiesced. "Your place or mine?"

"Make it mine. I'm a bit low on the old go-go juice for the car."

"Now why doesn't that surprise me?" Jess shook her head ruefully. "Okay, see you in half an hour or so."

"HEY SIS," NICK greeted Jess as she pulled into his driveway. He retrieved her kit from its usual storage place in the back of her car and led the way through the house and into the back garden. It was smaller than Jess's, but it afforded enough space for a respectable practice session, particularly as Nick had not bothered with plants.

They spent a few moments warming up in anticipation of the workout ahead. Nick looked at their weapons, lying side by side on the patio table. "I'm glad to see you're looking after my old sword," he noted approvingly.

Jess stretched both arms out behind her back, lifting them as high as she could to loosen her shoulders. "The way you fall for new kit I'm expecting more hand-me-downs soon." She couldn't resist the opportunity to tease him.

"No way, that sword cost me a fortune." Nick shook his head. "As for my bow, you know I'd never part with her. When will you embrace your heritage and get a longbow?"

She smiled as he rolled out the familiar argument. "Probably when you stop whining about my flatbow." Jess did a few star jumps to get her blood moving. "How's everyone at the club? It's been ages since I last saw them." They were both members of the same local archery group. It had been there that they discovered the world of re-enactment. Nick had fallen for it straightaway and had dragged his sister to enough events to spark her interest.

Nick did some squats, answering as he jumped. "Same old, they ask after you. I say how busy you are."

Jess chose not to get into their usual debate about her work ethic. Instead, she grabbed her sword and practiced her salute.

"Nice." Nick tried to mimic the sequence but dropped his blade on the grass part way through. "Obviously, I spend more time doing the serious stuff."

She smirked but decided to save his ego by changing the subject. "So, tell me about this cute girl," she demanded as they circled each other, blades ready.

"Tall, blonde, and beautiful." Nick lunged forward but Jess deflected his blade easily. "Not unlike my sister," he finished with a grin.

"Charmed, I'm sure." Jess parried another blow with ease, her body becoming accustomed to the substantial weight of the sword.

"Thanks for coming to help me practice." Nick said after a brief pause.

"No problem. I could do with a distraction anyway. I have a dinner I don't want to go to tonight," she admitted.

"With a lady, perchance?" Nick queried, feigning a right swing but pulling it into an upward move at the last minute.

"A stunning lady, to be precise," Jess replied. "And one who is both totally out of my league and a professional no-no."

Nick shifted his weight onto the balls of his feet. "No beautiful woman should be a no-no," he chastised.

"This one is." Jess swung her sword in an arc, the clash of metal confirming the blow had been met squarely. "My gut says she's trouble but I have to admit, other bits of me are quite keen."

Nick laughed. "Don't you ever get lonely waiting for Miss Perfect?" he asked, a serious question couched in his usual humour. "You can have a little fun while you're waiting, you know." He instigated a rapid series of moves, feinting twice before swinging the sword in a downward slicing move.

Jess realised what he was planning just in time, and raised her sword horizontally above her head, with a hand at each end. The force of the blow ricocheted down her arms but she ignored it. Knowing Nick would have used a valuable burst of energy, she went on the offensive. He parried her straight thrust but she rolled the blades around one another and pushed her whole body forward. With an impish grin, she stamped on his foot.

"Hey, foul!" Nick lowered his sword and pouted at her.

She grinned, panting. "You have to be ready for anything if you want to impress Cute Girl."

"I mean it," Nick said, doggedly returning to his point. "You don't have to save yourself for 'the one', you know. Having a little fun in the meantime won't kill you."

Jess shrugged. "Perhaps. But have you ever thought that

commitment might not be fatal?"

"Touché!" Nick exclaimed, brandishing his sword in mock salute. "Who knows? Maybe tall, blonde, and beautiful will be the one," he suggested, absorbing the impact of Jess's sword against his padded gambeson.

"You won't impress her if you fight like that," Jess jeered playfully. "Come on. I know you can do better, so focus."

Nick stuck his tongue out at her then knitted his eyebrows in a familiar expression of concentration. Preparing for an onslaught, Jess planted her feet more firmly and remembered to keep her knees flexible to maximise her manoeuvrability. It might be a gruelling way to spend a Saturday afternoon, she mused, but it was mercifully absorbing.

Chapter
Ten

JESS PULLED HER black Lexus into the restaurant car park at exactly seven-thirty. She had seen her host's sporty red soft-top already parked near the building's entrance. The exclusive restaurant was on the outskirts of Oxford and boasted expensive dishes and impeccable service. Although Jess had eaten here before on several business-related occasions, it was too pretentious for her tastes. Scanning the car park she was unsurprised to note that only the more costly car marques were present.

Steeling herself, she slid out of the SUV and smoothed the lines of her evening trouser ensemble. She was a little stiff from her afternoon exercise, but it had felt good to do it and helped to relieve some of her tension about this meeting. She clicked her key fob to lock up then headed into the restaurant, pausing in the foyer. "Hi. The table is in the name of Brannigan," she said to the usher with more confidence than she felt.

The man smiled his welcome. "Excellent. Please follow me." He led her through the main body of the restaurant to a more secluded corner table.

Rosalind was already seated, her back to the wall. She stood at Jess's approach and clasped her hand warmly, the contact feeling disproportionate to Jess's sensitised nerves. "I'm so glad you could make it," she enthused. "I know it was short notice but I felt I've hardly seen you all week."

Jess held the hand, momentarily speechless. Rosalind had

donned a slinky turquoise evening dress that clung enticingly to her curves. She would be a beautiful woman in a baggy tracksuit but tonight she was truly dazzling. With sudden embarrassment, Jess realised she was still clasping Rosalind's hand. She let go and mentally chided herself for staring. It seemed that her chances for making intelligent conversation over dinner had just become even less likely. "Thank you for inviting me," she responded politely, glad it sounded professional. She took her seat and forced her errant thoughts under control. "I understand your workload is heavy at the moment. It's very generous of you to give up precious free time for a dinner like this."

"Not at all." Rosalind smiled. "I'd like to help you in any way I can and it makes sense for us to be better acquainted if we're to work closely over the next few weeks."

Jess shifted in her seat. Rosalind's charm was palatable and her body language intimate. Jess felt herself responding but fought against it. She didn't know her companion well enough to understand her motives.

The waiter provided Jess with some breathing space as he approached to take their order. Rosalind ordered efficiently without using the menu. Clearly a regular, Jess thought as she scanned the choices. She decided upon a fairly innocuous salad followed by a steak. Rosalind added a bottle of red wine and a jug of iced water before dismissing him with an almost imperceptible wave of her hand.

"Lucy has been really helpful," Jess began, steering the conversation into safer waters. "She's responded to my numerous queries with the patience of a saint."

Rosalind eyed her companion curiously, the barest hint of a smile evident on her lips. "Lucy is a gem, it's true." Again, the waiter interrupted their conversation. This time he held out the bottle of wine for Rosalind's approval. She gave a subtle nod and he poured a splash into her glass. She picked up the glass and swirled the liquid, raising it to her nose to sniff. Satisfied, she tested a delicate sip, tasting the wine on her tongue with consideration. "Yes," she said finally. "Excellent."

The waiter filled Rosalind's glass and then her own. "Thank you," she murmured as he retreated.

"To new friends," Rosalind intoned, raising her glass.

"New friends," Jess echoed, watching as Rosalind put her glass to full lips. "So, how long have you worked for Image Conscious?" she enquired somewhat superfluously, as she already knew the information from the payroll report she had been studying the previous day.

Rosalind replaced the wine glass on the starched white

tablecloth and settled herself more comfortably in her chair. "About four years, although only two in my current role. Marcus and I are old friends. He introduced me to the company, because he knew I was looking for a career change."

"Do you enjoy it?" Jess asked, somewhat disappointed that Rosalind considered Marcus an old friend.

"Very much. It offers me the chance to meet many interesting people, and to work on different challenges with the various projects we take on. I imagine your role must be similar."

"Yes, you're right. Though my job is perhaps more mobile than yours, given that I can be given an assignment anywhere in the country."

"I suppose you must be used to staying in hotels, then?" Rosalind reached for her glass.

"I am, but they quickly lose their appeal when all you want is your home comforts. Even on far-flung projects I try to make it back home at least every other weekend. It helps to maintain perspective."

"Your absence must be very difficult for, say, a partner. . ." Rosalind left the comment hanging, instead choosing that moment to sip from her glass, her piercing blue eyes fixed unerringly on Jess, who flushed at the personal nature of the comment.

Jess had the distinct impression she was being hunted. "It would be, if I *had* a partner," she conceded. "It's also the reason I don't have pets."

"Sally, my ex, had a cat—a beautiful Persian called Cleopatra." Again, Rosalind regarded her.

Jess kept her expression nonchalant. The comment felt like a test and she was glad she'd already overheard the rumours to prepare her. She disliked intrigue and posturing, instead preferring straightforward honesty. Unfortunately, that was not in ready supply in her line of work. Still, at least she had the satisfaction of foiling Rosalind's attempt to evoke a reaction. She sidestepped the subject. "I like most animals, but I have a particular soft spot for dogs myself."

The arrival of the starters provided Jess with an opportunity to regroup. She was relieved to have seen Rosalind's apparent predatory streak. Although she could not deny that she found Rosalind incredibly attractive, this opportunity to spend some time with her—however brief it had been thus far— had demonstrated that her attraction was primarily physical with no depth. Such a superficial response was a lot easier for Jess to ignore.

"So," Jess said, taking the initiative, "tell me more about your role in the company. I understand you're a client manager, but what exactly does that involve on a day-to-day basis?" Rosalind may have taken it out of the office, but Jess was determined to still have her business meeting.

Rosalind looked at her thoughtfully for a moment before replying. "I think of myself as the interface between the company and the client. When a customer commits to employing us, we assign them a dedicated client manager. There are eight of us in total, although I tend to take on the clients with the highest spend." She paused for a moment and turned her attention to her dish of Chardonnay oysters. "Over the course of the project, multiple departments within the organisation will each perform their specialist tasks. One of the key aspects of my role is to ensure that the client enjoys continuity of service irrespective of which department they are working with at any given point in the project. Providing a reliable, single point of contact is one of the key ways we differentiate ourselves from competitors."

"That makes a lot of sense," Jess said, thinking that Rosalind sounded like an interactive company brochure. "So how many clients are you responsible for at a time?"

Rosalind rested a hand on the table, her nail polish shiny against the matt tablecloth. "That depends on the size of the projects we're working on. Obviously, we have to ensure that we can maintain the high levels of service we commit to, so a very large client might receive exclusive attention. Alternatively, one of us may manage three or four smaller projects."

"How many are you working on right now?" Jess took a bite of her Mediterranean salad.

Rosalind toyed with her napkin. "I have one small one and one large one, which is in the signoff stage, hence the frequent meetings. Do you know much about the public relations industry?"

"Not really, no," Jess admitted. "One of the great things about my job is the opportunity to work in different industries, which allows me to build up a wide base of information and experience. Having said that, I tend to believe that the fundamental components of business are generic across the board. Questions of competitive advantage, efficiency, customer service, innovation, and human resources are all crucial factors that companies should be focussed on whether the company makes cardboard or provides a worldwide telecommunications service." She reached for her own wineglass.

"Our roles certainly have similarities," Rosalind responded. "Our clients can be in very different markets but again, common denominators of marketing allow us to offer expertise they don't have. So you have a good point."

"Can you give me an overview of a recent case the company has worked on?" Jess asked, ignoring the attendant who was surreptitiously clearing their discarded crockery. "I know you probably can't be specific, but just the salient points, maybe?"

"Sure," Rosalind said, smiling. "Let me think. . .ah. I worked with a global toy manufacturer recently, mainly operating in US and UK markets. As with many companies, they had jumped on the globalisation bandwagon and had moved their manufacturing division to Asian countries, taking advantage of cheap labour and fewer restrictions. Their expenditure dropped dramatically but they were dogged by press reports of poor working conditions and use of workers who would be considered underage in Western economies."

Jess nodded. It was something she had limited experience with from her past placements. She refilled their water glasses and motioned for Rosalind to continue.

"Well, the company experienced a massive drop in its market share as a result of the attention. They had previously enjoyed a very strong position with a monopoly in one particular sector of the market. In most cases, a declining market share is the key driving force that makes clients decide to take action and approach us."

"That makes sense," Jess agreed. "Consumers hold the power and they tend to vote with their feet. It's logical to conclude that regaining their customers is a public relations issue."

"Exactly." Rosalind said with a smile, seemingly pleased by Jess's quick comprehension of the situation. "So going back to the toy manufacturer, we had to start by assessing their current position. It's only through understanding exactly where they are now that we can plan a meaningful route forward. We conducted consumer reviews, interviewing individuals about their perceptions of the company and of their main competitors. As we suspected, in this situation Joe Public believed exploitation of children was going on in the background."

"Pretty fatal for a toymaker," Jess commented dryly.

Rosalind raised an eyebrow. "Precisely. So we adopted a multidirectional approach. As well as the usual brand analysis, we reviewed the strategic direction of the business, and developed a new mission statement with a slant more toward humanity than commerce. This was complimented by a set of values touting corporate responsibility, integrity, and the like. These values were widely published in any appropriate promotional material."

"Surely it must be backed up with some action?" *Or did Image Conscious just do the old "smoke and mirrors" approach?* The thought galled Jess.

"Of course," Rosalind assured her. "In this scenario, the company developed an internal 'college' within its Asian manufacturing arm. By promoting free learning for all employees as well as multiple scholarships for unrelated individuals from the local community, they were recognised to be taking a more responsible role in the host country and accusations of exploitation ceased."

Two waiters brought in the main courses before they faded once again into the background. Jess ate slowly in the wake of her recent fast and tried to ignore the inner voices that told her she was still too fat to eat. Instead, she continued the conversation. At least Rosalind was proving interesting to talk to. "Has enough time passed to see any results?"

"It's still early days," Rosalind said, "but evidence to date shows a very positive result with the business recapturing lost market share and demonstrating healthy growth across all their divisions."

"And this was one of *your* projects?" Jess asked before taking another bite.

"Yes. With the size of the business, it was one I worked on exclusively."

"You must have gained a real satisfaction from those results." She refrained from saying "well done," since Rosalind might construe that as patronising.

Having reached the topic's natural conclusion, there was a brief pause in the conversation. When they began talking again, it was of more mundane matters.

A short while later, Jess leant back in her chair, full after the three-course meal. Despite her original misgivings and Rosalind's earlier personal enquiries, she had to admit that the evening had surpassed her expectations. Work had been the main topic of conversation, which suited Jess well, but Rosalind had turned out to be a fun, relaxed conversationalist and it had been surprisingly informative, providing Jess with a much deeper understanding of the business. Rosalind had also impressed her. Marcus undoubtedly used Rosalind's beauty and charisma to his maximum advantage but she clearly had undeniable business skills too.

"Thank you for a lovely meal," Jess said as they walked toward the exit. She wasn't sure if Rosalind had paid personally or would be adding it to her business expenses claim. She could probably check in the accounts next month.

"I wonder if I can impose upon you in return?" Rosalind asked, glancing at her.

Jess's stomach knotted with anxiety. Whatever this was, it wasn't in her plan. "Well, um…" she enquired, as noncommittally as she could.

"I think I had the lion's share of wine at dinner. I must have been distracted by the exceptional company." Rosalind giggled with feigned embarrassment.

Knowing where this was going, Jess tried not to show her reaction. She couldn't cause offence, after all. This was a professional relationship, ultimately, and refusing to give a potentially drunk colleague a lift home would probably make her job harder in the long run.

"Could I trouble you for a lift home?" Rosalind asked. "My house is very close but I suspect I am over the limit to drive."

Jess pushed down her anger, realising this had probably been Rosalind's plan all along. She had noticed her companion indulging in the Rioja whilst she herself had abstained from all but the taste, knowing she'd be driving home after dinner. She contemplated calling a taxi but realised there would probably be a long wait on a Saturday night. "Sure," she responded with a nicer tone than she felt, consoling herself with the fact that she would at least be in control as the driver.

Rosalind took Jess's arm and giggled again as they walked toward the Lexus. Once the car was moving, Rosalind issued directions lucidly enough, leading Jess to believe she could probably have managed another glass or two and still have remained perfectly in control, though not safe to drive.

Rosalind's directions eventually led them to a long, gravelled drive to a private home. Jess proceeded slowly, unfamiliar with the road. At the end, a large, brick house loomed in the darkness. The light by the front door had been left on, illuminating the doorstep and nearby topiary.

"Thank you." Rosalind smiled as they pulled up outside her front door. She swivelled in her seat so she was facing Jess and gently reached out and caressed her cheek.

Jess inhaled quickly, shocked by the unexpected advance. "Um—no problem. See you in the office on Monday." She rushed the words, a sloppy but unmistakable dismissal.

"Jess." Rosalind clearly had no intention of being dismissed, and instead bridged the gap between her and her quarry until their faces were millimetres apart. "Can't you feel the attraction between us?" She dropped her gaze and looked seductively at Jess's lips.

Jess certainly *could* feel something. It was undeniable, as forceful as giant magnets pulling their bodies closer. Shutting her eyes the moment their lips met, she succumbed to the kiss, desperation, passion, and panic fuelling their contact. The sound of a car horn on the nearby road startled her and Jess regained enough sensibility to pull back from the embrace. Belatedly taking control of the situation, she got out and circled the bonnet to open the passenger door. "Good night, Rosalind," she said simply, struggling to keep her voice free of emotion. *How did I let that happen?*

Rosalind looked sober and vaguely smug. "Good night," she said softly, getting out of the car.

Jess watched her safely into the house before driving away. Angry at her own lack of control, she spent the journey home speculating dismally on the fall-out she could expect.

Chapter
Eleven

MONDAY MORNING AND Jess had sequestered herself at her desk since seven. After the fateful dinner and subsequent kiss she had decided that arriving early gave her a slight advantage in what she anticipated would be an awkward meeting with Rosalind. At first she had been angry with herself and shocked by Rosalind's forwardness. The kiss had affected her, though, awakening responses she tried to keep buried. Part of her dared to hope for more, even though common sense warned her against it. She had tried to stop those feelings before they developed. This wasn't the first time individuals involved in her assignments had tried to form an attachment with her.

As always, she felt somewhat abused, a small part of her wondering if there was something wrong with her that advances only seemed to be made toward her by those motivated purely by self-interest. As usual, Jess had compounded her problems by consoling herself with comfort food. Her subsequent self-disgust and poor night's sleep had neither improved the situation nor calmed her roiling thoughts.

A part of Jess stubbornly refused to renounce the memory of the kiss. Albeit brief, it had been an exhilarating, passion-filled experience that she didn't want to relinquish readily. Repeatedly, she had speculated about her colleague's authenticity but each time returned to the fact that only Rosalind could know her true motivation. Despite her resolute efforts to maintain rationality, Jess kept reliving the sensation of their lips meeting, the inescapable pull that drew them together, and her undeniable arousal.

Jess glared at her computer screen, trying to focus. Her emotions cycled round to anger when she thought about the inevitable work-related consequences. The dynamic between them had been permanently changed and as a result, their working relationship had to be modified. How it would change she didn't know, since much depended on Rosalind's behaviour this morning.

Jess tried to imagine all possible scenarios. Would Rosalind ignore her? Would she be frosty to cover her own embarrassment? Maybe she would try and take things farther— particularly likely if there were other motivations in play. Would she keep the incident to herself? Perhaps she had already told people or maybe she had been instructed to do it in the first place? There were too many unknowns for Jess to identify a probable way forward.

After much deliberation Jess settled on her own approach, taking comfort in being proactive rather than reactive. Although the attraction was undeniable, Jess had found Rosalind's predatory side off-putting, ironically feeling most enchanted by the proficient confidence with which her companion described her work. So Jess concentrated on the predatory side of Rosalind, thus attempting to minimise the attraction and theoretically set professional limits on their relationship. Whether or not this method would work when face-to-face with the object of her desires was another matter.

One thing that had definitely surprised Jess was the intensity of her reaction to the kiss and the possibility of genuine emotion behind it. She recognised her own loneliness when she realised how much she wanted the advance to be real despite the complications it would create at work. She ruefully acknowledged that her brother might have had a point with his frequent accusations that she isolated herself through her career. As compensation, she told herself that if, in the unlikely event that Rosalind were genuine, then they could develop any relationship after the assignment had been completed. Still, she couldn't shake the feeling that in all probability, Rosalind's advances had more to do with business than pleasure. With this depressing thought, she went back to sifting through more information with regard to the investigation.

THE MIDMORNING KNOCK on her office door startled Jess out of her number-crunching trance. "Come in," she called.

The door opened and Rosalind entered, gorgeous even on a Monday morning. "Good morning," she said, smiling in greeting before closing the door quietly behind her. "I'm sorry I wasn't able to come and see you first thing. I had a breakfast meeting that only just finished."

"That's quite all right. What can I do for you?" Jess tried to keep her tone relatively brusque and professional, though her body was responding quite differently.

Rosalind pulled the visitor's chair out from under the desk and sat down, crossing her shapely legs at the knee. She cleared her throat, evidently uncomfortable. "I wanted to apologise for the other night. I was wrong to probe into your personal life, I was wrong to coerce you into driving me home, and I was wrong to take advantage of your kindness when you did." She paused, waiting for a reaction. When none was forthcoming, she continued, "I know it's not an excuse, but I'm very attracted to you. I wanted to get to know you better and I enjoyed your company so much that I let my feelings run away with me." She glanced down at her lap then up at Jess again. "I did plan the trick with the wine." Her voice was quiet, her eyes betraying a sense of shame. "It was wrong. I just thought if I asked you would turn me down, given the work dynamic."

"So you decided to force the issue?" Jess snapped.

"Yes, and I'm not proud of it." Rosalind seemed genuinely remorseful. "I don't want to pretend it didn't happen because regardless of what *you* might feel, it meant something to me. Something you don't come across every day."

Jess didn't know whether to trust her or not. She wanted to believe her so much, but what if it was all an elaborate pretence? After all, Rosalind had already admitted she was willing and able to manipulate a situation for her own end.

"I don't want you to feel uncomfortable and I certainly don't want to make our working relationship any more difficult." Rosalind shifted and leaned over. "Here, I want you to have this." She handed Jess a scrap of paper. "It's my phone number," she explained. "I would like to spend more time with you, outside the work environment. If you feel the same way then perhaps you can call me sometime. If not, then I assure you we can still have a most effective working relationship." Rosalind stood. "I'll say no more about this unless you bring it up first." She smiled wanly and left.

Jess watched Rosalind's retreating form. After a brief word with Lucy, Rosalind entered her own office opposite Jess's and shut the door. Blowing out a breath she had not realised she'd been holding, Jess studied the small piece of paper that held Rosalind's number. Relief, elation, suspicion, and hope warred within her. Time enough to deal with it later. Returning to the column of figures she had been working on, Jess let her subconscious worry about it for the time being.

FRIDAY ROLLED AROUND disconcertingly quickly. Jess had been spending long hours at the office trying to get a handle on her investigation. So far everyone she had spoken to had been cooperative, a fact that belied the existence of anything sinister. Even if nothing untoward were occurring, she knew her report would need to be comprehensive enough to reassure Theodore Willis. Therefore, until she had a specific area of concern, Jess had to continue her work on a broad front.

Jess had opted to focus on the company financials, which could tell her lots of different things. They covered performance, possible issues with consumers, or, if something seemed really odd, whether somebody on the inside was doing something questionable with the books or funds. She had studied the financial trends for Image Conscious over the last five years, a period that covered the end of Willis's tenure and the start of Gibson's. Jess found an increased turnover for the business and steadily falling profits. There were many possible reasons behind this — some probably innocent, others less so — the responsibility for all fell squarely on the shoulders of the management.

Some of the expense claims made Jess shake her head with disbelief. Thousands of pounds of restaurant bills, golfing days, and even a hot air balloon ride were put down as 'entertaining'. Technically, these examples were not illegal as long as the tax was dealt with appropriately, but they certainly showed a managerial conflict of interests. When they should be protecting the interests of the shareholders, the senior managers were instead living it up on the company. The one thing that bucked the trend seemed to be Gibson's Aston Martin, which surprisingly didn't appear on the company asset register.

Human resources told her a similar story, but nothing specifically damning. The business had a large payroll, most of whom Jess had been able to identify against the personnel database on the company intranet. Only a few employees, such as the ones working from home, were missing. Pay rates were reasonable though not generous and the company complied with necessary legislation.

Jess had also invested time observing some staff and she had held brief interviews with others. She never expected people to relax enough to speak freely but interviews still provided a valuable insight into the company. The culture of the organisation had changed significantly since Willis's departure, Jess discovered. People hinted at less trust in management and subsequently acted with more self-motivation. Morale seemed low and internal politics divided teams that should have been working together. The statistics showed both a higher rate of employee turnover and sickness. This didn't surprise Jess, since it was exactly what she would have predicted given the behaviour of senior management.

Meanwhile, customer feedback files made for dry reading. Although clients no longer gushed about the imagination and commitment they enjoyed in the heyday of Willis's leadership, the evidence suggested consistently high levels of customer satisfaction were being achieved.

Tapping her pencil against her lips, Jess furrowed her brow in thought. Although it was no longer the flourishing organisation Willis had retired from, there was nothing as yet to justify the former CEO's concern. Neither was there any evidence to suggest that people were attempting to hide anything. Gibson had promised her ready access to transparent information and everything she had encountered suggested his full compliance. As she shut down her laptop and prepared to leave for the day, she decided it was time for a different approach. Luckily, she had the whole weekend to come up with one.

Chapter
Twelve

JESS WATCHED NICK as he took his last shot of the round. She was glad she'd had the idea to invite him for a spontaneous archery session. The prospect of spending the weekend alone, agonising about Rosalind's intentions and her slow-moving investigation was not an appealing one. She felt herself smile as she saw Nick's tongue sticking out in concentration. He was taller but sometimes he reminded her so much of the little boy he used to be. Blond, gangly, and always looking guilty about something.

"Nice." Nick's shot complete, he complimented her tight clump of six arrows slightly to the left of the gold.

"Thanks." Jess accepted his compliment with pleasure. Before she had joined the archery club she had assumed that the best results were those where the arrow landed closest to the centre of the target. Technically, this was true, but she had since learnt the value of consistency. Archery was about being able to repeat your skill. It made sense when she thought about it. Anyone could fluke a shot, after all. Consistency was the real mark of proficiency. Placement could always be adjusted later.

"Okay." Nick's last shot had completed the round. The siblings walked to the boss and inspected their arrow placement more closely, each deciding what adjustments to make on the next round. They began to remove the arrows carefully. "So, how is your stunning lady?" Nick asked, flashing her a grin.

Jess shook her head and smiled. Nick would forget his own sister's birthday but could miraculously recall any conversation about attractive women. "I'd hoped you would have forgotten that," she retorted teasingly.

"No chance. 'Stunning' isn't a word you use regularly. So come on, spill it." He grinned again, this time with his most appealing boyish charm.

Nick was persistent but Jess could make him drop the subject if she really wanted to. The trouble was, her own mind was quite determined to think about Rosalind and she was getting bored with the same well-worn thought loops. In truth, she would be grateful to talk things through with an outsider. "All right," she relented as she slid the last of her arrows into her quiver and headed back to the shooting line. "We had dinner," she confided, "at Giovanni's."

"Jeez, Jessie, you don't hang around do you? And Giovanni's no less. So, what happened?"

"We talked about work a lot, she fished to see if I'm single and she let me know she's gay." Jess felt a small flush of embarrassment as she recalled the evening.

"Whoa," he said appreciatively. "She doesn't waste time, either. It looks like you guys are well suited. Did you say, 'take me, I'm yours'?" Nick grinned again, clearly entertained by his own joke.

"Of course not," Jess huffed. "I diverted her back to safer topics — work-related, I'll have you know. It was a useful, informative evening."

"Useful? Jessie, you went to that posh place and drank wine — I'm assuming you drank wine?" Nick looked at her questioningly.

She nodded.

"You drank wine, she's stunning, there were candles, romantic music. . ." he paused for dramatic effect. "All of that and you found it useful for work? Jessie, I worry." His theatrical outrage was partially based in truth, Jess knew. "You have to know when work stops and it's time to play."

"We did kiss," Jess blurted out in her own defence. "After the dinner I drove her home and we kissed."

"Who kissed whom?" Nick pressed.

"She kissed me."

"And what did you do?"

Jess paused while she drew her first arrow, aimed carefully and released it. She observed it shuddering in the gold before she replied. "I said good night."

"Why doesn't that surprise me?" Nick took the sting out of his words by the kindness in his voice. "Let me guess. Inappropriate with work, unprofessional distraction —"

"You're damned right it is. I've worked so hard in my career, Nick. Too hard to throw it away on some stupid crush."

Nick lowered his bow without shooting and put his hand on Jess's arm. "Hey, Jessie. This is me. You don't have to defend yourself. I'm sorry if I hit a nerve. I just want to see you happy and

I worry that your work makes you lonely." He paused before he lifted his bow once again. "So," he continued, talking as he shot his first arrow. "How have things been since?"

Jess took a deep breath and shot her second arrow before responding. "Dinner was on Saturday night," she elaborated. "Rosalind came to talk to me on Monday."

"Mmm?" Nick encouraged.

"She apologised for her inappropriate behaviour. It seemed pretty genuine but then, I don't really know her. She said that she was attracted to me, that she thought there was something special between us. She gave me her number and asked me to call her if I feel the same way."

Nick picked his words carefully. "Am I right to think you haven't called her?"

Jess nodded.

"But you do feel the same way, right?"

Jess nodded again.

"So it's the work thing getting in the way."

"Yes. Plus I don't know if it's genuine. She might just be looking for a fling. Or maybe she's a corporate pawn and wants to know what I find with regard to the company." Jess stopped and looked at him. "If it's not genuine, that's going to hurt. Badly. And I don't want to get hurt."

"I understand." He was unusually serious. "How has she been with you since that conversation?"

"Perfect," Jess admitted to her own surprise. "We have spent quite a bit of time together in the office. I can't fault anything since Saturday. She's been totally professional. She has kept her word and not even hinted at what happened."

There was a pause while they each shot another couple of arrows. The boss was beginning to resemble a vertical hedgehog. "That's pretty good, isn't it?" Nick said cautiously, perhaps afraid to put his opinion forward, recognising this as a sensitive subject.

"Yes."

"So, what's your plan?"

"I was thinking that maybe I would phone her after my work with the company is completed. That way I'll know right away if her interest is genuine or not." Jess waited for her brother's inevitable disagreement.

Nick lined up his last shot. "That sounds fair enough," he said, loosing the arrow.

Jess laughed, suddenly feeling better than she had done for days. "You don't mean that." She brandished her bow at him with mock severity. "You think I should go out there and grab the girl."

Nick shrugged and smiled. "I'm always in favour of grabbing

the girl, but I don't want to see you get hurt, either."

"Well, maybe you'll get both your wishes." Jess grinned coyly. "That was some kiss. Who knows if I'll be able to stick to my high morality and wait the project out!"

They both laughed as they collected the completed round of arrows. Jess studied her efforts critically, her sporadic performance a testament to her distraction. She consoled herself with the fact that Nick didn't appear up to his usual standard, either. "Fancy staying over?" She asked him. "I'll treat you to a takeaway if you want."

"Do I ever turn down free food?" He asked with another grin.

Jess walked back toward the house with a spring in her step. Talking through the Rosalind situation had helped clarify her feelings and her brother's support was invaluable. Now a relaxed evening in his company stretched out ahead of her, offering the perfect antidote to her frustrating week.

Chapter Thirteen

"MORNING, LUCY." JESS paused at the secretary's desk. "How was your weekend?"

"Lovely, thanks. How about you?"

"Good," Jess said, nodding. "My brother and I spent far too much time watching budget horror films, though."

Lucy laughed. "We spent too much time at the pub. Weekends are supposed to be fun, after all. We spend enough time doing what we're supposed to at work." After a momentary pause, she continued. "I'll be getting a coffee in a minute. Can I get one for you?"

Jess smiled gratefully. "That'd be fantastic, thanks. I need to have a word with Mr. Gibson in a minute so a little caffeine wouldn't go amiss."

Lucy wrinkled her nose in displeasure. "Oh, dear, maybe I should slip something stronger in there for you."

"Don't tempt me." Jess joked back as she started walking toward her office. She noted Lucy's opinion with interest. She was a bright young woman, exactly the sort of talent the organisation should be going out of its way to keep.

A short while later, Jess left her half-drunk coffee and made her way to Marcus's corner of the building. "Good morning,

Hilary," she said, smiling at the sour-faced assistant, thinking what a change she was to Lucy. "Any chance I can see Mr. Gibson for a quick five minutes?"

Hilary pressed the intercom button. "Mr. Gibson, Ms. Maddocks is here. She would like five minutes."

"Send her in." His electronically distorted response was clipped.

Jess nodded at the assistant in acknowledgement and brushed past her desk to enter Marcus's office.

Marcus's attention was on his computer screen. "Good morning," He muttered, without making eye contact. A few more seconds passed before he looked up. "You were lucky to catch me. I have a meeting at ten." He motioned toward the visitor's chair before pointedly checking the clock.

"I appreciate you seeing me and I won't keep you long." Jess had come to expect such displays of poor manners from him.

"What can I do for you?" Marcus smiled, showing two perfect rows of white teeth.

Jess sat back, making herself comfortable, hoping to disarm him a bit. "First, I wanted to thank you for ensuring such ready assistance from your team. Everyone has been most cooperative and efficient about responding to my requests for information. Quite a team you have here." She had a low opinion of the man in front of her, but she knew rudeness would get her nowhere. So she tried compliments, interested to see how he would respond.

"I'm pleased to hear it," Marcus replied, though his tone wasn't entirely convincing.

"My work here is progressing well," Jess said, embellishing the half-truth, "but I think it would be enhanced by a different approach."

"Did you have something specific in mind?" Marcus queried, looking sceptical.

"As a matter of fact," Jess said, "I'd like to be assigned to one of your client projects so that I can observe the customer interaction dynamic first-hand."

Marcus's eyes narrowed almost imperceptibly. He stiffened, and regarded her coolly. "Look, Ms. Maddocks—" he emphasised her title as though it were an insult. "I have every intention of cooperating with you. However, surely you can see that something like that just isn't workable." He frowned with poorly concealed irritation. It reminded her of the way adults looked when children repeatedly asked 'why'. "A very delicate relationship exists between us and our clients. We need them to see that we are professionals with whom their company image is safe. There are issues of confidentiality and business etiquette that, I'm sorry to say, your presence would undermine."

"I have no objection to signing a confidentiality contract," Jess pressed smoothly. "In fact, I would expect it."

"You don't seem to understand." Marcus sighed and shifted in his seat. "How am I supposed to explain your presence? You're not knowledgeable enough to be an expert and I can tell you now that we will haemorrhage business if we told the truth. I cannot think of a more effective way to lose client confidence." He punched his words out, as if trying to beat her into submission.

Jess smiled sweetly. "Perhaps you could tell them I'm a work experience student."

Marcus ignored the comment. "Ms. Maddocks, you evidently have no idea what you're asking of me. Please, reconsider your request. Surely briefing meetings with our client managers would achieve the same goal?"

That would be the perfect way to ensure filtered information. Jess regarded him, not entirely surprised by his reticence. It only made her want to sit in on client briefings more. She had intended to follow this idea through, but Marcus's heated response made her even more determined. "Mr. Gibson," she began, using a tone a school teacher might employ with misbehaving students, "I appreciate that this is clearly not something you wish me to pursue. Nonetheless, I believe this approach is necessary in order for me to provide a comprehensive report to my client. If you cannot agree, I will have no alternative but to approach him directly for approval, a move I would be loathe to make." She retained her relaxed posture for show, hoping fervently that this was not a threat she'd have to complete, as she had no idea if Willis would support her or not. Either way, her approach certainly didn't comply with the instruction she had been given to utilise sensitivity and minimise aggravation. Pity Gibson's the sticking point, she thought. Theodore would probably clear anything that didn't impact on Marcus and therefore his daughter.

"Fine. Have it your way," he said in a low, dangerous voice, unable to maintain his genial pretence any longer. "It's the old man's dividends that'll suffer from this interference."

"I'm *so* glad we could compromise." Jess was unable to resist the jibe.

Marcus ignored it. "Rosalind has just started a new project, and they have only had one introductory meeting, I believe. I'll ask her to treat you as her shadow from this point onwards." Jess didn't miss the sarcastic emphasis to his words or what he might be implying.

"Thank you," she said, having anticipated this outcome. She maintained her mask of professional detachment, hoping it irritated him further. "I shall take up no more of your valuable time, Mr. Gibson. Good day."

Jess paused as she closed the office door behind her. Sure enough, she heard Marcus speak.

"I need you in my office. Now."

She gave Hilary a pleasant smile on her way past and retraced her steps back to her office. On the way, she passed Rosalind in the corridor. "Good morning."

"Morning, Jess." Rosalind replied, looking harried.

Jess mulled over the brief encounter as she paused at the coffee machine. She would have put money on meeting Rosalind in the corridor. What surprised her was the expression on her face. Whatever she was feeling, it wasn't pleasant. It was the first time she had seen anything negative on that beautiful face. A little flame of hope sparked within her. *So they're not such good friends, then.*

ROSALIND IGNORED HILARY and walked straight to Marcus's door. She rapped sharply on the wood and immediately let herself in.

"Come," Marcus demanded, somewhat superfluously.

She crossed the familiar room and seated herself without prompting. "You called?" she said sarcastically, irritated at being summoned in such a discourteous manner.

"You won't believe what that bitch wants now." He got to his feet and paced with agitation. "She wants to sit in on client meetings to observe our customer service. She evidently has no idea of the effect this ill-conceived attempt at involvement will have on our clients."

Rosalind prudently remained silent, her alert gaze following Marcus's rhythmic, fractious pacing. Not a bad idea, she thought, appreciating the tack Jess was taking.

"I tried to put her off but she threatened to take it to Willis. I had no choice but to concede." He glared at her, as if willing her to disagree so he could vent his anger.

"Of course," Rosalind responded, sensing how close she might come to copious amounts of his misdirected rage. "Am I right to think you intend to assign her to the PetZone project with me?" She kept her tone level, hoping to keep him calm. Marcus's temper could be volcanic.

"Yes," Marcus deflated suddenly and sank back into his seat. "I need you to look out for us here."

She held his gaze and nodded.

"This woman's trouble," Marcus continued. "She could blow us out of the water. Keep her busy, distract her with the small stuff if you have to, but just keep her away from anything big."

"So am I on my usual remit with PetZone?"

"Yes, you have to be. I have commitments…" he let the sentence trail off. "Have you netted her yet?" He asked suddenly, his gaze intense, almost lascivious.

"No," Rosalind admitted. "She's taking longer than I expected, but it's just a matter of time." She studied her fingernails, perfectly manicured. "They always fold." She looked up at him. "As you know."

"Well show a bit more leg, or whatever it is you do," his tone was dismissive, in a way that signalled to Rosalind that these days, he saw her in terms of the advantages she offered, no longer susceptible to her physical charms himself. "We need her under our control."

Rosalind's resentment built, but she bit back her retort. Marcus was nothing without her. He may hold power, but the looks, the talent, and the intelligence of their combination were all hers. This was a power struggle she knew instinctively that they would have, but today was not the time for it. "I understand." Her vocal response was one of capitulation but her mind had already begun plotting her revenge.

"JESS?" THE CALL echoed oddly in the empty corridor.

Jess paused and looked around. Lucy's desk was empty. She was presumably out at lunch. Rosalind was in her office, though, beckoning at her. Jess altered direction, suddenly apprehensive.

"Sorry to shout, I've been trying to come and see you for days but things keep coming up. Do you have a second?" Rosalind looked hopeful.

"Sure," Jess said simply, conscious she was holding the sandwiches that gave away her next activity.

"I don't know where the week's going." Rosalind laughed lightly. "It's Wednesday already and I still haven't finished the things I wanted to get done on Monday." She shook her head, a rueful smile on her face. "It's usually like this when a major new project starts but you'd think I'd have got used to it by now."

Jess smiled politely, still unsure of what Rosalind wanted.

"Marcus has said you'll be joining me on the PetZone assignment?" She paused, looking at Jess expectantly.

"That's right. I'll simply be an observer."

"It'll be good to have you around." Rosalind smiled though she still seemed quite tense. "I need to find some time to get you up to speed but things seem to be conspiring against me." As if to prove her point, her desk phone began to ring. Rosalind gave the device an exasperated look.

"Take it. We'll talk later." Jess urged. She hated it when people ignored ringing telephones. It made her nervous.

Rosalind shook her head. "I'm in a meeting with consumer research for the rest of the day. Any chance you can come to my place for an early dinner on Saturday? I need to be able to brief you without all these distractions."

A familiar sense of dread overwhelmed Jess. She tried to think rationally but the ringing phone distracted her. With great effort, she managed to form a coherent sentence. "I really don't think that's a good idea."

"Please, think about it at least?" Rosalind looked pathetic rather than predatory. "I'd appreciate the chance to talk to you freely." She gave her a pointed look.

Sensing the hint at intrigue, Jess couldn't help but be tempted. Rosalind had certainly looked unhappy when Marcus had summoned her the other day, maybe she was feeling ready to be a little more open. One could only hope.

Rosalind pressed her. "You have my word that nothing untoward will happen. Shall we say seven again? You remember where it is, right?" She reached her hand toward the telephone, still looking hopefully at Jess.

Tense and outmanoeuvred, Jess nodded. As Rosalind answered the phone, she returned to her own quiet office wondering what she had just committed herself to.

Chapter
Fourteen

FOLLOWING THE INSTRUCTIONS issued by the prim, feminine voice of the route guidance system, Jess navigated her Lexus steadily toward her destination. She was still undecided whether accepting Rosalind's invitation to dinner at her home was a good idea. It was two weeks to the day since that fateful kiss and her subsequent commitment not to let herself get into the same situation again. The irony wasn't lost on her. She'd come close to cancelling the arrangement on more than one occasion, but each time she remembered the note of anxiety in Rosalind's voice as she advised Jess that her home was the ideal location for talking freely. Of course, there was an element of confidentiality surrounding the PetZone case, but still. An office at work would have sufficed. It was Rosalind's intimation that she wanted to discuss Image Conscious itself that had hooked Jess once and for all. The possibility of making significant progress in her assignment was a temptation she could not resist.

On a personal level, Jess had made a resolution to worry less. Rosalind had been the epitome of professionalism over the last two weeks, whatever her intentions. She had proven she was capable of controlling herself. Jess smiled wryly as she turned up Rosalind's driveway. Now if only she could say the same about herself...

She pulled up in front of Rosalind's home and tried to settle the butterflies in her stomach. This is just a business meeting, she reminded herself. But she couldn't stop reliving that amazing, sensuous kiss.

Rosalind greeted her before she had chance to ring the bell. "Hi," she said, smiling. "I'm so glad you could make it tonight."

"Thank you for the invite." Jess responded mechanically, the vision of her hostess in snug jeans rather than her usual business attire proving a considerable distraction.

"Please, come in." Rosalind led the way into the house. "What can I get you to drink? Tea? Coffee? Something stronger?" Her voice held a teasing hint of hope at the last suggestion.

"Coffee, please. White with two." Jess said, taking a seat on the sofa where Rosalind had indicated. Left alone, she busied herself liberating pens, paper, and reports from her briefcase, preparing the tools of her trade, and setting her boundaries. Her arrangements complete to her satisfaction, Jess took the opportunity to look around more closely. One thing was for certain, Rosalind had impeccable taste. The room was decorated in complementary neutral tones. Two large leather sofas dominated, their luxuriously tanned hide and enveloping softness stating their quality. A bronze figurine took pride of place in the centre of the mantelpiece, the theme repeated in smaller versions placed at strategic locations around the room. The effect was aesthetically pleasing but revealed little of Rosalind other than her fine taste. It looks like a scene from an interior design magazine, Jess reflected. *Beautiful but hollow.*

Rosalind returned with two steaming mugs and placed one on an etched glass coaster on the coffee table in front of Jess. She put her own mug on a twin coaster next to the second sofa, before moving to the expensive looking stereo. Quiet, inoffensive music filled the room from hidden, surround-sound speakers. "I hope you don't mind," Rosalind said with another smile as she settled onto the sofa. "I find it easier to concentrate with some background noise."

"No, it's fine." Jess smiled back. "Thanks for the coffee."

Rosalind inclined her head and regarded Jess frankly. "Marcus wasn't too happy that you requested to be included in a client project."

Jess relaxed, reassured by Rosalind's beeline toward work topics. "No," she admitted. "I hope he didn't take his bad mood out on you." That sentiment was genuine. One of the worst failings she came across in her line of work was a manager who skirted responsibility and vented petty frustrations on subordinates.

Rosalind smiled wryly. "He *was* a little testy."

"I'm sorry. He has a lot on his mind, I'm sure." Jess took a sip of coffee, unwilling to voice any negativity toward Marcus, since Rosalind had said two weeks ago that she and he were friends.

"Marcus has changed since Mr Willis stepped down," Rosalind confided as though she could read her guest's thoughts. "We used to get on quite well but these days I find myself disagreeing with him more and more."

"In what ways?" Jess asked, hoping she sounded noncommittal.

Rosalind took a sip from her cup before she responded. "He doesn't treat the team as well as I would like," she began, sounding a little reluctant to discuss it. "I think he finds this role much more stressful than he expected. He certainly puts in long hours." After another brief pause she continued, "I've seen him snap at people for nothing and it's really taken its toll on the motivation of the workforce."

Jess nodded sympathetically. *Tough position for Rosalind to be in.* "It's always hard for the employees when there's such a crucial change of leadership. So many things have to change as the newcomer adapts the business to their way of doing things."

"Exactly," Rosalind agreed. "I had just hoped that we would have passed through this phase by now. If he doesn't take care, Marcus may face losing some of the most talented members of the group. I already know headhunters are calling for them."

Jess didn't want to ask how she knew such information, although she was curious. She simply nodded again, storing the information for future reference but refusing to be baited into offering an opinion.

Rosalind let the pause linger before continuing. "That's one of the things I wanted to make sure you knew about," she explained. "One of the things I didn't feel I could talk about in the office. I know it may seem trivial but if Image Conscious loses these key staff to competitors, then I believe its future to be in serious jeopardy. We have all worked too hard for that."

Though still unwilling to voice her opinions, Jess pressed the issue a little, wanting to see how much information Rosalind was willing to divulge and whether it was something she could believe. "Have you spoken to Marcus about this?"

Rosalind shook her head sadly. "No. He values my opinion when it comes to some things, but he makes sure I know my place. To raise issues like these would be overstepping my boundaries, and that's not something I'm tempted to do."

"It's certainly a difficult situation," Jess said neutrally, not sure she could even believe Rosalind. For all she knew, she was just planting information.

"There are other things I wanted you to know about. I didn't want to tell you at first because I thought things were best dealt with internally. Marcus has reacted so badly to you, though, that I don't know anymore if he has what it takes to sort things out." Rosalind appeared in a genuine quandary, her allegiance to her boss warring with her loyalty to the company. "In the end, I realised that if problems aren't fixed, there will eventually be redundancies and I really don't want that to happen." She raised her gaze and searched Jess's face hopefully. "If I tell you these things, then you can make sure that doesn't happen?"

Jess nodded, cautious but intrigued. "I'll do what I can, but I can't make promises. Still, it's always much easier to solve a problem before it grows too big."

"Okay." Rosalind sighed with resignation. "I told you about Marcus and how he treats the staff. Sometimes he can be a little too friendly with some of the women, if you know what I mean." She looked at her companion, her serious expression adding weight to her words. "Not long ago one of his favourites left suddenly. It was odd because she was well liked but she didn't tell anyone. There was no leaving party or anything. We just came in one Monday morning and her desk had been emptied. I asked Marcus about her but he just said she had been offered an opportunity she couldn't turn down and he let her out of her notice period so that she wouldn't miss out. Who knows?" Rosalind shrugged. "Maybe that's all there was to it, but it just seemed rather odd to me."

"I think you're right," Jess looked at her, encouraging. "It does sound strange. Does Marcus have any favourites at the moment?"

"No. Not since Moira left. None that I know about, anyway." The music was the only sound for a few moments. "I also thought you should know that some people are exaggerating their expense claims. Again, it doesn't sound like much, but from what I hear, the claims are getting worse and eventually, I'm sure it'll start to make a difference. I heard about one the other day—I don't think it's appropriate for me to name the person, but they took the whole family to a race day. You know, one of those driving experience days?" She raised her eyebrows, questioning.

Jess nodded in comprehension and Rosalind continued, "I know those things are pretty pricey but they put it through on expenses as 'corporate entertaining'."

This was old news to Jess, since she had inspected the expense claims closely and had identified certain abusers. Even though Rosalind was confiding in her, she was not ready to reciprocate, still somewhat unsure of her confidant. "Interesting. Is Marcus aware of it?"

Rosalind shrugged. "I don't know. Not that he has mentioned to me anyway. I suppose it's all part of the bigger picture," she mused aloud. "Marcus squashes people down so they respond by taking unjustified sick leave and try and get as much out of the company while they can. I suppose I can understand it but don't they realise that they're only hurting themselves and their colleagues in the long run?"

Jess eyed Rosalind. Either her hostess was a fantastic actress or she genuinely cared about the company and its employees. Of course, it was always possible she was playing the game for her own purposes. Perhaps she wanted a stab at Marcus's job. Rosalind was certainly qualified. Whatever the answer, the bottom line remained. Jess just didn't know her well enough to make that call.

"Anyway," Rosalind spoke, breaking the silence. "I've told you what I needed to. I hope you don't think of me as a telltale, and that you can understand I have made my choice for the greater good?" Her tone lifted at the end, demonstrating a need for reassurance on the subject.

Jess obliged. "No, I don't think that at all. As you say, if the company suffers, then so will its staff. Hopefully, with your help, I can make sure that these things are brought to the attention of those who need to know before the problems become unmanageable."

Rosalind smiled, her relief obvious. "Thank you. It really means a lot to me to have your support." She hesitated, as if she wanted to say something more, then decided against it. "Now," she began, checking her watch. "I must attend to dinner for a few moments. I've gathered together all my information to date on PetZone. I thought you may want to familiarise yourself."

Jess accepted the proffered file, pleasantly surprised by the readiness with which Rosalind had volunteered the information. "This is great. Thank you."

With a gratified smile, Rosalind stood up. "Just call me if you need anything. I'll probably be fifteen minutes or so."

Jess nodded in confirmation, already beginning to read as Rosalind left the room.

Chapter
Fifteen

ROSALIND'S BACKGROUND REPORT on PetZone was comprehensive, even by Jess's high standards. It had been created with a combination of research that Rosalind herself had done independently and bolstered by information provided by the company itself. Given her present circumstances, Jess read through it quickly, but even with the cursory overview, she was reassured by the thorough briefing.

PetZone was a name she was already familiar with. Even without owning a pet, few people could be unaware of the multinational animal care giant. From the file, Jess learned that the company had been established a little over eight years ago and had built up to its current size through multiple acquisitions of smaller competitor chains. Although quite an aggressive tactic, the continually swelling number of outlets had given the organisation the opportunity to take the lion's share of the market. The company had floated its shares on the stock market the third year of its existence, using the funds generated to facilitate the largest of its acquisitions. Since then, it had proved a perennial favourite with investors, popular for its considerable dividend payouts.

The company touted itself as "all things pet care", complementing its vast product ranges of foodstuffs and accessories with in-store grooming and veterinary drop-in centres. Consumer reports had demonstrated increasing confidence in PetZone's credentials with regard to pet care and the company seemed to have recognised the opportunity this presented, so it then pursued a strategy of vertical integration. Two years ago PetZone purchased a pet food manufacturer and rebranded the product range as their own. Reinvesting a significant proportion of their profits into their new manufacturing arm, the company then did substantial research and development, with the aim of producing a premier range of pet foods.

Jess sat back, thinking. Perhaps it was working so hard to implement this new strategy, which had distracted PetZone. Whatever the reason, they had failed to recognise the severity of the threat provided by Al's Animals, a formerly insignificant competitor. Al's Animals had embraced a small minority of dissatisfied PetZone customers, winning their loyalty with high quality personal attention. Word spread and Al's expanded rapidly. The company marketed itself as committed to animals rather than profits, thus subtly questioning PetZone's priorities in the eyes of consumers. A rapid swing in fortune occurred and soon, Al's Animals had taken the majority market share from PetZone.

Forced to report performance consistently below historic results, PetZone lost the confidence of investors and suffered a corresponding drop in share price. Best efforts to date had failed to rectify the situation and unless profits could be improved dramatically in the next six months, the company would be forced to reduce dividends to its investors.

Such a step would only be taken as a last resort but could still prove fatal for PetZone. Recognising this, company officials had approached Image Conscious with the hope of revitalising their flagging name. The project with Image Conscious dovetailed with the imminent release of Delta, PetZone's much-anticipated premier pet food range. The new food, which PetZone claimed was scientifically enhanced to promote long and healthy lives for pets, was to form the cornerstone of the campaign, demonstrating once and for all PetZone's genuine commitment to animals.

"So, what do you think?" Rosalind reappeared in the living room and settled back into her spot on the sofa.

"Fascinating," Jess answered, enthusiastic. "It looks like it's going to be an interesting project."

Rosalind nodded her agreement. "I'm glad you think so. As you've no doubt realised, they are a particularly large client and this could be very important for us."

"Have you had clients this large before?" Jess set the file on the coffee table and glanced over at Rosalind.

"No. The closest was the toy manufacturer I told you about at dinner the other night. It may well be the positive outcome from that case that attracted PetZone's attention."

"If that's the reason, then you should be very proud."

Rosalind's smile confirmed she was, though she seemed too modest to pass much comment. "Thank you," she said simply. "The PetZone project certainly is a challenge I'm looking forward to." Checking her watch again, she stood. "If you would—it's time we move to the dining room for dinner." She motioned with her hand toward the doorway and Jess stood, forcing her eyes away from Rosalind's denim-clad backside. Instead, she gritted her teeth and tried to think about PetZone as she followed her hostess to the dining room.

BY HALF PAST ten, Rosalind and Jess had returned to the living room. Jess was pleasantly surprised at how easy it was to share an enjoyable meal and conversation with Rosalind. She'd been expecting a much more stressful event, given the last time they'd had dinner.

"Thank you, Rosalind. That really was delicious. I had no idea you were such a talented cook." As Jess settled back into the sumptuous leather, a sense of slow-burning excitement washed over her. Stealing a surreptitious glance at Rosalind, she decided the feeling could be attributed to her. Everything Jess found most attractive about Rosalind was present this evening. Not only her physical features, but her confidence, intelligence, and humour. Jess had long ago recognised confidence as one of the traits that she found most irresistible in a woman, possibly because of the contrast to her own insecurities.

"I'm glad you enjoyed it." Rosalind's smile held genuine warmth. "It's a hobby I enjoy, though I rarely get an opportunity to cook for someone else."

"You must have no shortage of offers." The comment had left Jess's mouth before she had time to censor it and she winced. *And things were going so well.*

Rosalind laughed and Jess relaxed. "The trouble is," Rosalind explained, half in humour, half in truth, "that to have dinner with someone means conversation. It's rare indeed that I find a meal companion whose interests complement mine and who values decent conversation in the same way I do. When I do discover such a person—" her gaze rested intently on Jess's face, "that's a valuable find indeed."

Jess's ears burned at the implied compliment. Her pulse was thumping through her body, responding to the underlying message Rosalind had supplied in her sultry voice. "Indeed," Jess echoed, simultaneously chiding herself for the inane comment.

Rosalind smiled again, her expression free of condescension. Retrieving the PetZone file from the nearby coffee table, she moved to sit on the sofa next to Jess. Opening the folder, Rosalind flipped through the pages until she came to several graphs. "Did you see these?" she asked, resting the file across both her own lap and Jess's.

The warm weight of Rosalind's body pressing against her own distracted Jess from the question even though she gazed diligently at the pages. Her companion appeared to be studying the page intently, her fingers tracing lines on the graph that corresponded with her words. Jess heard Rosalind's words, but they might as well have been in a foreign language. Jess had been lonely for too long, isolating herself from nearly everyone. Now, the object of her desire was pressed against her and her own body was rebelling, yearning to break down the barriers that Jess had purposefully erected between them. A war raged within her, her logical self fighting to concentrate on the work in front of her, utilising years of discipline in its favour, yet her long subdued dreamer refused to be silenced.

"Everything okay?" Rosalind looked into Jess's face, her expression one of concern.

Jess lifted her gaze to meet Rosalind's, knowing she was overdue to say something, expectation settling upon her. This was her moment. If she was ever going to take a chance, it was now. "Kiss me," she demanded before she could change her mind.

Rosalind didn't hesitate. She leaned in and their lips met tenderly. Reaching out, she caressed the side of Jess's face. Jess returned the kiss hesitantly at first, pushing back all the contradictory voices in her head that clamoured for her attention. This was about her and Rosalind and the purity of this moment. Rosalind must have sensed her hunger and dropped her hand to Jess's neck, pulling her deeper into the kiss.

Heat rose in Jess's torso as her body reacted to Rosalind. Every sense seemed heightened, and exquisite sensations washed over her, leaving her desperate for more. She placed her hand on Rosalind's midriff, and moved it quickly to the enticing curve of her breast when she encountered no opposition.

Rosalind's breathing was ragged now too, her own body responding to passion. Their kisses became forceful, even bruising as they sought to fulfil a need that escalated in intensity. Rosalind's hands moved over Jess's body, constantly in motion, as if trying to be everywhere at once.

Jess shifted position, affording Rosalind maximum contact.

Pulling back suddenly, Rosalind broke the kiss, "Jess," she gasped, her voice husky with desire. "We can't. Not like this."

Jess pulled back as if burnt and retreated to her corner of the sofa. Before she could formulate a defence and try to gather her composure, Rosalind spoke again.

"Don't distance yourself," she commanded, capturing Jess's chin with her hand and forcing Jess to make eye contact with her. She crossed the newly created space on the sofa and rested her body comfortingly against Jess's. "You misunderstand. I want you very much. I want *this* very much." She stroked Jess's face tenderly.

Jess wanted to melt into the touch, wanted to lose herself with Rosalind.

"I need you to take enough time to be sure," Rosalind continued, her tone gentle. "I don't want this to be a one night thing."

Nodding silently, awash with emotion, Jess grasped what Rosalind was saying. *She's not rejecting but protecting me.*

Rosalind must have seen comprehension in Jess's eyes and she smiled as she leant closer and kissed Jess again, sweetly and slowly as though they had all the time in the world.

Chapter
Sixteen

SUNDAY EVENING AND Jess was curled up in the familiar comfort of her own sofa. She had spent much of the day grinning despite the relatively mundane activity of going over the PetZone information. Her aim had been to familiarise herself with a lot of the details of the report that she had not had time to absorb the previous evening. The theory behind this plan was sound, but Jess's best efforts at sticking to it failed because she spent so much time gazing into space, daydreaming about Rosalind. She was caught in another memory of the night before when the telephone rang, interrupting her reverie.

"Hey, Jessie." Nick's greeting was as enthusiastic as always. "How'd it go last night?" He got straight to the point, his enthusiasm evident.

"Hey yourself." Jess smiled. "It was very...productive."

"Aw, come on," he cajoled, knowing she was teasing. "What happened?"

"We kissed again." Jess cut to the chase, unable to draw it out any longer. She had wanted to talk about it all day.

"About time, too. I take it you didn't freak out this time?"

"Very funny," Jess replied dryly. "Actually, I instigated it."

"Did you —" Nick paused, not sure of the most appropriate phrasing, "*you* know?" he finished, obviously embarrassed.

Jess almost laughed at his reticence, given some of the stories he had regaled her with in the past. "No, but things did get quite heated, in a good way." She grinned again. They were close, but some things she was not going to tell her brother.

"Fantastic!" Nick's voice betrayed his excitement. "So, come on, tell me more. This is like trying to draw blood from a stone! Did she wine you and dine you in her bijou residence?"

Jess laughed at his chiding but complied. "She's a great cook, she has a gorgeous house, and she said she thought we had something pretty special. I had wondered," Jess admitted, "if she was just trying to take advantage, you know, with the work dynamic and everything. Anyway, last night she stopped it going too fast, she said she wanted it to have more of a future."

"Not exactly the approach you take if you just want wham, bam, result." He mused with characteristic practicality.

"Yeah, and I certainly feel reassured about her intentions. I mean, she could have pushed it last night but she didn't. I really felt like she was genuinely wanting to do what's right." Jess fiddled with the hem of her pyjama top, rolling it absent-mindedly between her fingers as she spoke.

"So where do you go from here?"

"We have planned to do something together next weekend although we haven't decided what. I know, I know," Jess said in response to Nick's laugh. "I said I wouldn't get involved until the project is over. I suppose I just realised that life is too short, and you have to grab on when you find something good. You have to find the right balance between work and life." She paused, hearing the familiar content of her words. "You don't need to say 'I told you so, either'."

Nick laughed. "Would I? So, any ideas for your first proper date?"

"A few. I wanted to check some things on the Internet first. It'll be weird because we haven't really spoken socially, and we hardly know anything about each other. I don't know what sorts of things she likes doing in her free time or even if we'll have anything other than work to talk about."

"Don't start worrying, Jessie, I know what you're like. Just relax and have a good time. Everything will flow along okay."

"Oh, listen to my younger brother, the sage of dating! So who's *your* girlfriend at the moment, then?" She teased.

"As you well know, I am working to attract the attentions of Cute Girl." He adopted a tone of mock indignation.

"Don't you even know her name yet?" For all his bluster, her younger brother was surprisingly shy when it came to approaching women.

"Not yet," he admitted. "I thought it would be more impressive to introduce myself after I'm announced the champion of the tournament."

Jess recognised his bravado for the screen it was. Nick was putting off approaching the woman he was interested in. "Just make sure you don't miss out." The jibe was deliberate, as she enjoyed the opportunity to turn the tables on him. "Any luck with the job-hunting?"

"Nope, not yet." Nick already had a job at the local garage to pay his way but he had long wanted something more challenging.

"Have you been cracking jokes at interview again?" Jess chided, knowing he tended to resort to humour when he was nervous.

"What's wrong with a few jokes?" He sounded a little defensive.

Jess softened her tone. "They're probably just better for after you get the job. Let them see what a mechanical wizard you are before you unleash your sense of humour."

"Yeah, maybe." His tone was despondent.

"Well, if you want a fresh pair of eyes to look over your CV or anything, just let me know."

"Thanks. I might well take you up on that," he responded, sounding buoyed by her support. "Well, I think I'm going to get some extra training in before it gets too dark. Maybe we can get together for a practice session and some dinner later in the week?"

A panic seized her. The thought of possible physical intimacy with Rosalind had sent Jess's negative body image into overdrive. Subsequently, she had committed to a strict diet that didn't allow carbohydrates, meat, or dairy products, let alone the indulgent meals Nick tended to favour. "I've got a lot planned this week," she hedged, "so I'll have to take a rain check on that one." She tried to keep her voice as nonchalant as possible. "I'll definitely phone you mid-week though."

"Okay, Jessie," he replied simply, a note of sadness in his voice. "You have a good week."

"You, too." Jess hung up and flopped her head against the back of the sofa. She recognised the cloud that now shadowed her previously elated mood. She knew Nick didn't understand her need to control her weight, and she also knew that the subject usually upset him. She loved him more than anyone else in the world but he could not know what it was like to live with such self-hatred. Like it or not, she had to get her weight under control or she would never be able to have a relationship with Rosalind. Or anyone else, for that matter. With resignation, she retrieved the PetZone file and continued reading.

Chapter
Seventeen

ROSALIND HAD HER audience captivated. Men and women alike were mesmerised by her magnetism as she paced the meeting room with seemingly boundless energy. Jess had identified her almost constant movement as a method of control, because it focused the attention of the meeting attendees on her as a source of dynamism and interest. There was no mindless window gazing in Rosalind's meetings. She spoke confidently and articulately, utilising body language and reinforcing her points with gestures. The effect was a perfectly choreographed business performance.

Watching Rosalind work, Jess's professional ethics were in

serious jeopardy. Rosalind sported her usual tailored business suit but had shed the jacket seemingly in response to the heat. Her silk blouse emphasised her physique perfectly. Jess's imagination had taken her on a passionate tangent that had nothing to do with PetZone or corporate branding. The kisses they had shared three nights ago served only to fuel her imagination further. After many minutes of distraction, Jess forced her attention back to the matter at hand, realising she had failed to absorb anything that was being said. Since then, she had focussed on the other inhabitants of the room in an effort to concentrate.

Vernon Meyer was the strategic director of PetZone International and the assigned representative for the crucial Image Conscious project. He struck Jess as charismatic and shrewd and seemed to have a talent for obtaining information whilst offering minimal in return. His assistant had accompanied him to the meeting. She was organisation personified and Jess suspected that the plain, diminutive woman was key to facilitating Meyer's success. The two others, Andy and Lydia, were both Image Conscious employees, responsible for the specialist consumer research that Rosalind was now presenting. They were in attendance more to give Image Conscious the advantage of presence than out of necessity, as Rosalind had grilled them thoroughly on their findings in an earlier internal meeting.

Rosalind had insisted on issuing a disclaimer against the report given the absurdly brief timescale the Image Conscious team had been expected to work within. Andy, Lydia, and their colleagues had put in many hours of overtime over the last fortnight and Jess saw the strain in the lines on their faces. The results of the report supported the original research that Rosalind had conducted. Consumers viewed PetZone as a corporate giant, focussed more on investor relations than animal welfare. Most of the advantages the company was known for, such as its comprehensive product lines and low prices, were not enough to sway an increasing number of customers, particularly in the face of growing competition.

Meyer bristled at the critique, but the ease with which he was mollified suggested to Jess that he wasn't actually surprised. Rosalind had quickly refocussed his attention on the way forward with a line of questioning that was clearly designed to ascertain a greater understanding of the image the company desired.

"So you wish to keep the PetZone name but undergo an exercise on both sides of the Atlantic that will make it synonymous with compassion, respect, and knowledge regarding domestic animals?" Rosalind paraphrased Meyer's responses back to him to ensure clear communication.

"Yes," Meyer answered. "But it must be believable enough to reassure the public without unsettling investors. We're committed to maintaining our appeal as a sound investment opportunity."

"You do realise—" Rosalind paused, planted her hands on the table and eyed Meyer determinedly, "that people are increasingly aware consumers, armed as they are with the ready availability of information that has arisen from technological advancements? If they do not see sincerity in your new image, they'll leave you at an even greater rate than they currently are."

Jess studied the combatants with the relief of one not directly involved. Rosalind had certainly taken a gamble speaking brazenly to a man with an ego so large it was tangible. The resultant silence seemed to stretch unbearably for the bystanders though it was probably only a few seconds.

Meyer flicked his tongue across his top lip, his face showing irritation. "Come now, we all know the general public are easily influenced sheep, following the herd and transfixed by clever marketing."

Rosalind's gaze did not leave his face. "On the contrary, Mr. Meyer. They demonstrate increasing cognisance of the tools of the marketer and will recognise insincerity with startling precision." She illustrated her point by the examples of several well-known businesses that had met such a fate in the last five years. "We are here to help you in the long term, not to facilitate a more spectacular downfall than you are already experiencing. Or do you fail to see that PetZone's problems are also a result of a more savvy consumer?"

Unexpectedly, the PetZone director laughed. "I appreciate your candour, Ms. Brannigan. Perhaps there is some middle ground to our impasse?"

"Call me Rosalind." Her full charm permeated her words. "I assure you that we can develop an approach that will be equally appealing to both customer and investor, without lacking sincerity for either." Retaining the initiative she continued, "I can get our creative teams working on ideas this afternoon and we can meet again in say, two weeks to review the suggestions?" She raised an eyebrow, a gesture Jess knew Meyer wouldn't be able to resist. She was right.

"That will be fine," he said. "Please sort out the arrangements with my assistant at the end of the meeting. Oh, before we adjourn I must advise you that we are having minor difficulties with regard to the Delta food range we discussed at the previous meeting."

Jess looked over at him. Delta was supposed to be their enhanced "superfood" and it was set to be PetZone's flagship product. Rosalind had said that PetZone wanted Delta to form the cornerstone of their new image, demonstrating the company's intent to "put its money where its mouth is" when it came to dedication to pet health. And now here was Meyer, saying there were some problems with Delta. *This doesn't sound good.*

"We have yet to ascertain the full extent of the problem, but it appears we have some vocal, if unsubstantiated, opposition to the product. We're currently investigating the possibility of suing for slander but I wanted to take the opportunity to both inform you of it and reassure you that it's a temporary and minor problem." Though he seemed forthcoming, the expression on his face indicated that Meyer was unhappy volunteering such information.

"I understand," Rosalind said, her tone light. Jess suspected she had simply opted to play down the potential of the situation for the time being. "Let me know promptly should the difficulty escalate."

JESS RETURNED TO her office after the morning meeting and typed up some brief notes for her own reference. Though she was pursuing the client involvement approach, she continued her more traditional activities with regard to her assignment at the same time. This afternoon she intended to look for trends in employee turnover by department and see if she could glean anything by linking the results to manager appraisal records. Not the most exciting thing she could be doing, but then again, she never knew what an investigation might turn up.

Without realising, she had shifted her gaze from the papers on her desk to the redheaded beauty in the office opposite her. Rosalind was speaking on the telephone, leaning back in her chair and moving her free hand with animated gestures. Unexpectedly, she lifted her eyes and met Jess's gaze. A surge of embarrassment heated Jess's face because she knew she hadn't guarded her emotions.

Rosalind offered a sexy grin and held the eye contact long enough to be intimate. When she swung her chair around to concentrate on her telephone conversation, a lingering heat suffused Jess's body. There had been a few similar episodes so far this week, but much to Jess's relief, Rosalind had been consistently careful in her efforts to protect their privacy. Smiling, Jess forced her eyes and mind back to the personnel reports on her desk, though Rosalind was an infinitely more attractive distraction.

After a few minutes, a familiar knock breached the silence of her office. "Come in," Jess called, an unbidden but unavoidable sense of anticipation welling within her.

Rosalind closed the door behind her. She placed a steaming

mug on Jess's desk before she settled herself in her usual seat. "I thought you might like a coffee."

Jess grinned, feeling like a small child with a fantastic secret. "Thank you. I would, actually."

"Having a good week?" Rosalind said it innocently enough, but Jess heard an undercurrent of teasing in her voice and it sent a little spark down her spine.

"Not bad, though I have to admit that I'm looking forward to the weekend." Jess smirked playfully, something she would never have previously allowed herself to do during business hours.

Rosalind smiled in response. "How about a trip to the seaside? It's been too long since I felt the sand between my toes."

"Sounds great." An image of Rosalind in a bikini brought another flush to Jess's face. *Luckily, this is England so I don't have to worry about that. Mind you, Rosalind could probably make a duffle coat look sexy.* She cleared her throat and forced her mind back from its tangent.

"Good. Let's finalise the arrangements on Friday. So what did you think of the meeting this morning?" Rosalind changed the subject, seemingly keen for feedback given her independent nature.

"It was worthwhile." Jess switched to business mode as well. Even though it wasn't as exciting a subject as the weekend, work was still a topic that she felt more comfortable with. "Meyer accepted the consumer results more readily than I expected."

"I thought so, too." Rosalind nodded thoughtfully. "That always makes things easier. With some clients you have to waste valuable time persuading them that these are consumer opinions, not ours. Until they can accept that, we can't make any progress."

"Do you anticipate difficulties with the Delta situation?" Jess tapped the end of her pen against her lips. Something about the Delta problem wasn't sitting well with her.

"I'm not sure," Rosalind said. "He didn't strike me as the sort of person to volunteer information like that unnecessarily so there is a strong possibility that it's worse than he's willing to say. It's a crucial point, though, given the role he wants the brand to play in the company going forward. I'll see if I can find anything about it on the Internet. That would be the ideal medium for someone trying to transmit a negative message about a large corporation."

Jess nodded before taking a swig of her coffee. It occurred to her that Rosalind must have memorised her beverage preferences, a small attention that brought a smile to her face. "Do you think he understands the need for marketing sincerity or are you expecting that to be an ongoing difficulty?"

Rosalind's brow furrowed slightly. "If he doesn't change his thinking, it will certainly make our job a lot harder," she admitted.

"It's still possible, of course. Having said that, we are judged by long term results, and we would be at a considerable disadvantage if our client's subsequent actions undermine our work."

"Would you ever refuse to work with someone on such a basis?" Jess gently pried, wanting to draw out Rosalind's visit, but also wanting to know, out of general interest.

"It hasn't happened yet, but perhaps, if there seemed no other alternative." She shrugged, as if deciding not to think too far ahead on that path. "Would you like to spend some time next week looking at the internal idea generation process?" She rolled her eyes. "Oh, my, who needs wining and dining with an offer like that on the table?"

Jess laughed, enjoying the way Rosalind seemed to be opening up to her. The opportunity to study the company in action rather than from historic reports was a valuable one. Plus, she'd get to work closer with Rosalind. A benefit all around. "That would be excellent," she said in as professional a tone as she could muster. "Thank you."

"Of course. I'll copy you in on the arrangements. And now, I must get on, if you'll excuse me."

"Absolutely." Jess smiled and nodded. "Thank you again for the coffee."

Rosalind returned the smile. "Any time. Besides, the chance for some time alone with you makes it well worth it." The look she favoured Jess with as she departed proved a major distraction for the rest of the afternoon.

Chapter
Eighteen

SEAGULLS CRIED AS they circled overhead, buffeted by the strong ocean breeze. The summer had been temperate so far, gently caressing the English countryside rather than scorching it into submission. Consequently, the landscape retained its vibrant green hues of spring. The path on top of the cliff afforded both a grand vista of rolling countryside and of the seemingly unending ocean below. Walking hand in hand with Rosalind, Jess enjoyed a contentment that she had not known for a long time.

Having arrived at the relatively secluded beach they had selected, they had decided to take a walk along the cliff tops to invigorate themselves after being cooped up in the car. Though long, it had been a pleasant journey, and conversation had been easy. Their jobs were common ground but they frequently strayed into hobbies, holiday memories, and other random things as the conversation evolved.

"This was an excellent idea," Jess said enthusiastically. "Something about the sea is so invigorating. Perhaps because I so rarely see it."

"I'm always awed when I see the ocean. It helps to put things in perspective," Rosalind responded. "I can get too focused — on work, particularly — but then to come out here and feel so small. . .it makes me look at things in a different way."

Jess thought she detected a note of sadness in Rosalind's voice but she didn't yet know her well enough to question it. Instead, she said, "Perhaps it's a good thing not to live too close to it. Usually you stop really seeing the things that are around you all the time."

"Very true," Rosalind said with a smile at Jess. "When I lived in London I rarely did tourist things. In fact, I've probably seen more of the attractions in London since then than I did during the whole seven years I actually lived there."

Jess attempted in vain to tuck her windswept hair behind her ears as she navigated a narrower section of the path that demanded single file. The track rose steadily, twisting to a sharp left bend. It was slightly rocky, which led to a lull in conversation as they concentrated on their footing. At one point Jess swayed, a disturbingly frequent side effect of her intensive dieting. Gritting her teeth, she focused on each step, determined not to alarm Rosalind. The light-headedness passed as Jess cleared the corner and she was immediately distracted by what looked to be a derelict lookout post constructed of stone. It was set back a little from the path but there was a well-worn track in the heather from previous visitors.

"Look." Rosalind had seen it at the same time. "Let's go and investigate."

Jess led the way toward the deserted structure, placing her feet carefully so as not to twist an ankle in one of the multitude of rabbit burrows. As they got closer, she noted the inevitable graffiti markings with disappointment. It always reminded her of tomcats who were driven to mark their territory. *And they say humans are supposed to be the higher beings.* She looked back and watched Rosalind picking her way through the heather. A sudden sense of unreality overcame her, was she really out on a date with Rosalind? *Wow.*

Rosalind stepped forward and looked in the open doorway. "It looks like a hit with the kids." Her nose was wrinkled with distaste.

Jess peered in too. It was a small, circular building, the floor strewn with newspapers and empty bottles. Rough stone steps curved around to the level above. "Let's go up." She suggested, hoping the upper floor would be clearer.

Rosalind went first. "Fantastic view," she called back as she reached the top of the steps.

Just a few steps behind, Jess emerged back into the sunlight with relief. There was no roof to the upper floor but the walls were built up to about shoulder-height to provide some shelter from the wind. Rosalind was right. The view was fantastic. Jess let her thoughts wander, imagining the lonely lot it would have been for the scout posted here. She didn't know what era it originated from and she found herself pondering whether the inhabitant would have communicated by beacon or radio. Her daydream ran away with her as she visualised the surrounding countryside infiltrated by enemies, this small stone shelter the last bastion defending her home from invaders—two arms snaked around her waist from behind, and Jess jumped violently.

"Sorry," Rosalind apologised without breaking the embrace. "I didn't mean to startle you." Her words were low near Jess's ear.

Jess grinned sheepishly. "It's all right. I'd just let my imagination get out of hand." She leant back into Rosalind's arms, relishing the feel of their bodies pressed together in this lonely place.

"It's been so hard not to touch you at work," Rosalind said softly. "There have been so many times I've wanted to charge through to your office and pick up where we left off last weekend."

Flushing at the memory, Jess turned slightly so she could see Rosalind's face. "I was finding it pretty hard to concentrate in that PetZone meeting. Your business attire is quite distracting." A familiar heat returned at the memory of Rosalind's enticing silk-clad torso.

Rosalind read Jess's expression accurately and took full advantage by leaning in to kiss her. It was a sumptuously slow kiss, penetrating and arousing. Both women allowed their hands to wander, making delicious and long overdue contact with one another's bodies before voices from the path pulled their attention back to the real world. Stepping away from each other they took a moment to regain their composure before retracing their steps to the track.

"How about some lunch?" Rosalind suggested. "I saw a nice-looking pub on the promenade near where we parked the car."

"Sounds great." Jess wasn't keen to deviate from her diet, but she was definitely hungry and didn't want to be distracted by any more light-headedness.

Rosalind turned and held her hand out toward Jess. "Come on, then."

ONE OF THE best things about a British summer, Jess mused as she watched the scenery stream past the car window, is how late it is before it gets dark. They had been able to enjoy a long day at the beach with an afternoon of unhurried beachcombing and paddling after their leisurely lunch. It was early evening before they settled themselves into Rosalind's Mercedes for the drive home. Though the car seemed small inside, as often the case with sporty convertibles, it was surprisingly comfortable.

"Did you find anything out about that PetZone anti-Delta thing?" Jess asked, referring to Rosalind's intended Internet research.

"A little," she responded without taking her eyes from the road ahead. "The only pages I came across were by a Doctor Willoughby. The arguments against it look quite scientific, one of those things where it's impossible for anyone other than experts to form a meaningful conclusion."

"So it looks like just one person? That shouldn't be too much of a PR problem." Jess had been worried about scores of angry protestors chanting and waving banners outside the PetZone headquarters. "I wonder if there *is* anything wrong with the product?"

"The way it's written, Doctor Willoughby sounds like an ex-employee." Rosalind pulled out to overtake a lorry in the slow lane. "It could easily be a grudge or something, not related to the product itself," she speculated.

Jess giggled a little. "You've just reminded me. I was on an assignment a while ago and there was an awful smell in the offices. They had called out plumbers and even contracted in some industrial cleaners before they discovered a disgruntled leaver had shoved prawn sandwiches down the back of a radiator."

Rosalind laughed. "Oh, no, that must've been dreadful."

"Yes," Jess agreed, "I spent a lot of time working from my hotel room on that one." At the lull in conversation, she returned her gaze to the countryside outside the vehicle, pleasantly surprised to see they weren't far from Rosalind's house. She had driven over to Rosalind's that morning, as her own home was in the opposite direction from the beach they had settled on. Jess sighed. She would be pleased to see the end of the journey but she wasn't ready for their date to be over.

"Would you like to come in for a coffee?" Rosalind asked, her tone hopeful.

Jess looked at her, relieved. "Thank you, yes. That would be lovely." She was silent for the last few minutes of the journey, trying to remember when she had last enjoyed a date so much.

Rosalind turned into the familiar driveway and pulled up

behind the Lexus. "Come in and make yourself at home," she instructed with a smile. She stretched as she got out of the car then crunched across the gravel to open the front door. Dropping her keys into a dish near the front door, she moved toward the kitchen.

Jess followed her, interested to see more of her beautiful home. She stood in the doorway of the cavernous, well-equipped kitchen, gazing at the impressive-looking appliances. "Did you design the kitchen or was it already here?" She asked, curious.

"We had it remodelled." Rosalind confirmed as she made the drinks with practiced movements. "Sally was a chef with one of the local restaurants and we had batted around the idea that she would start her own catering business working from home."

The mention of Rosalind's ex seemed incongruous after their day together but Jess's curiosity increased. "What happened?"

"With Sally or the catering company?"

"Both."

"The catering company didn't work out," Rosalind explained, focused on the mugs. "The spikes in demand meant that sometimes she had to turn work down and other times she had nothing to do. We managed the cash flow but I think she just got frustrated." She poured boiling water into the two mugs and the pungent aroma of coffee filled the room. "Sally and I were together for six years. She was offered a job at one of the best restaurants in the country. It was an opportunity she didn't feel she could miss. I didn't want to move away from my life here so we agreed to live apart for a while. I don't think either of us intended it to be the end of our relationship, but that's how it worked out."

"Sorry." Jess commiserated automatically, unsure of the appropriate response. "Sometimes I guess these things just aren't meant to be." It sounded like the old cliché it was, so she decided to just stop talking.

"How about you?" Rosalind asked, handing a mug to Jess. She leant back against the counter and took a sip of coffee.

"Not much to say." Jess shrugged. "I had someone special when I was much younger. When I came out to my folks, they reacted pretty badly, and when I told my girlfriend about that, I think she panicked. She broke things off the same week and I never heard from her again. I guess it was just me that thought it was something special." Her voice betrayed the hurt she still carried even though it had happened years ago.

"Nobody of consequence since then?" Rosalind looked at Jess over the rim of her mug.

"Nope." Jess shook her head. "A few dalliances here and there, but I focussed on my career after that." She could trace each goal she had striven for since then that had led her to her current role.

The problem was, there always seemed to be another goal and the cycle continued. Increasingly, she found that despite her career success, she had a growing void in her life that often left her lonely.

Rosalind studied Jess thoughtfully. "Would you like to see the rest of the house?" she asked, perhaps in attempt to lighten the mood.

"Please," Jess said, relieved to change the subject but also intrigued to see more of the house.

Rosalind led them through multiple rooms, all styled and equipped to the high level of the kitchen and living room. The downstairs also contained the dining room they had eaten in previously, a conservatory that overlooked the large garden, and a decent-sized utility room. Upstairs there were four bedrooms, two of which had private bathrooms and two that used shared facilities. Rosalind used one of the smaller rooms as a gym and the other as a study. The second largest bedroom was apparently set aside for guests and Rosalind slept in the master room overlooking the garden.

It occurred to Jess with sudden clarity that she was in Rosalind's bedroom with her, a thought that brought a flush to her face and turned her ears pink.

"Are you uncomfortable?" Rosalind asked, apparently concerned.

"A little," she admitted.

"Would you like to go downstairs?"

"Not really." Jess's breathing was shallow with fear but she ignored it. Life outside work, she reminded herself. *Ignore the insecurities.*

Rosalind closed the distance between them, and took Jess's hands in hers. "May I kiss you?" Her voice held a husky edge.

Jess simply nodded. She knew where she wanted this to go, but she feared it. Rosalind meant something more than any of the brief romances over the last few years, and it had been so long since she had pursued intimacy with any emotional attachment that she worried she would freeze with panic.

Gently, for the second time that day, Rosalind leant in to kiss her. This time there were no interruptions and Jess sensed that Rosalind had every intention of letting things go as far as Jess wanted. She enjoyed Rosalind's enthusiastic response and the now familiar arousal that built quickly between them. A combined effort from them both resulted in a trail of discarded clothing leading to the oversized bed.

Jess groaned as their entwined, naked bodies slid against the cool sheets. Forcing all thoughts of body image, questioned intentions, and work complications from her mind, she surrendered to Rosalind and their mutual pleasure.

Chapter
Nineteen

"GOOD MORNING, ROSALIND, Vernon Meyer here."

Rosalind settled the telephone handset more comfortably against her ear. "Good morning." She returned the salutation. "I hope you're well?"

"Yes, thank you, though I do have some rather troubling news."

"I'm sorry to hear that. How can I help?" Looking up, Rosalind checked to ensure her office door was fully shut and she noticed Jess's blonde head bent intently over a spread of papers in the office opposite.

"Unfortunately," Vernon began, "the embarrassment I referred to regarding the Delta problem has escalated. It's only one person, an ex-employee, but she's well-respected and annoyingly persistent." Frustration was evident in his voice. "We had hoped it would be possible to ignore her but she's managed to get the attention of some influential people and it looks like we're going to face a hearing."

"What are the accusations based on?" Rosalind asked, though she had an overview from her earlier research.

"Doctor Willoughby holds a veterinary qualification but worked with us as a research scientist on the Delta product," he explained. "As I think you know, we have harnessed scientific advancements to make the product a pet superfood. It's comparable with a human meal that contains all the recommended vitamins, minerals, and chemical compounds that have been proven to increase health and well-being."

"So eating Delta everyday means the pet has an optimised diet." Rosalind knew all this. She just wanted to make sure she kept Vernon talking, to give her a chance to discern a solution during the course of their conversation.

"Exactly. The evidence demonstrates consistently higher levels of health in all domestic animals we've tested."

"So where exactly does Doctor Willoughby fit in? Is she pursuing a vendetta?"

"She has no reason to do so." Meyer's anger filtered through the line. "She chose to resign her post with us despite the fact that she had a long-term opportunity. The trouble came up because she did some unauthorised tests. She claimed the results demonstrated the presence of carcinogenic compounds in the product and even though animal health was boosted in the short term, it would be counterbalanced by a significant drop in life expectancy."

"Is that the basis of her current accusations?" Apprehension knotted in Rosalind's chest. *Damn.* If true, this critical flaw could undermine everything they were currently working on.

"In summary, yes." His response was clipped.

"How likely is it that the accusations are factually correct?" she pressed.

"I don't know. I'm a businessman, not a scientist." He paused and when he continued it was in a more reasonable tone. "My advisors say there is a chance it could be true, but the methodology she used to get these results was unproven, even radical. Experienced scientists using traditional methods cannot duplicate the results."

"Would you like us to reconsider our approach, and take Delta out of the equation?" Rosalind drummed her fingers on her desk, considering options.

"No. We've invested far too much in the Delta project to stop on the basis of some unsubstantiated scientific minutiae. On the slim chance that Willoughby is correct, we'll still take the product to market. We can use the income it generates to research the issue more thoroughly and rectify any problems that do exist before any long-term damage is done."

Rosalind furrowed her brow. *This* was certainly a questionable way forward. "What happens if things don't go well at the hearing?"

"Let *me* worry about the hearing." He was dismissive. "You carry on with the project as per the original terms we agreed. Just buff Delta extra brightly and don't let your staff become distracted by any negative rumours they may encounter. I look forward to reviewing your progress next week."

"I understand." Rosalind closed the call and replaced the telephone handset. She leant back in her chair and stared out of the window with unseeing eyes, her mind churning over the potential ramifications of this latest development.

ROSALIND KNOCKED ON Marcus's door and paused, eager for acknowledgement.

"Enter."

She let herself in and closed the door before she crossed the office toward him. "I'm glad you're free," she wasted no time with formalities. "The PetZone case has taken an interesting turn."

"Grab a seat and fill me in." Marcus put down his pen and graced her with his full attention.

Rosalind settled herself in the leather chair, crossing her legs at the knee. "I've just finished speaking with Vernon Meyer. It seems there's a problem with their flagship product."

"What sort of problem?"

"The pet food that is supposed to prolong life might actually shorten it." She looked at him triumphantly, watching his face for dawning realisation.

"So?" He seemed irritable. "Is the project under threat?"

Rosalind took a deep breath. "No—"

"Well, can't you deal with it? I have enough to do already."

A large part of her wanted to get up and walk out but Rosalind forced herself to stay. If she played this right then maybe she could start to think about a change of scenery. She smiled sweetly, "Actually, I see *potential* in this situation."

Marcus raised his eyebrows in realisation. After a short pause, he narrowed his eyes suspiciously. "How?"

Rosalind resisted the urge to roll her eyes. "Well, for one thing, Meyer just told me that even if it were true, they would still roll it out. Surely a sound bite like that would offer some valuable blackmail potential?"

A greedy expression appeared on Marcus's face. "Could you get him to repeat it?"

"Perhaps, but more importantly, he is a desperate man and principles don't seem to be too high on his agenda. I suspect if we play this right, we could get something bigger." She smiled with predatory satisfaction, knowing she had his full attention.

"Any particular angle?" Marcus asked.

Rosalind nodded. "There is a single voice of objection to the pet food. If they could find a way to silence that voice for a while then their work would be a lot easier."

"I see." Marcus grinned at her conspiratorially. "This could be exactly what we've been looking for." He paused, his eyes narrowing with suspicion. "Does Blondie know about this turn of events?"

"No. I was alone in my office when the call came through." She consciously adopted a more deferential manner now he had grasped the situation.

"Make sure it stays that way," he instructed tersely. "She is quite adept at asking awkward questions. Have you managed to get yourself in her confidence yet?"

Rosalind felt a twinge of shame though she hid it from Marcus's prying eyes. "Yes." This time there was no glory in her achievement, just a sense of sadness. Reminding herself that this was not the time for such thoughts, she moved the conversation on. "How would you like me to proceed?"

"What do you know about Meyer?" Marcus answered the

question with one of his own.

"He's talented and egotistical with an old-school mentality. I wouldn't trust him as far as I could throw him." She spoke bluntly, knowing Marcus expected her to.

Marcus grinned. "He strikes me as my sort of guy. Perhaps he would like to partake in a round of golf with me? Of course," he said, voice cocky and expression self-assured, "the best thing to do with that hearing is make sure it's a non-starter."

Rosalind stared at him, surprised he was so unaware he couldn't even tell she despised him. She had planted the seed of the plan but in his arrogance he assumed he had thought of it and was now dropping hints, attempting to tantalise her with his strategic brilliance. When they had first met his ambition and charm had blinded her. Looking back, she realised he had wanted to tame her, to posses her from the start but his romantic attentions had bolstered her ego at a time when Sally had been all but ignoring her. Though their affair had been short-lived, it had given him a hold over her and involved her in some of his shadier dealings. Somewhere along the line, a clean break had become impossible.

"Keep me posted on this, Rosalind." He grimaced. "This would be so much easier if that woman wasn't watching me so closely. Perhaps you should try and involve her. If she's implemented too, then she may be wise enough to keep her mouth shut."

As she left the office Rosalind promised herself that was one thing she wouldn't do. She had already lined Jess up for enough heartache. She wouldn't stand by and let her fall into the same trap she herself was in.

Chapter
Twenty

JESS ADJUSTED THE blinds in her office to ensure the room was as private as she could make it. After she returned to her desk she pushed her laptop well out of the way and replaced it with a simple pad of paper and a pen. Having a laptop on the table could be seen as a barrier and for these interviews she wanted to make the environment as conducive to information sharing as possible. She had tried some brief employee interviews earlier in this assignment, but had only received simplistic, stunted answers to her questions. Now, in the absence of other leads, she was ready to give it another chance. Hopefully, by now she was a more familiar sight around the office and because she had a better grasp of internal politics, she might have more success. A knock on the office door preempted any further rearranging of her desk.

"Come on in," Jess called.

"You wanted to see me?" A young man, probably in his early twenties, leaned into the room hesitantly.

"Hi, John," she said warmly, trying to encourage him. "I did. Please, come in and grab a seat."

He closed the door behind him and settled himself nervously into place opposite her.

"Is there some problem with my work?" He asked, concern evident in his voice.

Jess smiled at him. "No, not at all. This is a non-personal chat. I just wanted to have a talk to some people and find out how they feel about their jobs and the company in order to try and understand what we're doing right and how we could improve things. You're here because I did a random selection on the payroll and you were one of the ten people who came up. If you would rather not take part, though, that's your choice." She ended the last sentence questioningly, leaving the option to him.

John paused for a couple of moments, before shrugging. "No, I don't mind."

"Thank you. I really appreciate that." Jess smiled again, reassuring. "Now, I want you to know that I am writing a report based on all the information I gather from these conversations. Other people, including Image Conscious managers, will read that report but it will not be possible to trace comments back to the individuals who made them. I want you to feel free to tell me honestly what you think about any of the issues we discuss. My aim is simply to help make this company be the best it can be."

John nodded. "I understand."

"Okay, perhaps we could start with you telling me what you particularly like about your job." Jess's pen hovered above the paper. She would make notes about whatever was said even if she knew it to be irrelevant to her assignment. It was a technique she used to prevent interviewees from concerning themselves about what was or wasn't noteworthy.

He paused before responding. "I guess I like the creativity and learning from some people who have been in the business a long time."

"You work in one of the design teams don't you?" Jess queried, trying to maintain the flow of the conversation. "How do you get on with the other members of the group?"

John shrugged, obviously uncomfortable with the question. "Everyone gets on okay, I think."

She needed a different tack. "I saw in your records that you started as a trainee and you have been promoted quite recently. What was your training like?"

"It was good," he replied simply. "My mentor, Dave, was a great bloke." The young man's face animated suddenly as he reminisced about his colleague.

"I suppose the mentoring finished when you completed your traineeship?"

"Yes, but Dave had left before that. He said he couldn't stay any longer."

Now we're getting somewhere. "Why was that? Do you know?"

John evidently felt he had said too much already and resorted to shrugging once again.

The remainder of the interview continued in much the same way. Whenever Jess felt that she was making progress, stumbling upon the more contentious issues of life at Image Conscious, John seemed to hesitate and forestall any further discussion. After about half an hour it became evident that there was nothing more he could or would volunteer so Jess called an end to the meeting.

"Thank you, John. I appreciate your time and help." Jess smiled at him as he stood to leave.

"No problem." John smiled weakly back at her and then scurried out of the meeting room as quickly as possible.

Jess placed her head in her hands, resting for a bit. She studied the pages of pointless notes that marked all she had achieved in that last thirty minutes. By the time she had made herself a fresh cup of coffee and returned to her desk, she was beginning to question the wisdom of these extended interviews. However, before her negative thoughts could develop further, a knock sounded on her door.

"Come in," Jess called, unsure of whom her visitor would be.

"Hello, I'm Pauline." A middle-aged woman strode confidently into the room with an expectant look on her face. She had a no-nonsense demeanour and reminded Jess of a schoolmistress from her youth. "I'm here for the interview?"

Jess smiled and gestured to the chair. "Take a seat." Searching through her papers she concluded what she had already known. There was no Pauline on her list of randomly picked interviewees.

"You won't find my name on your list." Pauline commented shrewdly. "John mentioned what you were up to and I thought it was about time you had someone who wasn't afraid of offering an opinion or two."

"Well Pauline, you're very welcome and your help would be much appreciated."

"I think it's a good thing, what you're doing. I've been in this place for over twenty-five years and it has gone downhill fast in the last couple of years. I think we should all take on the responsibility and do our bit to get it back to something we can be proud of."

"What do you think has caused this change?" Jess asked, writing on her notepad.

"Well, the change in management of course," Pauline responded impatiently. "In the days when old Willis was in charge, you knew where you were. Now that the company is saddled with his son-in-law, it's going from bad to worse. I have a bad feeling about him you know. Something needs to be done." She looked at Jess expectantly.

Resisting the urge to smile at Pauline's forthrightness, Jess encouraged her to elaborate. "Can you be any more specific?"

Pauline settled more comfortably into her chair. "There's the staff, for one thing. We're losing good people because nobody wants to work here."

"Why not?"

"Bickering between managers, power struggles, impossible deadlines, understaffing...the list goes on. Then you have the fact that there have been no bonuses since Willis left and only minimal pay rises. There is nothing for anyone to strive for."

"I see." Jess jotted down notes as fast as she could. "What about customers? Do you think *they* have been affected by the change?"

Pauline studied her with intelligent grey eyes. "How could they not be? The more good people we lose, the lower the quality of service we can provide to clients. The people with initiative, creativity, and ambition are going to our competitors, leaving us with mediocre people and mediocre service."

"Why are *you* still here?" It was a direct question but one Jess had to ask of someone so cognisant of the problems.

Pauline appeared to consider the question. "Probably some misguided sense of loyalty to Willis. I have had about enough, though, and I'm this close to leaving." She held up her index finger and thumb about an inch apart. "I just heard about what you are doing and I thought it worth one last shot."

That made sense. "So if you were in charge, what would you do?"

A devilish grin spread across Pauline's face. "Get rid of Marcus and Rosalind, for a start."

Jess's stomach lurched at the unexpected mention of Rosalind's name. It was interesting and worrying that Pauline, who seemed to be so right on the other opinions she had stated, evidently thought so little of Rosalind. She pushed the thought away. There wasn't time to think about it now and it was probably only a case of jealousy, anyway.

"Then up the pay and training to attract and maintain some good people. Someone needs to figure out why we don't have repeat customers anymore. We used to have high levels of it and the industry is inclined toward it in general. It's a rarity for us now, so something isn't right somewhere. Then maybe try and get a really top-notch job done for a high-profile client. Something that will get us back in the game."

Jess completed her notes and smiled at her. "All very good points, which I will make sure I consider fully. Thank you for your candid opinions."

Pauline nodded and stood. "I suppose that is enough for you to be going on with. Come and ask if you need anything else. I really wouldn't bother with the young ones if I were you. John's a nice enough lad but you won't get much use out of him and the others —" she shook her head with disapproval. "They're too fond of the sounds of their own voices, if you ask me. More hot air than sense, I'm afraid."

Jess nodded, again trying to suppress a smile. "Thanks again," she said to Pauline as she left the office.

Chapter
Twenty-one

MARCUS STOOD WHEN he recognised Vernon Meyer as he entered the clubhouse. Since his conversation with Rosalind, Marcus had invested a generous amount of time performing background research into the PetZone strategic director, including familiarising himself with the subjects his quarry felt strongly about and information regarding his hobbies.

Marcus prided himself on how well he played the business social game. He attended all the functions that mattered and was on first-name terms with more than his fair share of commercial heavyweights. His networking had paid off when one mutual acquaintance had introduced him to Meyer at the latter's golf club. With the charm he was famed for, Marcus had quickly ingratiated himself with his client. After a command performance, the PetZone executive seemed only too happy to accept the invitation to join him for a round of golf at Marcus's club. In truth, Marcus hated golf but he took pains to make sure nobody knew that. Participating in the game was rather like holding a passport and he knew there were many successes he could attribute primarily to networking on the green.

"Mr. Meyer." Marcus stood and extended his right hand. "I'm so glad you could join me."

Meyer shook the proffered hand firmly and looked his host directly in the eye, his expression ambiguous. "I appreciate the invite. Nice weather for it, too."

"Absolutely." Marcus smiled widely. "Shall we?"

After a few minutes the pair were teeing off at the first hole. They had opted to forgo caddies, instead utilising a golf cart to transport their equipment around the extensive grounds.

"Nicely maintained course, this," Meyer complimented. "Do you play here often?" He stepped up to the tee and lined up his shot.

"Not as often as I would like," Marcus responded. "I do find it hard to get away from the office. You know how it is, I'm sure."

"Indeed." Meyer muttered the comment into his moustache.

By the fifth hole Meyer was well in the lead. Marcus bent over and placed his ball carefully on the tee. Straightening up, he squinted toward the hole centred in the green a little below and to the left of where he currently stood. His competitor's ball had landed well, not far from the flag, and he felt pressure mounting on him to prove a worthy opponent. He could feel Meyer's eyes on him, evaluating his posture and technique. With as much composure as he could muster, Marcus planted his feet, raised his club, and swung.

"Good shot," Meyer congratulated him, a note of surprise in his voice.

With anticipation, Marcus watched as the ball landed close to the flag and continued to roll congenially toward it. Then the ball disappeared from view and he knew the satisfaction of an ideally timed hole-in-one.

The two players crossed the distance to the green and inspected the state of play. Marcus retrieved his ball from the hole and politely held the flag for his opponent.

"So," Meyer began, pulling the putter from his bag, "what is it you wished to discuss with me?"

Although slightly taken aback by the direct question, Marcus maintained his external cool. "I'll be frank," he began, knowing it would be the approach his client would prefer. "I've heard about the opposition to your Delta product. I'm concerned about the damage that could do both to your business and one working explicitly to enhance your corporate image."

Meyer hit the ball successfully and noted his score on his card before he replied. "It is a justifiable concern, Mr. Gibson. However,

I am not accustomed to being questioned. You may have confidence that I have matters well in hand."

"Of course," Marcus said hastily. "I had no intention of questioning your ability to deal with this issue. I simply wanted to assure you of two things."

The PetZone representative remained silent but raised his eyebrows in query.

"Firstly, we as a company do not have any desire to get involved or question how organisations we may be linked with conduct their affairs. We have been employed to deal with corporate image as it exists in the pubic domain. We do not interfere or judge matters that are out of public awareness."

"I see," Meyer's response was noncommittal. "What was your second assurance?"

Marcus settled himself into the golf cart and transported them to the tee box for the next hole before answering. "I wanted you to know that we sympathise with your situation. We understand that such—" he paused, searching for the correct term, "shall we say 'cantankerous' difficulties, often require creative remedies." Marcus prolonged eye contact to emphasise the depth to his comment.

Meyer was silent for a time. When he did speak, his voice held a note of camaraderie that had been missing until now. "I suppose you have thought of at least one such creative measure?" His enquiry was issued with interest, laced with humour.

Taking a breath, Marcus mentally reassured himself. This was the risky bit. Long ago he had learnt that risk and reward went hand in hand in business. The greater the risk, the better the reward. He thrived on it, just as a different person would thrive on extreme sports. "Yes, I have." He committed himself with a confident smile. "If it were me, I would simply undermine the credibility of my accuser."

"Interesting." Meyer said slowly. The duo were going through the motions of the golf game but their full attention was on each other. "Scientific questionability, perhaps?"

Marcus shrugged. "Perhaps. A simple non-appearance would achieve the same result, and would probably be more cost efficient to boot."

"I like it." For the first time, Meyer seemed genuinely excited. "By the time it was all rescheduled, we could have the next line of defence in place."

"If it ever *was* rescheduled." Marcus grinned conspiratorially. "I believe we are ready to move on. Shall we?"

"Lead on, Gibson," Meyer replied, giving Marcus a slap on the back.

Chapter
Twenty-two

"I CAN'T BELIEVE how many stands there are," Rosalind exclaimed as they turned a corner and saw more stalls stretching out.

"I know," Jess agreed. "The first time I came here I was really surprised. I knew there were other people into re-enactment as a hobby but when you see it all put together like this," she said with a shrug, "it's impressive."

"How many of these festivals have you been to?" Rosalind asked as they began walking down another of the thoroughfares.

"This is my third. One thing that still amazes me is the attention to detail of it all. The costumes are obvious but it isn't just a surface thing. If you look closely you'll see that the stands and pavilions are held together with wooden pegs and dowel pins. Not a metal screw in sight." Jess looked around with admiration.

"They take it very seriously." Rosalind kept her face free of expression, leaving Jess to speculate on her true feelings.

Jess was nervous. It was two weeks since their beach date though they had spent some time together since. She had really wanted to share something more personal with her new lover. "They're good people." She couldn't keep the defensive note from her voice.

"Of course," Rosalind agreed with a smile. "What's that?" She asked, gesturing toward a crowd of visitors grouped together. They went to investigate and found an arrow-making demonstration taking place.

"Do you do this?" Rosalind asked, probably because Jess had told her a bit about her hobby in the car while en route to the show.

"Yes. I have made my own arrows, but I use modern tools." She smiled. "It's easier." She then watched with interest as the demonstrator utilised little more than a knife. "I use a fletching jig for attaching the feathers. It's a specially designed clamp that holds everything in place until the adhesive can set. It also keeps placement of the fletchings equidistant on the same shaft and constant across all the arrows that you make." Jess realised she had been preaching. *Uh oh, too nerdy.* She shrugged and attempted to lighten her tone. "It's intensive, but it's worth it when I come to shoot them and I know that I made them from scratch. It's a bit like a traditional art form with a point. If you'll excuse the pun." She grinned.

Rosalind rolled her eyes exaggeratedly before they moved

away to survey another stand. "So where is your brother going to be fighting?"

Jess looked at the programme. "There are several rings in the centre. Nick will be in one of them."

"Do you know when he's on?" She checked her watch.

"The tournament runs through the day but Nick said he was in the afternoon heats so he should be starting soon. Let's head in that direction. I'd hate to miss him." As always, Jess was a little worried about Nick competing but she knew how much he enjoyed it.

Rosalind looked at a dressmaker's stand as they passed. "Do you dress up?" She asked curiously. "I'd rather like to see you in one of those buxom wench outfits." She gave Jess a sultry smile.

Jess laughed and a blush heated her neck. "No. I've resisted the urge so far. I still can't decide which gender I prefer in terms of outfits. There are some really gorgeous dresses and they appeal to my girly side. You may have noticed that I don't wear dresses as a rule but sometimes it's fun to break your own mould. On the other hand, the men get swords and boots." She shrugged and grinned.

"Tough call. But I suspect you'd look good in either outfit."

"Well, I do have my own sword." Jess flicked a glance over at Rosalind, relieved that she seemed to be entering into the spirit of the fair.

"Really?" Rosalind asked, obviously surprised. "That's not something I would have imagined. It seems a little incongruous, given the professional side I've seen so far." She paused, apparently getting used to the idea. "Do you compete like Nick?"

"No," Jess said as she stopped at a brightly coloured tent and looked over the displays of daggers. "He tried to get me to at first but the matches are too real for my taste." She took her attention from the weaponry and looked around for a moment, "You see that helmet over there?" She pointed to an armoury stand that displayed a highly polished, domed metal helmet.

"Yes."

"They hit each other so hard they put great big dents in those."

"Doesn't anyone get hurt?" Rosalind's eyes widened in concern.

"Every now and then, but there are obviously lots of rules. Come on," Jess encouraged as she gently gripped Rosalind's arm, the sword tournament arena in sight. "Nick should be on soon."

As they approached the back of the crowd the repeated sound of metal striking metal reached Jess's ears. Finding an area relatively free of spectators, they settled down to watch.

"Is Nick fighting now?" Rosalind asked.

"Nope." Jess didn't recognise the armour of either combatant currently battling. As she waited for him to appear, she scanned the crowd for Cute Girl. Her search was brief and fruitless. "Blonde and gorgeous" wasn't a particularly helpful description from Nick and there were a few women in the crowd who, allowing for the vagaries of taste, could be considered to qualify.

The bouts didn't last long because the full medieval armour was extremely heavy, and just moving around in it was a tiring exercise. They had watched two more fights before Nick entered the arena.

"That's him, on the right," Jess said, excited.

"Excellent. Let's hope he does well."

The fight was similar to the previous two. The men began by circling each other, assessing each other's height, weight, and manoeuvrability. Nick was the first to strike, but his sword was readily deflected. He followed up swiftly with an arcing downward slice, forcing his opponent into an upward block. They both took a step back and circled again, this time each having a better idea of the strength and capability of the other.

Nick's opponent was the first to break the stalemate, and he launched a powerful series of blows that Jess knew would have left both men sweating. Nick deflected each, then stepped in on the last one, positioning himself in such a way that he could shove his opponent bodily backward. They paced the perimeter of the ring, sizing each other up. Nick took the initiative, moving as swiftly as his armour would allow, using his momentum to add power to his blow. The audience shouted their appreciation and encouragement as Nick's opponent stumbled. He quickly regained his footing, performing an impressive rising attack that drove Nick backward a little. Their next parry locked their sword hilts overhead and the opponents circled each other underneath. Nick twisted his blade free and landed a solid blow with his fist against his opponent's midriff. The referee, also dressed in traditional costume, ordered them back, giving each man time to regain his footing.

Jess leaned forward, caught up in the action. Both were tired. She saw it in their slowed movements, and she knew the end of the bout was close. Nick charged at his opponent again, sending him to his knees. This time Nick followed his blow with an armoured knee to the other man's side. He recovered and swung his blade in a wide arc that would have connected painfully with Nick's helmet had Nick not ducked. Taking advantage of his low position, Nick swung the flat of his own blade against the other man's knee, bringing him to the ground. As he levelled his blade at his opponent's throat the referee announced him the victor of the bout.

SEVERAL HOURS LATER, the tournament complete, Jess and Rosalind were celebrating with Nick in the nearby beer tent. Although he had not won the cup, Nick had earned his best placing yet and was justifiably proud of his achievement.

"So what did you think of it all?" Nick looked at Rosalind with an eager expression. He had barely stopped ogling since Jess had introduced her.

"Fantastic," Rosalind said with genuine enthusiasm. "I thought it would be full of old geeks." She grinned at the stereotype. "But there are young geeks, too."

Nick laughed at the jibe and amusement showed in his eyes as he met his sister's gaze.

Jess knew what he was thinking. His approval of Rosalind wasn't necessary but it was welcome nonetheless. "So, have you seen you-know-who?" she prodded.

"Yes, actually, she's over there." He nodded his head toward his left. "Don't look," he said in a low voice as both Jess and Rosalind simultaneously turned to stare.

"The one in the red top?" Jess asked.

Nick stole a quick glance. "No, the one to her right, in the stripy jumper."

Jess spotted the woman he meant and smiled. She looked a little younger than Nick and her face was animated in laughter. "Cute" was definitely an appropriate description for her.

"If you want something done. . ." she muttered, pushing her chair back to stand.

"Jessie," Nick said in a warning tone.

She ignored him and headed directly toward the subject of their conversation.

"Jessie. Jess!" Nick's theatrical whispers became more desperate.

Jess turned and put her finger to her lips to silence him. "Hi," she greeted Cute Girl with a friendly smile. "I think you're in the same archery club as my brother, Nick." She pointed back to their table.

The girl smiled with recognition. "Yes, we haven't spoken but I've seen him around. I saw him competing today too. He's pretty good."

Jess couldn't help but grin. "I'm sure he'd love to hear the praise direct. Would you like to join us?"

Cute Girl looked at her companions then nodded, "Sure, why not."

"Great. I'm Jess, by the way." She said as she led the way back to the table.

"Marie."

Jess gave her brother a pointed look as they approached. He seemed to get the hint and transformed his expression from worry to friendliness.

"Nick, this is Marie." Jess introduced, torn between pity and delight at the abject horror evident in his eyes. "She remembers you from the club but it seems you always run off so quickly that she's never had a chance to introduce herself." The temptation to embarrass her brother further was great but Jess let him off the hook.

"Hi," Nick said shyly, shifting his weight and looking like he'd like to crawl under the table.

"Hi," Marie smiled at him. "I saw you in the tournament. You did really well."

"Thanks." He grinned and relaxed a bit. "Wanna see my sword?"

Jess stifled a laugh and cleared her throat instead. She and Rosalind exchanged glances but both managed to keep straight faces.

"Sure," Marie agreed with another smile, evidently finding his bashfulness appealing.

"We'll, er, see you guys later?" Nick addressed both Rosalind and Jess as he prepared to leave the tent with Marie.

"Sure. Nice to meet you, Marie." Jess said warmly, hoping they'd hit it off.

"Take care," Rosalind said, amusement in her voice as Nick whisked Marie away even before the introductions were complete.

With a wave, Nick escorted his new charge from the table and headed in the direction of the tournament ring.

"They make a cute couple," Rosalind commented, her gaze on the retreating pair.

"Possibly the worst chat-up line in the history of the world, though," Jess replied dryly.

Rosalind glanced at her and burst into laughter. It was contagious, because Jess soon joined her in the mirth.

"Will you stay over tonight?" Rosalind asked after a few moments, and there was a hopeful undertone to her question.

"Sure," Jess agreed, taking Rosalind's hand in hers. "I'd like that." She looked back to check they hadn't left any belongings then followed Rosalind out of the marquee.

Chapter
Twenty-three

DESPITE THE FACT it was nearly eight o'clock on a Wednesday morning, Jess was lounging contentedly in Rosalind's bed. She had decided to work from home for the day and was celebrating her freedom by taking the opportunity to watch Rosalind perform her morning ablutions. Rosalind had just disappeared downstairs, promising to return soon with freshly brewed coffee to help them get the day started.

Shifting her position slightly, Jess rested her hand on her newly flattened midriff. Peering at it with interest, she noted that her rigorous diet was having a surprisingly rapid effect. She had managed to hide her unusual eating habits from Rosalind, despite the fact they had been spending an increasing amount of time together in the three weeks since the re-enactment festival. Rosalind loved to cook, so Jess tried to indulge in her creations as much as she felt comfortable doing. Sometimes she refused to let herself eat anything the following day, believing that such abstinence should even it out. There had been times when Jess considered taking more drastic measures after a meal but her sense of self-preservation had so far won the struggle.

Her reflective mood continued and she thought about work. It was hard to believe that she had been on the Image Conscious project for nearly two months. The time was coming for her to conclude the investigation and report her findings. Indeed, her ability to partially work from home was due to this change. Overall, she had mixed feelings about this assignment. It had been a catalyst for important changes in her life, both in her own mentality and through the introduction of Rosalind. Still, finishing the project did not mean the end of the relationship with her, and Jess looked forward to her finishing as a way to put them on more equal footing. An added bonus would be that she did not have to work with Marcus Gibson any longer, nor would she have to feel dragged down by the lethargy of his uninspired team. Despite all these positives, Jess was not ready to leave Image Conscious from a professional standpoint. The project felt unfinished without a clear-cut resolution to report.

She rolled over in bed, troubled by the assignment. Eight weeks of intensive digging had obtained disproportionately meagre results. The problems she had encountered early on that related to poorly motivated staff and a flippant mentality toward company expenditure had been repeatedly demonstrated. These points and the evidence supporting them would form the crux of the negatives in her report. Pauline's comment about fewer repeat customers had seemed a key issue and one that Jess had proven statistically. Frustratingly, she had been unable to find any explanation, let alone suggest a remedy.

Despite Rosalind's early warnings, Marcus had not made any improper advances to his female staff during Jess's subtle but lengthy surveillance. Although she didn't doubt Rosalind's testimony, issuing such unsubstantiated allegations against Marcus to his father-in-law wasn't an approach Jess wanted to take. Not for the first time, she wished she could continue working on the project longer, because she was convinced of Marcus's guilt and believed it was just a matter of time before she could prove it. Unfortunately, the fee for her placement prohibited her staying much longer so, frustrating as it was, she knew a line needed to be drawn.

Rosalind's return to the bedroom distracted Jess from all further thoughts of work. Instead, she admired Rosalind's body as she moved seductively across the room, enticingly encased in her silk robe. "Why don't you call in sick today?" Jess asked, letting her amorous thoughts show clearly on her face.

"Believe me, I'd like to," Rosalind replied as she set the coffee mugs on the bedside table next to her. She neatly evaded Jess's exploratory hands. "No, you don't," she chastised with a grin. "Some of us have to go out and earn an honest living!" Rosalind moved toward the bathroom and let her robe slide tantalisingly to the floor in preparation for a shower. She threw a self-satisfied smirk over her shoulder in the wake of her obvious taunt.

Jess groaned at the sight of Rosalind naked and smiled at the horseplay before taking a tentative sip from the steaming mug beside her. Before long she heard the shower start up and decided she must force herself into action. Although she only had to throw some clothes on, she needed to be ready to leave the house at the same time as Rosalind. Jess had taken to carrying a change of clothes in the boot of her car, as the decision to stay over was often a spontaneous one. Forcing herself out of the comfort of the bed she retrieved her overnight bag and began pulling garments out. She smiled slightly as she pulled her jeans on, noting that they now fitted much more loosely on her considerably reduced frame.

The shrill ring of the telephone interrupted her thoughts. She debated answering and glanced at the bathroom door. Rosalind probably couldn't hear it in the shower, and she was quite defensive of her privacy. Jess didn't want to upset her by answering. Torn with indecision, she glared at the handset, willing whomever it was to give up and ring off. Her quandary settled itself when the call diverted to the answerphone. Rosalind's voice sounded on the recorded greeting, slightly distorted through the electronic speakers.

"It's me," Marcus said when the greeting stopped. His voice was unmistakable. "Meyer called. The hearing's today. Get Perkins to Archie's Farm as soon as possible, usual precautions." The long bleep marked the end of the message.

Jess stood staring at the phone, struggling to make sense of the message and failing in the face of her emotional turmoil. Marcus's tone had been clandestine, and whatever he was up to it looked like Rosalind was in on it, too. Jess guessed it was Meyer from PetZone but the rest of the message meant nothing. She couldn't think of any genuine situation where Marcus would leave a message like that about a client. *Is this the secret that Marcus has been hiding*? If so, the stakes had been raised. This investigation had become personal as well as professional. Not only was she duty bound to pursue this unexpected lead, but she also needed to know what it was and to what extent Rosalind was involved. Jess looked from the phone to the bathroom door, uneasy. What would she do or say if Rosalind realised she had heard the message? Simultaneously she recognised the need to feign ignorance and saw her only plausible excuse in doing just that. Hastily grabbing her toiletry bag she made her way to the shower in the guest bathroom, peeling her recently donned clothing off en route.

"HEY," A CLEAN, fully clothed Jess re-entered the master bedroom some time later. "I hope you don't mind, but I really wanted a shower and I didn't want to hold you up."

Rosalind tried to keep her anxiety from showing. When she had emerged after her own shower, she had found the answerphone light flashing and heard the incriminating message from Marcus. From personal experience, she knew it was not possible to hear the phone from the shower but the question still remained as to whether Jess had left the room before or after the call. "Of course," she reassured Jess with a smile. "I've always told you to make yourself at home."

Jess towel-dried her damp hair. "I still say that we should save time by showering together in the morning." She eyed Rosalind, an impish grin crossing her face.

Relief washed over her. If Jess had heard the message, she would then know there was something going on and realise that she was involved just as deeply as Marcus. Jess would almost certainly feel confused and betrayed, but at this point, she demonstrated no such emotions. It was the reassuringly familiar Jess who Rosalind had always known, playful and amorous yet with an appealing hint of innocence. At that moment Rosalind decided she had played this game far too long. Over the last month she had found something she had never expected to with Jess and she wished with all her being to protect that. She would get this one last thing done and behind her then she would leave Image Conscious and start afresh somewhere else, with Jess. "You know as well as I do," she returned to the playful conversation, "that joint showers have many commendable features, but by no stretch of the imagination could 'time-saving' be considered one of them!"

They continued their banter as they hurried through their remaining tasks before parting company in driveway. "Have a good day," Jess said, leaning in to kiss Rosalind good bye.

Rosalind returned the kiss with feeling. "You too. Don't work too hard." She winked and started her car's engine.

They drove in convoy to the end of the drive where Rosalind turned right toward the Image Conscious offices and Jess turned left toward Chipping Bibury, her home village.

Chapter
Twenty-four

AS SOON AS she was sure she was neither being followed nor anywhere near a route Rosalind would use to get to work, Jess pulled into the nearest lay-by and cut power to the engine. It had taken a huge effort to act normally in front of her, to kiss her good bye without arousing any suspicion. It was clear that Rosalind had picked up the message after she finished in the bathroom and Jess had felt Rosalind's intense scrutiny raking over her.

She forced herself to take several deep breaths, and tried to calm her fractious mind. So many questions were whirling through her thoughts but before she could consider any one of them, another interrupted. She shut her eyes and allowed her head to fall back against the car seat as she tried to think logically.

There was no point in rushing ahead into 'what if' territory. What she needed were more facts so she could deal with the situation rationally. There would be time enough for dealing with whatever the situation proved itself to be later. The only information Jess had was that Perkins had to go to Archie's Farm. Who was Perkins and where was Archie's Farm? She took her handheld PC from her briefcase. Using her mobile phone to secure an Internet connection, she keyed the name "Archie's Farm" into her preferred search engine.

The page loaded tantalisingly slowly. It was a long shot, Jess admitted to herself ruefully, but the name was an unusual one and she really needed to find out what or where it was. She tapped the screen impatiently with the stylus, backtracking when the links led to a dead end. Eventually she struck lucky with a register of accredited vets. One entry listed Dr. G. Willoughby, Archie's Farm. Jess sat for a minute, thinking. She couldn't place the name, though it was one that felt familiar in a recent context. Jess noted the postcode the site detailed for the listing and entered it into her satnav. Within a few moments the screen displayed a route from her current position. Grateful for the opportunity for meaningful action, she restarted the engine and headed in the direction suggested.

It proved to be a lengthy journey that took the best part of two hours. Jess stopped briefly to fill the car with petrol and to get herself some food, as she was unsure of what the day ahead might bring. Giving in to her unease, she included copious amounts of chocolate in her purchases and had been snacking on it nervously as she drove. The journey had inevitably given her too much time to think and her paranoia was in overdrive. Her speculation about the rendezvous ranged from something as innocent as a long-awaited interview opportunity to something as sinister as the location for a drug delivery. She tried to subdue her overactive imagination, but invariably her thoughts returned to Rosalind.

Jess repeatedly reminded herself that she didn't know what this was all about, that Rosalind may not be implicated too badly, that it didn't necessarily mean her relationship was crumbling around her ears. The reassurances were hollow though, and Marcus's message had sown a big seed of doubt in her mind. Rosalind's behaviour afterward simply served to confirm her guilt. If the message had been innocent, why hadn't she mentioned it? Why had she suddenly started acting so nervously when she had been fine before the shower? Jess pushed away the thoughts of betrayal that loomed over her, forcing her attention toward anything that had the power to distract her for the remainder of the journey.

"YOU HAVE ARRIVED at your destination," the automated female voice of the satnav announced primly. "Route guidance will now cease."

Jess looked at the farm track. It was a long drive. She could just see the corner of the building at the other end. Isolated as it was, it would be difficult to approach it without being seen but on the other hand, approaching it by foot would look even more odd if she was spotted. A hand-painted sign for fresh eggs gave her a ready excuse and she opted for the more cautious but subtle approach. Parking her Lexus in a nearby track out of sight of the road, she switched her mobile to silent and slid the device into her pocket, then began her trek toward the farmhouse.

When she was considerably closer she paused and observed the house from the cover of some shrubbery. It was a beautiful old building constructed of rich red bricks. The glossy green paintwork on the doors and window frames looked recently done and, combined with the carefully tended flower borders, gave the impression that the property enjoyed the caring ministrations of its owners. Jess watched the house for some time but could discern no sign of activity, though that didn't necessarily mean the building was unoccupied. Keeping a wary eye on the house, she looked around the rest of the area more closely.

A collection of happily clucking chickens moved around a large yard, bordered by several outbuildings. From her vantage point, Jess could see into a few but others were closed up. From what she could tell, they mostly seemed to contain farming machinery although there was a car parked under the cover of one of the newer-looking structures.

As she was about to move closer, she heard the engine of a vehicle slowing on the nearby country road. She couldn't see it from her hiding place but she heard the car getting progressively closer so she knew it must have been approaching the house. Wondering whether this was the farmer returning home she decided to stay where she was until she knew more.

As soon as she saw the car, she decided it wasn't a farmer of any sort. For one thing, the vehicle was far too impractical to belong here. Clean and luxurious, it was definitely a city-dweller's car. Furthermore, it approached the building slowly as though the driver was unsure about where to go. Eventually, the car stopped not far from the mouth of the drive and the door opened, revealing a young, dark-haired man who was vaguely familiar to Jess.

She watched the man's movements, irritated by her inability to place him. Despite her best efforts at reasoning, today felt like a day when everyone else in the world knew something she didn't. As the man retrieved a large black object from the back seat of his car, Jess suddenly remembered who he was – a photographer in the press department of Image Conscious. The realisations were simultaneous: this must be Perkins.

He shut the doors of his car quietly and opted for a path that kept him close to the hedge as he approached the house. Evidently, whatever he was doing was not something he felt relaxed about. He paused to check for signs of activity before creeping to the nearest window of the house and peering in. He moved stealthily and without certainty, presumably not knowing what was on the other side of the glass. Whatever he saw, it wasn't what he was looking for because he rapidly moved on to the next set of windows. When these evidently proved fruitless as well, he proceeded around the corner of the house and looked in again. Suddenly, he recoiled from the glass as though burned, squatted down, and waited a few moments. There was no obvious reaction from inside the house and after a minute or two he stood up and looked cautiously in again. This time, he raised the camera to the glass, presumably taking photos although there was no flash to attract attention. It appeared that this completed his mission, as he returned hastily to his car and retraced his route away from the house.

Totally puzzled by his behaviour, Jess sought in vain for a rational explanation. The only conclusion she came to was that she would have to look through the window also if she wanted to know more. Perkins's prior approach had reassured her that there was no dog or other alarm system that would alert people to her presence. Nevertheless, she still decided to approach the building as surreptitiously as possible, remaining close to cover should she need to hide on short notice.

Her heart hammered in her chest as she approached the deserted yard. All her senses strained to identify any indication that her intrusion had been detected but all remained unnervingly calm. The chickens went about their business of scratching the ground. A few noticed her but apart from giving her a wide berth, they showed no other response. She hurried across the yard from her last patch of cover to a section of wall near her target window. Crouching down as Perkins had done, she paused to catch her breath and summon her courage.

Very slowly, Jess moved her face toward the window. Now that she was so close to the house, she could hear noises from inside the room, the majority of which sounded like an overly loud television. Dreading the shout that would signify she had been spotted, she moved close enough to allow her to see inside the room. Panic rose in her chest at what she saw.

A dark-haired woman was sitting on an upright chair side-on to the window. Each foot was tied to a leg of the chair and her hands were bound together behind her back. Some sort of cloth had been used to gag her though it was not possible to see her face properly because her head lolled against her chest. Standing near the woman was a large, rough-looking man. He had what looked like a large kitchen knife stashed in his belt and a beer bottle in his hand. Though he was on his feet, his attention was more focused on the sports game on the television than on her.

As Jess watched, the woman stirred slightly, raising her face to the man and squirming against her bonds. He looked at her with irritation, obviously annoyed to have his attention distracted from the sport. He shouted something at her and threatened her with the knife, smiling when her ready acquiescence proved her fear of him.

Jess pulled back from the window and returned to her squatting position. Though she had little idea of the reasons behind the scene, it was patently obvious that the woman was being held against her will. Even if she were a criminal it was wrong to treat her like that and Jess felt the need to do something. She quickly considered her options.

Obviously, she needed to get police support. What worried her was that the isolated location of the house would leave the woman vulnerable to her captor, who already seemed irritable, and was in the process of impairing his judgement with alcohol. In addition, he was armed with a knife. A plan forming in her mind, Jess moved quickly away from the house and back toward her car.

She dialled the emergency number from her mobile, notifying the authorities of the situation. As expected, they advised her to remain hidden until the police arrived — an instruction Jess had no intention of complying with. Back at her car, she manoeuvred it from the track to the drive of the farmhouse, where she proceeded to advance toward the building very slowly. The almost silent battery powered engine of the hybrid allowed her to get closer to the house than Perkins. If she needed to escape with the woman, the car would need to be as close as possible.

When she reached the top of the drive she cut the engine and prepared for the next stage of her plan. Trying not to think too much about the potential flaws in her idea, Jess retrieved her re-enactment sword from the back of the car and strapped it firmly to her hip. She then crept back toward the window to check on the status of the inhabitants.

Although she tried to be subtle, Jess didn't waste time in approaching the window. This time she had a much better idea of what the room contained, where the people were positioned, and the advantage the distracting television afforded. The woman seemed unchanged but the man was pacing and shouting at the television with agitation. Jess looked for the interior doors into the room and tried to assess the room's location within the context of the rest of the house. Once she felt she had plotted it in her mind, she crouched below the windows and made her way around the perimeter of the house to seek a way in.

She rounded the next corner of the building, and spotted the back door. Wrapping her fingers securely around the hilt of her sword, she pulled the blade silently from its scabbard and flexed her wrist, adjusting to the familiar weight. She tried the door handle carefully, relieved when it opened silently, admitting her into what looked like a utility area. Quickly taking in information about her surroundings, she moved through the house in search of her quarry. The noise from the television guided her toward another door, semi-ajar. Putting her eye to the gap, she peered into the room.

The man was close to her, but his attention was focussed on his hostage. She was struggling again and this time she continued even when he threatened her.

"I said, shut up," he shouted, anger evident in his aggressive posture.

The woman wriggled and swayed on her chair, emitting muffled noises that would have been shouts if it hadn't been for the gag.

He took two strides forward and backhanded her harshly across the side of the face. Jess flinched. "Shut up, or I'll do much worse." The tone in his voice and knife in his hand left little doubt that he would.

"No, you won't." Jess entered the room. A patch of sunlight streamed in from the nearby window, striking her blade to magnificent effect.

The man spun around, surprise on his features. "Who the hell are you?"

"It doesn't matter who I am." Jess said, conjuring all the bravado she could muster. "I just want the woman."

The man laughed, obviously considering the whole thing to be a big joke. "Yeah, well, why don't you come on over here and get her? The football was getting boring anyway." The gleeful look on his face made it clear he welcomed the diversion. Knife drawn, he started to move toward the newcomer.

"I wouldn't do that," Jess warned, not believing for a second that he would heed her advice.

"And how exactly are you going to stop me?"

Jess was surprisingly calm in the midst of this most bizarre situation. All her experience sparring with her brother came to her aid. She lunged forward quickly, seizing the initiative, and sent the knife flying from his hands.

"Bitch," he spat at her, shaking his stinging hand. His face flushed with rage and humiliation, but Jess didn't trust that the fight was out of him.

"Get over there," Jess motioned with her free hand to an area of the room away from both the woman and the fallen knife.

He paused for a moment but soon complied, evidently

deciding that her sword trumped his lack of a knife. He watched her through narrowed eyes, no doubt waiting for his chance to regain control.

Keeping a wary eye on him, Jess moved toward the bound woman, her sword in hand. She had been prepared to reassure the stranger but found her head once again lolling against her chest. Apparently the recent blow had knocked her unconscious and an unnerving trickle of blood ran down her face from her eyebrow. A sickening bout of worry clenched at Jess's chest but she pressed on, knowing she would be no help if she panicked. Grasping her sword, she attacked the bonds that tied the woman to the chair. The sword wasn't the optimum tool for cutting ropes but Jess didn't want to relinquish the weapon and the advantage it gave her.

The man appeared to be increasingly restless at the unexpected change in his fortunes. Jess tried to watch him but she had to work carefully to ensure she didn't injure the woman while trying to free her. As she struggled to cut the last section of rope, he made a desperate dive and retrieved his knife. He charged at her, swinging the knife viciously.

Jess saw the attack coming too late. She tried to twist out of the way but a searing stab of pain in her upper thigh confirmed the knife had found its mark. She pulled back into a defensive posture and tried to ignore the pain until the immediate threat had passed.

"Bitch!" The man shouted, running at her again.

This time Jess was ready. She parried the blow easily, an advantage her longer weapon ensured. She tried to ignore the blood she could see on the blade of his knife, knowing it was hers.

He regained his balance and struck again, this time jabbing the weapon toward her face.

Jess blocked the move and followed quickly with a blow of her own that set the knife once again sliding across the carpet.

Resorting to brute strength, he raised his fists and began to advance.

Anger replaced fear. Jess's leg hurt and she wanted this to all be over. "Back off," she said in an icy tone. "You know you can't win this."

He ignored her and rushed forward, preparing to strike.

Instincts forged from months of practice guided Jess's movements and she wielded her sword in a controlled arc. The impact of her sword connecting with his shoulder reverberated through her own body.

Screaming with pain and hatred, he clutched his shoulder and fell back, defeated.

Chapter
Twenty-five

THE MAN MUST have heard the approaching sirens at the same time as Jess. An expression of panic crossed his face and he gathered himself as if to run.

"Oh, no you don't!" Jess exclaimed, springing forward to block his exit. She raised her sword and eyed him menacingly, hoping that her expression would be enough of a deterrent.

Apparently it was and he sank down against the wall and resorted to glaring at her.

The sound of car doors slamming in the yard was quickly followed by the arrival of two uniformed police officers. Jess almost fainted with relief. Lowering her sword before they got the wrong idea, she addressed the first officer. "He's the bad guy," she nodded at the sullen man. "This woman needs medical attention." She paused. "Well, actually, we all do but I think she is most serious."

The first officer nodded at his colleague who proceeded to use her shoulder radio to call for an ambulance. In the meantime he approached the hostage. "Hello, can you hear me?"

The woman raised her head and looked at him. She seemed confused.

"It's all right, I'm a police officer. We're here to help." When she didn't respond he continued. "Can you follow my finger?" He held his finger up and moved it slowly across the range of her vision.

"Yes." She replied, her voice quiet.

"That's great. You just sit quietly. The ambulance will be here soon." He smiled at her soothingly before turning to Jess. "Can you tell me what happened?"

"I don't know much, I'm afraid," she admitted. "When I got here she was tied up and the man had a knife. He was holding her hostage. I don't know why."

"Are you a friend or relative?"

Jess shook her head. "No, I was just passing and saw the sign for eggs." She felt a little guilty at not mentioning Perkins but this seemed simpler for the time being. The main thing was to get the woman treated and the man secure.

He nodded at his colleague for her to check on the intruder. "How did these injuries occur?" He asked, his arm movement taking in all three of them.

"She was barely conscious when I got here. I saw him hit her in the face. We fought and he stabbed me with a knife. I tried to get him to back off but he kept coming. In the end I hit him with the sword." Jess suddenly realised how bad the whole thing looked. "I just wanted to protect her. He was drinking and threatened to really hurt her."

The sound of more sirens preempted further questions. The female officer went out and returned a few moments later with two paramedics. One of them went straight to the hostage while the other checked Jess and the man in turn.

After some brief discussion, the lead police officer separated them. As requested, Jess followed the female paramedic into the kitchen.

The paramedic looked at the large patch of blood on Jess's jeans where she had been stabbed. "I need to have a closer look at that wound. Can you drop your trousers?"

Jess avoided her eyes but complied. *I'm glad I've been dieting.*

"It's quite deep, I'm afraid. It'll need stitches. Have you had a tetanus shot recently?"

"Yes," Jess nodded.

"That's good. I'll just clean the area then sew you up. You'll be better in no time." She smiled reassuringly.

The policewoman knocked before putting her head around the kitchen door. "Is this a good moment to ask some questions?"

The paramedic looked up at Jess and gave her a nod, indicating the choice was hers.

"Sure," Jess replied, "I'd welcome any distraction at the moment." She gave a tight smile.

"Great." The policewoman pulled up a chair near Jess. "I gather you were just passing by?"

"Yes, but I'm afraid I don't know what any of this is about."

"It seems you're not the only one." The police officer smiled ruefully. "The lady is Doctor Grace Willoughby. She lives here. She doesn't know the man or what prompted the attack. The man is refusing to say anything at all."

"Is his shoulder okay?" Jess asked, dreading a negative answer.

The officer looked serious. "It needs stitches but it seems to be relatively minor considering the weapon. Where did the sword come from?"

"It's mine. One of my hobbies is re-enactment, I tend to carry it in the car."

"I see," the policewoman made a note in her pad. She refrained from further comment.

Jess tried not to look down at the stitching. "Is Doctor Willoughby going to be all right?"

The policewoman nodded. "The paramedic's worried about potential concussion. He wants her to go to hospital but when I came through she was still refusing."

"There you are," the paramedic interrupted, signalling the end of her work. "Now you need to keep the leg rested. Make an appointment to see your GP in ten days. They'll need to check whether the stitches are ready to come out. The more you can rest your leg the better the healing process will be. If you have any trouble in the meantime, call your doctor and get an appointment."

"Thank you," Jess said automatically.

"No problem." She began cleaning up her kit. "No more heroics for a while, okay?"

Jess grinned sheepishly.

"If you are finished here, I think you're free to go." The constable said with a smile. "We'll need a formal statement from you but you can do it tomorrow if that is easier? I can arrange for your local bobby to make a house call to save you going out on that leg."

Jess sighed with relief. "That would be good, thank you." The pain in her leg seemed to be getting worse and all she wanted was to go home and spend some quality time with her duvet.

The three women returned to the living room. Jess was pleased to see the man was handcuffed. When the police officers had taken contact details from both Jess and Doctor Willoughby, they escorted the man out of the house.

The male paramedic turned to Doctor Willoughby. "Remember, take it easy but no more than two hours sleep at a time. If you experience any dizziness or disorientation you'll need to go straight to the hospital whether you like it or not." He gave her a grin.

"Thank you," she said, watching as they left.

Jess felt suddenly awkward, like the last one at a party. "Well, I suppose I had better go, too," she said. She was physically and emotionally drained after her terrifying ordeal.

"Please don't." Grace responded quickly.

Jess looked at her, puzzled, but somehow relieved that this stranger would reach out to her in such a way. "Is there someone I can call for you? I can stay till they get here."

Grace shook her head and looked away.

Imagining what Grace must be feeling after the attack and recalling the advice of the paramedic, Jess blurted, "I don't live locally, but you're welcome to come and stay with me for a while." It was a strange suggestion, a part of her thought, but she was too drained to analyse, and for whatever reasons, it seemed like the right thing to do. "I know you don't know me at all, but at least you wouldn't be as isolated as you are out here." Jess was running on instinct now.

Grace smiled, obvious relief softening her features. "That is such a kind offer. Are you sure?"

"Yes." Jess smiled back, completely sure.

"Thank you, then. I would greatly appreciate a change of scenery." Her quick acceptance demonstrated the gratitude she felt. "I'm Grace, by the way, in case you didn't hear that while the police were here." Her comment was slightly redundant given the police procedure but it seemed somehow appropriate.

"Jess." She extended her hand and took Grace's, squeezing gently, and it didn't seem odd at all, inviting this stranger to her home. In fact, it seemed perfectly natural and reasonable. "Well, then. Shall we get some things together for you?"

THE JOURNEY TO Jess's cottage was quiet. Grace had slept most of the way, and Jess decided it was probably a natural reaction to the trauma she had experienced. She had kept a close eye on her companion, aware of the caution the paramedic had urged regarding delayed effects. However, she seemed peaceful and her breathing was steady, both of which Jess took to be reassuring signs.

Grace was still asleep when Jess manoeuvred the car carefully into her own driveway. She stopped and looked over at Grace, torn between not wanting to disturb her but knowing that she was due to wake her to check on her. She seized the opportunity to spend a few moments studying the sleeping form, since she hadn't had the chance during the rapidly unfolding events of the day. She estimated Grace was in her mid-thirties though the lack of animation on her sleeping face made it harder to tell. Her dark, chestnut hair was cut to about shoulder-length and held out of her face in a ponytail. Jess knew her to be a little shorter than herself from their earlier meeting, and Grace's body suggested a lithe athleticism. Her features were attractive though not in the traditional sense of beauty. Instead there was a more appealing friendliness, suggested by subtle features like the laughter lines around her eyes. Jess gazed at Grace's eyelids, wondering what colour her eyes were, when they suddenly opened. She started a little with surprise and embarrassment at having been caught staring.

"Hey," Grace greeted her sleepily. "Are we there?"

"Um...yes," Jess managed, transfixed at the answer to her silent question. Grace's eyes were a rich brown, reminiscent of chocolate, flecked with gold that seemed to spark in the evening sunlight. Her thick black lashes framed them perfectly. Jess knew she shouldn't stare, but she was unable to break the contact.

"Shall we go inside then?" Grace asked, ending the moment.

Jess pulled her attention back to the practical. "Not so fast. I need to quiz you first. I don't want you getting out and falling over." She grinned to keep the subject light.

Grace groaned. "Okay, fire away."

"Tell me the date and who's President."

Grace squinted as she thought for a moment. "Sixteenth of July and shouldn't you be asking who the Prime Minister is?"

"Good, excellent reasoning and recall." Jess nodded with mock seriousness. "Okay, let's go." Wincing as she got out of the car, she retrieved her visitor's bag from the back seat and limped toward the front door of the cottage. "Come in and make yourself at home. I'm sorry it's a bit of a mess. I wasn't expecting visitors." She smiled apologetically.

"It's wonderful," Grace complimented, looking around with interest.

Jess paused to look, too. She was pleased with the work she had done in the cottage. She had tried to make the most of the traditional features. She had started by opening up the inglenook fireplace and installing a wrought iron fire basket she had designed herself. Then she'd taken up the worn carpet and replaced it with sturdy grey flagstones, using colourful rugs to add some warmth. The collection of furniture was the result of many weekends scouring antique fairs. She smiled as she remembered how much Nick had grumbled about going with her.

The ceilings were low with beautifully aged, irregular wooden beams that had undoubtedly seen many lifetimes. She found the thought comforting and she often speculated on the momentous moments of human lives that the cottage had housed. She nodded lightly with satisfaction. "Thank you. I like it." Jess hobbled in the direction of the kitchen. "Would you like something to drink?"

Grace looked at her with evident concern. "No offence, but you look awful. Sit down," she commanded. "I'll get us settled. You need to rest for a while."

Jess was too tired to argue. Her leg hurt and the rest of her body felt like it had been through an assault course. Her mind was packed with worries and questions but she felt too overwhelmed to think about any of them. "Thank you." She let her head flop back against the chair and shut her eyes.

She could hear Grace opening and closing cupboards in the kitchen which was soon followed by the sound of china clinking. Evidently her unexpected houseguest was finding what she needed by trial and error. Consciously forcing her breathing to deepen, Jess encouraged her body to relax. It was such a relief to be back in the sanctuary of her own home after the physical and emotional turmoil of the day. Surprisingly, the noises from the kitchen were reassuringly homey rather than invasive.

"Here you are," Grace said as returned a few minutes later. "This will get you feeling better in no time."

Jess smiled at the comfort the first sip of hot chocolate provided. She would probably have gone for coffee herself but Grace was right. The chocolate was soothing rather than invigorating. "Thank you, Grace," she said again. Before she could say anything else, the telephone rang.

"Would you like me to get that?"

"No, thanks." Jess sighed, not wishing to talk to anyone just yet.

"Hi, darling, it's me." Rosalind's voice greeted the answerphone. "I just wanted to catch up and see how your day's been but I guess you're out. I'll try you again another time. Take care."

Belatedly, Jess wondered if she should have taken steps to avoid such a scenario but decided it was too late to worry. Rosalind had just inadvertently outed her to Grace. Jess glanced over at her, bracing for a reaction.

"Should you phone her back? Will she be worried?" Grace asked, her tone revealing nothing but concern.

A sense of relief settled over Jess, followed too quickly by the shadows raised by thoughts of Rosalind. *Well, at least Grace doesn't seem to have an issue with the whole gay thing.* "No. I—I'm actually not entirely sure where we stand at the moment." She stopped, kicking herself mentally for revealing so much to a woman who was basically a stranger in her house.

"I see." Grace responded, taking a sip of her drink. She said nothing further, and Jess silently thanked her for not pressing the awkward subject.

"I need to ask you something," Jess started, "about today." She wasn't sure if it was too soon to be talking about the harrowing events but she needed to find out if her suspicions were right and she needed to do so preferably before she gave her statement to the police the next day.

"I have questions for you, too." Grace said.

"I'm sure you do. So, you first. Fire away."

Grace shook her head. "You can't sit there in those jeans," she said. "If the material dries to the wound, you'll re-open it when you get undressed. Here—" she passed Jess the blanket from the back of the sofa, "take your jeans off and cover the rest of your legs with this. Make sure you leave the wound open to the air, though."

A flush of embarrassment coloured Jess's face. She appreciated the common sense, but was loathe to take her trousers off in front of her guest.

Grace seemed to read Jess's thoughts. "I'm a vet," she reassured. "Nothing I haven't seen already, albeit on animals."

Jess stared at her for a long moment then laughed. "Of course. The finest thoroughbred horses probably have cellulite and leg stubble, too."

Grace smiled then started laughing as well and the cosy living room filled with heartfelt, cathartic merriment.

Chapter
Twenty-six

WHEN JESS DROPPED her trousers it proved more of a distraction than either woman expected.

"Cute," Grace said with a smile when she saw Jess's boxer shorts. "Can't say I've ever seen a horse wearing *those*."

"They'll be all the rage at Ascot next year," Jess said sagely, drawing a giggle from Grace. Jess looked up at her, and Grace dropped her gaze, clearing her throat. She wouldn't meet Jess's eyes, and for reasons that weren't entirely clear, Jess flushed again.

"Yes, well...thanks." Jess turned her attention to the wound. The state of her own thigh was a shock. She had avoided looking at it when the paramedic had stitched it earlier, knowing she had to keep her composure until she reached the sanctuary of her own home. The stab mark itself was only about as long as her little finger but the skin surrounding it was red and swollen. A mixture of dried and fresh blood made the whole thing look even more grisly and the regimented black stitches seemed alien on such a familiar patch of skin.

"We need to clean that up," Grace said matter-of-factly. "Where do you keep your medical supplies?" She followed Jess's instructions and soon returned with cotton wool and a suitable antiseptic solution. Kneeling down next to Jess, she carefully began to clean away the blood.

Jess sucked her breath in and flinched involuntarily at the sting of the liquid as it made contact with her skin.

"Sorry," Grace apologised, looking up at her sympathetically before continuing her ministrations with dogged determination.

Jess watched Grace work, thinking that she would ordinarily

be embarrassed to have anyone paying such close attention to her thighs. Somehow, with Grace, it didn't seem so bad, perhaps because of the professionalism of her movements.

"There you go," Grace said, leaning back and looking critically at the wound. "Try to sit still for a while." She removed the items she had been using and cleaned up before returning to the sofa. "So, do you feel up to continuing our conversation?"

Jess arranged her position more comfortably and draped the blanket over her legs. "Actually, I do. Thanks for—" she motioned vaguely at the blanket.

"Absolutely. So. What was it you wanted to ask?"

Jess hesitated. A large part of her didn't want to know the answer to the questions even though she had little doubt that her suspicions were correct. "Was there something important you were supposed to be doing today?"

Grace looked surprised and then her expression changed to one of dawning realisation. "The hearing," she said slowly. "I had completely forgotten. Wait—how did you know?"

"One more question, did the man do anything or take anything?"

Grace shook her head. "No, it was odd. He just seemed to be waiting."

Her fears confirmed, Jess exhaled, an exhaustion overtaking her that was only partially related to the day's events. She knew it was time to tell her story. "My job is to investigate companies," she began, knowing she was about to breach confidentiality. "And my current assignment led me to you today. The company I'm investigating, Image Conscious, recently began a consultancy project with PetZone."

Grace's eyebrows rose but she didn't comment and Jess took her silence as encouragement to continue.

"I've known for some time that things with Image Conscious weren't adding up but I couldn't put my finger on it. Little things gave it away, issues that proved nothing in isolation, but that eventually combined to paint a clear picture."

She paused, knowing she had to talk about Rosalind and their relationship. "Soon after I started the placement, I—" she stopped again, searching for the right words. "I realised my growing attraction to Rosalind Brannigan, the senior employee who had been assigned to mentor me. I have a personal rule not to mix business with pleasure but this time, I broke it. I really thought Rosalind and I had something—" she paused again, not wanting to utter the cliché. "Anyway, evidently I was wrong." Jess tried to keep the bitterness and hurt from her voice, but she knew she wasn't successful. "Anyway, PetZone mentioned they had been having trouble with a campaigner and Rosalind did some research on the Internet. She told me that the only information she could find was by Dr. Willoughby. I might have made the connection sooner," Jess admitted, "but I wrongly assumed Dr. Willoughby to be a man.

"I thought nothing more about it until this morning, when I overheard a message on Rosalind's answerphone." Had it just been that morning that she had been lying in Rosalind's bed, blissfully unaware of the events that were about to unfold? "The message was from her boss, Marcus Gibson, a man I have long suspected of being at the heart of whatever trouble was happening at Image Conscious. Anyway, he instructed her to send someone to Archie's Farm today. I didn't know whom he meant but it was such an unusual message and his voice was so cagey that I was immediately suspicious. Knowing I couldn't let Rosalind realise I suspected something, I managed to convince her that I hadn't heard the message and we went our separate ways for the day."

Grace sat quietly, listening intently. She didn't offer comment and Jess forged ahead.

"I found out where Archie's Farm was and drove there on spec, hoping that I would find out what was going on. The Web site I used gave your name against the address but even though it was familiar, I didn't see the connection till later. Soon after I got there, a photographer from Image Conscious arrived and took photos of the room you were in from outside. I couldn't understand what he was doing so I just waited till he left then went to see for myself. Obviously, I saw you and that man inside the room." Jess looked up, relieved to see Grace still looked composed.

"I knew you needed help so I phoned the police. I didn't want to leave you with him any longer and luckily, I was able to help you." She allowed herself to gloss over most of this section, modesty preventing her from providing much detail. "I was in the house when he hit you, but I didn't realise that you were unconscious at first. I got him under control and untied you, then luckily the police turned up."

Jess paused for a few moments to order her thoughts. "I had a chance to think things through in the car on the way home. After you told the police your name, I realised you must be the same person as the one involved with PetZone. That told me what the link was between Image Conscious and the farmhouse. The photographs strongly suggest blackmail, but I don't know how any human being could see such a situation and walk away." The heat of anger raced across her face at the thought of Perkins's cowardly and selfish actions.

Jess spoke slowly, seeing the components of the puzzle in her mind. "Blackmail makes sense. That's how Gibson can afford a brand new Aston Martin on his mediocre salary. PetZone is Rosalind's client. She must have been feeding Marcus information. That's right," she was excited by a sudden realisation. "Willis said that ex-employee was a photographer. Blackmail would ruin a reputation. Maybe we can get him to open up now we know specifics." The pieces were coming together. With hindsight, Jess could see the whole thing.

Grace looked confused. "I'm having trouble following this. Who is blackmailing whom?"

"I don't know for sure," Jess warned, "but I suspect Gibson is blackmailing the company clients. He finds out something they wouldn't want publicised, collects evidence, then offers to keep quiet for a sum."

"But it wasn't him who took the photos, was it?"

Jess shook her head. "No, you can bet that Gibson is safe in his ivory tower, pulling strings and ensuring nothing can be traced back to him." *Rosalind must be one of the puppets.*

Grace nodded slowly. "Okay, but why would PetZone do this in the first place? I missed the hearing but they must know I'll arrange another one."

"True. Maybe they are trying to buy themselves time to disprove your claims?"

Grace's expression hardened. "That's despicable."

"Yes," Jess agreed.

After a meditative silence, Grace spoke again. "There are still some things I'm curious about."

Jess looked at her, waiting.

"I remember that thug hitting me and I remember being terrified. Things did get blurry after that but I had some relatively lucid moments. I saw you, fighting him with a sword. You defended me even when he injured you. I just had this feeling that I was safe, then I blacked out again. The next thing I knew, the police were in the room." She paused then continued. "How was I so lucky to have someone like you around just when I needed you?" It was a rhetorical question but one she apparently needed to voice. "Seriously, Jess, I don't know how to begin to thank you for your bravery today."

Jess shifted her position, deeply relieved. Grace hadn't said anything about Rosalind. Maybe she wouldn't judge her too harshly for that lapse. *I'll do enough of that for both of us.* Jess did wonder on the drive home if she could have prevented the attack completely by somehow uncovering the plot sooner. Guilt through association weighed on her and she had been unsure how Grace would feel about her once she knew the full story. Jess regretted trusting Rosalind, and she winced inwardly at the fact that she had been sleeping with her. At the same time, she knew that if it hadn't been for her lucky placement this morning, she wouldn't have known anything was happening. Grace may still have been under the control of her attacker and worse could have happened to her. "I'm just glad I could help," she answered eventually.

They were quiet for a few moments before Grace spoke, her tone thoughtful. "Jess?"

"Hmm?"

"Where did the sword come from?"

Jess grinned, considering how the scene must look from a stranger's perspective. "My brother and I both like archery and re-enactment. I still had the sword in my car from duelling him the other day."

Grace stared at her for a moment then smiled. "I always thought that was a pretty nerdy hobby," she admitted. "That'll teach me, huh?"

"I should hope so," Jess huffed, though she was teasing. "Otherwise it's the last time I come riding to your rescue."

"Are boxers part of the modern knight uniform?" Grace asked innocently.

Jess raised her eyebrows with surprise before fixing a serious expression on her face. "They are recommended in the handbook for ease of movement. There's quite a lot of lunging involved. Who knows, maybe the round table would still be going if they had worn boxers instead of those horse hair smalls."

Grace started laughing and a few seconds later, Jess joined her.

Chapter
Twenty-seven

"THANK YOU." P.C. Johnson accepted his cup of tea graciously and added sugar and milk from the tray Jess had provided. He and his colleague had arrived at Jess's home as arranged, mid-morning the day after the incident.

"I'm sorry we haven't given you much time to recover," he began, "but I wanted to get the details of your statements while they were fresh in your minds." He was brusque and burly but his mannerisms showed sensitivity to their recent ordeal. "I can tell you that the man we are holding in custody has been refreshingly forthcoming, although he seems to be a fairly ignorant hired hand.

It makes our jobs a lot easier and allows this process —" he gestured around the room in general, "to be slightly more informal."

Jess was aware of her position as host to the party though she knew that the men would wish to interview both herself and Grace. "Would you like me to leave while you talk to Dr. Willoughby?"

Johnson shook his head. "I don't think that's necessary, given the circumstances." Both he and his colleague had their notebooks out and were prepared to write. "Dr. Willoughby," Johnson started, "if I could just ask to you recount your statement with regard to yesterday's incident? I'll ask questions as we go."

Grace nodded then retold her version of the events of the previous day. Much of it she had volunteered yesterday informally but she covered it again as requested. In the tone of her voice and her body language, it was obvious that she still felt shaken by the experience and it would be quite some time before she would be able to put it behind her. The senior constable did what he could, offering her a referral to the police victim support unit where she would have access to specialist counselling. As her statement progressed both men asked her to clarify a few points and scribbled her answers rapidly in their notepads.

Tension radiated through Jess's body as she sat in silence, awaiting her turn, and thinking about what had happened. For the first time in her life, she had caused bodily harm to another human being, even though it was in self defence. The informal approach the police had adopted reassured her to some extent, but she knew she could face charges for her actions. The Rosalind element to this whole situation also worried her. Jess knew she couldn't avoid implicating Image Conscious or Rosalind when she gave her account of events, as much as she wished she could. Trying to keep her nerves under control, she listened as Grace completed her statement. *Such a lovely voice.* She mentally rolled her eyes at herself. *Jess, focus.*

"Thank you, Doctor," Johnson said, smiling reassuringly at her. "That completes the questions I wanted to ask you. P.C. Jones will type up a copy of the statement that I would ask you to check, sign, and return as soon as possible."

"Of course," Grace said, clearly relieved that her part of the interview was complete.

"Now, Ms. Maddocks." The senior officer shifted in his chair to face Jess. "Please, can we turn to your testimony? Again, if you would recount events as they occurred — we'll ask questions as necessary." He watched her with alert, intelligent eyes, his pen poised to take notes.

Jess repeated the lengthy story she had told Grace the previous day, trying to keep the account as dispassionate and rational as possible. The police had more questions for Jess than they had for Grace, which was logical given her unusual and complex involvement. They chastised her for disobeying police instructions and proceeding into the building alone, but Jess sensed it was a token complaint, the shining commendation Johnson subsequently gave her for her bravery seemed much more in earnest. Jess reiterated that she suspected PetZone as the ultimate intelligence behind the incident but that she couldn't prove it, explaining that it was somewhat circumstantial evidence based on the link between Dr. Willoughby and Image Conscious.

"It certainly sounds as though PetZone are the ones we need to be talking to next," Johnson confirmed, "although I'm not sure what, if any, case we have against the Image Conscious individuals. I suspect we may be limited to a rap across the knuckles for them as I doubt there will be anything actually criminal we can charge them with." He checked the details he had written down in his notebook. "I'll contact the relevant parties this afternoon," he said. "I'll also have a chat with our man in custody and see if the name PetZone rings any bells."

Jess nodded and tugged at the hem of her T-shirt, dreading the answer to her next question. "Where do I stand, since I'm the one who injured him?"

P.C. Johnson studied her as she gazed at him, nervously waiting for his response. "It's too early to say, Ms. Maddocks," he replied, his voice genuinely remorseful. "All those involved here have the utmost respect for the courage you have shown but the letter of the law must be adhered to. Much of it depends on the attacker and whether he wants to press charges against you."

"I see," Jess responded quietly. "When will I know?"

Grace forestalled the officer's response. "That's ridiculous," she exclaimed. "Jess is the heroine of the situation, not a criminal!"

"Believe me," Johnson said, sincere, "I fully agree with you and we are doing everything in our power to minimise the risk of charges being brought against Ms. Maddocks. However, we cannot be seen to ignore the law when it seems convenient for us to do so." His voice was grave but resolute. "I'll make sure we clear the matter up one way or another as soon as possible."

Jess sighed and glanced over at Grace. Clearly that was as much reassurance as the officer was going to provide, so Jess didn't pursue the topic any further and neither did Grace. Soon, satisfied that they had obtained all the information they needed for the time being, the police officers departed, leaving Jess and Grace alone once again.

GRACE REPLACED HER mobile on the side and went to locate Jess. She found her in the kitchen, loading the dishwasher. "Hey, great news!"

Still clutching a dirty saucepan, Jess turned around, her expression hopeful. "Yeah?"

Grace caught her breath. *Damn, she's cute.* "The new date for the hearing has been set for next Wednesday. It would normally take a couple of months but they had a cancellation." Grace grinned. "That should scupper PetZone's plans, don't you think?"

Jess returned the grin. "Absolutely. That's great news. Will you be ready in time? That's less than a week."

Grace nodded. "I was prepared before the attack. I'll go over my notes again but only to refresh myself."

The house phone rang, interrupting the conversation. Grace stepped out of the doorway but Jess made no move to answer. Instead they both stood in silence waiting for the inevitable message.

"Jess? It's me." Grace recognised Rosalind's voice from the first message. "I was surprised not to see you at the office today. I hope everything's okay. Give me a call when you get back in. I've been thinking about you a lot."

Grace studied her shoes for the duration of the message, feeling like some kind of voyeur. She looked up, sad to see the tension in Jess's body language. She wanted to offer her a hug but it seemed improper considering they barely knew each other. "Have you decided what you're going to do?" she asked instead, hoping that Jess would feel better if she talked it through.

Jess sighed and leant back against the counter. "Yeah. Things are over between us. I think I knew that as soon as I heard Marcus's voice on that message." She paused before continuing. "I'm not sure how to tell her. I guess I don't feel like I know her at all anymore. Who knows? Maybe she'll laugh that she had me fooled for so long." Jess retrieved the nearby tea towel and twisted it absently between her fingers.

"I doubt it," Grace said with conviction. "It would have to be someone pretty blind not to see how special you are." She looked at her companion with deliberate objectivity. Although they hadn't talked about ages, she guessed Jess to be mid to late twenties. She had a slight curl to her bobbed blond hair, a smattering of freckles and a slightly upturned nose that combined to give her an appealingly impish look. She was slightly taller than Grace with an attractively curvaceous body that she had found herself appreciating on more than one occasion over the last forty-eight hours.

More importantly than any of that, Jess had proved herself to be a true hero. She had acted with courage and honour in her actions to defend a stranger. She had been sensitive enough to recognise Grace's fear of remaining at the scene of the attack and generous enough to welcome her into her own home instead. Her sense of humour and slightly quirky outlook on life made her fun to be with even in difficult times but despite all this she seemed genuinely unaware of her own appeal. "I mean it," she reiterated, responding to the scepticism she saw on Jess's face. "If I were Rosalind I would be kicking myself that I made the choice I did."

Jess smiled though she still didn't look convinced. "Thank you."

"I know," Grace started, wanting to lighten the rather sombre atmosphere. "Let's change into our pyjamas and lounge about reading. I do love a good spell of self-indulgence every now and then."

Jess smiled. "It's a deal. I'm exhausted after having to check on you every two hours. I knew there was a reason I never wanted children."

"Not as exhausted as I am from having to answer trivia questions at all hours of the night." Grace batted the jibe back. Still, she could think of worse things than Jess waking her up in the night. *Preferably not to test her mental faculties.* "Come on, let's be decadent." She led the way out of the kitchen and headed for the stairs.

Chapter
Twenty-eight

"YOU STUPID BITCH." Marcus spat the words at Rosalind as soon as she entered his office. "What did you do, write it all out for her in a signed confession?" He was pacing around the room exuding an air of menace.

Stunned by the unexpected tirade, Rosalind marched toward him but continued to stand. "Be careful, Marcus. I'm getting pretty fed up with the way you speak to me these days, and insulting me for something I know nothing about won't improve the situation." Her voice was calm but icy. The brittleness of her own emotions lingered just below the surface and she wasn't sure she wanted to rein them in anymore.

"Maddocks," Marcus said with derision. "You told her everything, didn't you?" His face was flushed red. "The boys in blue paid me a visit this morning. They wanted to discuss PetZone and a kidnapping incident with me."

Rosalind sat down suddenly, shocked at his revelation and disconcerted by the subsequent unsteadiness of her legs. She tried in vain to see the link, knowing she had taken pains to protect Jess from all knowledge of the scheme. The only two people she had discussed the situation with were Marcus and Vernon Meyer.

"Don't play dumb," he accused. "The police reported that Maddocks had been there. She even saved Willoughby." He reported the last piece of news with theatrical drama, belittling Jess's endeavours.

"Jess was there?" Rosalind looked up at him, disbelieving. *How could that be? She saved her? Of course, Jess wouldn't just walk away.*

"They knew everything." Marcus continued, oblivious to Rosalind's confusion. "They knew about the photos, the blackmail, everything. I would've thought that *you* more than anyone would have known not to allow work confidences to slip in the bedroom."

Rosalind bridled at his smutty accusation. Her newly rekindled sense of self would not allow anyone, let alone someone like Marcus, to besmirch her relationship with Jess. Before she had a chance to retort, realisation dawned on her in a chain reaction. "It was you," she said, standing again and pointing her finger accusingly at his chest. "You left the message on my answerphone, which she must have heard." The implications sickened her. Jess had known. For days she had known, and that was why she hadn't been able to reach her. *Oh, Jess.*

"My message?" Marcus's voice was dangerously quiet. "What was she doing in your house at that time of the morning?"

"She slept over, which is exactly what you've been pushing me to do for weeks. The problem is, you're too stupid to think these things through." She unleashed the anger and resentment that had been building for months, and spoke with the contempt she truly felt for him.

Marcus glared at her with hatred. "On the contrary. I'm intelligent enough to have let myself into your house and deleted that message from your phone system. Personally, I would have said keeping the spare key in the same place you did years ago was stupid."

A wave of nausea coursed through her stomach at the thought of this man, whom she despised so thoroughly, letting himself into her home, her sanctuary. She resolved to have the locks changed at the earliest opportunity. "Bastard."

"Perhaps, but now there is nothing to link me with this whole thing. So, just like I told the police, I'll make my own internal investigations to find the real perpetrator." He looked at her like a predator might eye quarry.

"You *are* involved in this," Rosalind exclaimed. "Up to your neck. Do you think I'll just stand by while you sink everyone else around you to let yourself off the hook?"

"Oh, I'm sure you'll bleat to anyone who'll listen," Marcus responded with venom, "but the bottom line is, it's your word against mine. You were the one who instructed Perkins. Both his testimony and the mobile call registers will confirm that. You're the guilty one and it's only to be expected that someone like you would try to bring down innocent people if you thought it would improve your own situation."

Fear clenched in her chest. At no point had she trusted Marcus, but she had obviously overestimated his integrity. This was a level even she wouldn't have expected him to sink to.

"First things first," he said. "I'll do what any responsible manager would do upon discovering his employee had been pursuing such activities. Consider yourself sacked." He laughed at her shocked intake of breath. "I'll inform the police of my discovery this afternoon, so enjoy your freedom while you can," he taunted. "Now get out, I want your desk cleared and you off the premises within five minutes."

Reeling with shock, Rosalind walked to the door. She needed air and space away from him. She needed to talk to Jess.

"Oh, Rosalind?" He waited until she had her hand on the door handle before issuing his final blow. "You can warn your girlfriend that she's next."

ROSALIND DROVE HOME in a state of shock after her meeting with Marcus. Not sure what else to do, she engaged in a punishing workout in her home gym. The repetitive physical exertion was reassuring in its familiarity and as usual, allowed her brain to work on the issues troubling her.

Though she was intensely angry with Marcus and the injustice of the situation, she also had a sense of foreboding about her relationship with Jess. She had foolishly believed that Jess hadn't heard the message. Wishful thinking, Rosalind thought. With her new knowledge, it was pretty obvious that Jess was not inclined to speak to her but she wasn't sure if that was a short-term situation or not.

Bitterness roiled through her thoughts. That it should be now, when she had been on the cusp of reaching out for something that really mattered to her, that the ramifications of her actions should catch up with her. She really *had* meant to start afresh after this one last thing was done, but fate had not given her the opportunity to prove it. With her feet pounding stationary miles on the treadmill, Rosalind realised that Jess would probably never believe her now, anyway.

The loss of her job didn't bother her so much as the injustice of it all. In truth, she probably did deserve it but the point was that Marcus did, too. Ironically, she didn't mind a fall from grace if he took it with her. It wouldn't be too hard for her to find a new position. She was self-confident enough to know her looks would gain her entry to many businesses even if her intelligence were a secondary thought. Job-hunting could distract her later. In the meantime she increased the speed of the treadmill and turned her keen mind to bringing her former boss down to her new level.

Presumably, the police would call on her soon. She felt uneasy at the prospect but knew there was little they could accuse her of. Meyer had arranged for the hostage situation to take place so he was the true criminal behind the scenes. She knew Marcus had encouraged him but she had no doubt her former boss would've covered his tracks. The evidence against her suggested she was preparing to blackmail but without any threat being issued it was impossible to prove. Reporting Marcus to the police with so little evidence would probably mean he got away with little else than a warning. Sweating freely, she increased the speed of the treadmill, her heart pounding with the exertion. *I need something out of left field, something he won't see coming.* An expression of grim resolution set on her features. *I'm going to bring him down.*

THE SUNDAY SUMMER barbeque at the Willis mansion was a family tradition. It was the only point in the year when the large extended family could all be found together. Theodore and Elspeth Willis had six children and fourteen grandchildren so the event was always a lively affair with much laughter and tearful good byes.

Currently seated in his favourite garden chair, Theodore surveyed his residence and family with pride. His feelings soon changed when he recognised the familiar form of his least favourite son-in-law approaching him. "Marcus." His greeting was polite but it lacked any warmth.

"Theodore." Marcus returned the greeting with a similar tone before settling himself into the vacant chair next to his previous mentor. "Fine weather." He commented banally.

"What do you want?" Theodore asked, unwilling to bear further false niceties. Each knew of their deep-rooted dislike for one another and though there were times they were civil for the sake of family peace, today there was nobody else in earshot.

"Is that any way to greet a beloved family member?" Marcus's tone was sarcastic. "I wanted to talk to you about that little stunt you pulled at the offices." The smile was pasted to his face in case of onlookers but his voice held no humour.

"I did what I deemed necessary," Theodore replied calmly. He had expected this topic to arise.

"Did you not think of the good of the company?" Marcus asked in a low voice. "I know we have had our share of differences but I always believed in your dedication to the business."

"Of course I did, you fool." Theodore tried to keep his temper in check and remain civil. "That is why I had to do it. The company name is worth more than you realise."

"Oh, but I do realise," Marcus said with an undercurrent that might have been gleeful. "I just don't know how far the ramifications of your misguided actions will go. That little dyke did a lot of damage before she left."

Theodore gritted his teeth and kept his gaze focused on the activities around him rather than on Marcus. He wasn't sure what Marcus was trying to goad him with but by the confidence in his tone, it was something big.

Marcus continued, relentless. "Of course, she drove Rosalind away with her perverted overtures. It'll take the company a long time to recover from that loss. As you know, Rosalind was our most successful client manager." He paused, perhaps giving his words time to sink in before continuing. "Then there was her insistence that she liaise directly with the clients. From what I have heard, it was her advances toward the PetZone representative's assistant that lost us that case. All the work that had been put in by the team, and we're left with nothing to show for it."

Theodore clenched his jaw, sickened by the news Marcus seemed so delighted to share. He hoped there was some mistake but he knew his son-in-law too well. Marcus wouldn't have humiliated him like this without making sure of his facts first. "Of course, I always thought you abhorred that type of perversion. You can imagine my surprise when I realised what you had unleashed on us." Marcus shook his head with implied fatalism. "Well, I promised my little nieces a round of croquet and I would hate to keep them waiting. Thank you for such a lovely lunch."

JESS SPENT MONDAY working from home. She knew that after recent events she would not be returning to the Image Conscious office and she was grateful that she had not left any personal belongings there. Still, she would have liked to say good bye to Lucy in person.

Her final report for the assignment was proving difficult. The only certainties she could report were minor and she was loathe to add the more circumstantial issues. *By the way Willis, your son-in-law is a sexist, womanising blackmailer who is funding his pretentious lifestyle by threatening company clients. Evidence? Oh none, sorry, he's a slimy little sod who can wriggle out of anything.* She grinned at the mental image of Willis's reaction. *Yeah, maybe not.*

She turned away from her laptop screen and looked out the nearby window instead and thought of far more pleasant things. Like Grace, who had asked to stay with Jess until after the hearing was over.

Funny, that. It didn't strike Jess as odd at all, that Grace was practically living with her. They had both agreed it would be highly unlikely for any further incidents to occur at Archie's Farm, but Jess understood Grace's apprehension. In fact, she very much liked having her company at the cottage. Grace had been working as a locum vet, covering holidays and sickness for other similar professionals near her home. It was therefore quite easy for her to take a break and decline any more placements until she was ready to return to work, and she seemed to have turned her attention to repaying Jess's hospitality. The kitchen positively gleamed in testimony to the elbow grease Grace had invested in it. Today she was outside in the sunshine, kneeling down and weeding the flower borders. She had borrowed Jess's iPod and was wiggling her backside to the music.

Jess watched Grace for a while, unobserved, and wondered idly which song she was enjoying so much. Grace seemed to fit with Jess's home and routine surprisingly well. In real terms, it had only been a few days but they got on with natural ease. Grace seemed grateful for the change of scenery and it worked well for Jess too. Having some companionship had distracted her a little from thoughts of Rosalind.

Jess was honest enough to recognise her attraction to her house guest. Grace was intelligent and fun to be around. Jess smirked. *She's pretty sexy, too.* She knew Grace was single but the way she'd said it didn't make it clear whether she dated men or women. Probably a good thing, Jess decided. The last thing she needed was to ruin a budding friendship with some rebound crush. They had met in an unconventional way but she hoped the friendship could be long term. She was determined not to go back to her self-imposed isolation.

Ironically, the friendship developing between Grace and Jess was almost the polar opposite of Jess's relationship with Rosalind. Grace was easygoing and straightforward. She said what she thought and not what she believed her audience wanted to hear. Jess was able to really relax with her and as a result, they had spent much time chatting and laughing as though they had known each other for years. Rosalind was a totally different animal. Stunning and proud, ambitious but ruthless, sensual yet distant. Looking back on the time they'd spent together, Jess was hard-pressed to identify what, if anything, about her relationship with Rosalind had been real.

As though she sensed she was being watched, Grace looked up from her work and met Jess's gaze. She smiled broadly and waved an uprooted dandelion triumphantly at her host.

Jess grinned back, making a 'T' with her hands and raising her eyebrows questioningly. At the grateful nod Grace gave her, Jess pushed her laptop away with relief and trotted to the kitchen to put the kettle on.

Chapter
Twenty-nine

THE DAY OF the hearing arrived faster than Jess expected. Grace expressed grim satisfaction that the bruises on her face were still visible, a testament to the violence she had received at PetZone's instruction. Jess went to the hearing with Grace, both to offer moral support and because she was interested in the outcome. It started promptly at nine that morning in a room that struck Jess as surprisingly normal. Having little experience in such matters, Jess had expected it to be more like a scene from *Judge Judy*. Instead, there were three tables arranged in a horseshoe shape. The panel of three experts, headed by an adjudicator, were seated in a line along the top table. Grace was seated alone on the right hand table and two PetZone representatives occupied the left. A few rows of seats had been arranged at the back of the room for observers.

Jess's attention wandered during the initial stages of the meeting. Grace presented her findings with confident eloquence but the complexity of the subject made it almost completely incomprehensible to Jess. Instead, she admired Grace's passion about the subject and reflected on why she found professionally dressed women so irresistible.

Grace had collected the suit from home yesterday when Jess drove her back to Archie's Farm to get the documents she needed for the hearing. It was strange, Jess thought, returning to the farmhouse, but she was glad she had been there for Grace, who had been apprehensive about how she would feel. The reality of her panic surprised even her. Jess minimised the length of their stay as much as possible and she had protectively shadowed Grace around the building.

The trip was necessary, though, and had given Grace a chance to reassure herself that her neighbour was indeed looking after the chickens well. Jess helped Grace check the outbuildings, silently wondering what her long-term accommodation plans were, given the severity of her reaction, but she decided not to broach the subject, not wanting Grace to think she had outstayed her welcome.

Jess snapped back to the present just as Grace completed her presentation. The adjudicator thanked her and opened the forum to questions. Jess was unable to prevent herself from silently shaking her head at PetZone's approach. Presumably, Grace's arguments must have been scientifically sound, as the pet company representatives seemed to be basing their defence on discrediting their ex-employee.

"I do accept that I did not follow procedure," Grace responded to the latest allegation against her, "but I understood this hearing to be about the results of my experiments, not the correctness with which I pursued company regulations." A general murmur of support from the panel confirmed she had made a good point.

"Perhaps," the PetZone representative responded, "but you must admit that you knowingly countermanded instructions from senior staff when you indulged your scientific whims. Can the results gained by such an eccentric, undisciplined person really be relied upon?" His question was rhetorical, aimed at the panel of experts.

Grace maintained her smooth, professional veneer. "I did ignore the instructions, yes. However, those instructions were intended to prevent further investigation into the critical concerns that had arisen from my earlier research." She spoke with the confidence of a person who ultimately knows that what she did was morally right. "It was my understanding that my role at PetZone was to undertake scientific research in order to enhance an existing product. I believed it was the will of the company to infuse that product with any harmless component that would enhance the well-being of the animal ingesting it. Based on this remit, I believed that finding evidence of carcinogenic compounds was suitably serious to warrant immediate investigation. Had I known that my job was actually to improve the product's saleability rather than the pet's health, I would not have accepted the role."

"I have to agree with Dr. Willoughby," the adjudicator said, forestalling the imminent PetZone response. "This hearing is about the scientific validity of the findings she has presented and whether or not there is sufficient concern to ban the product until such time as any flaws have been proven to be rectified. Any dissatisfaction with Dr. Willoughby's performance while she was employed by the company is of no interest to this panel."

Jess suppressed a sudden urge to applaud. Smugly, she watched the reprimanded PetZone representative shuffle his papers, no doubt preparing to pursue an alternate approach. His next question dealt with a purely scientific query that related to Grace's methodology and once again, Jess's attention wandered away from the discussion. She instead occupied herself by monitoring the body language of those involved in the meeting and trying to ascertain the inclinations of the panel. They looked serious but she had no idea which side they leant toward. Her gaze shifted to Grace, and for some reason, she felt a fluttering in her stomach. She shifted in her seat and tried to watch the panel again, but again her eyes tracked back to Grace. *Wow, she's cute when she gets all feisty like that.* Jess stopped that train of thought before it started, and instead tried to focus on the questions.

After another thirty minutes or so, it became evident that the PetZone representatives were running out of questions. The members of the panel had also queried Grace on specific points where they wanted clarification, but overall, they generally seemed satisfied with her responses. The adjudicator called for the meeting to be adjourned as the panel discussed their decision.

"How are you holding up?" Jess asked Grace during the temporary reprieve. They had retreated to a corner to talk.

Grace smiled at her, tired. "Okay. I *am* glad the end is in sight," she admitted. "And some of the accusations of scientific impropriety were pretty hard to take."

"They were hard to hear, too," Jess reassured her, "to anyone who knows you." She squeezed Grace's arm. "Hang in there. You're nearly done."

Further conversation was interrupted as the panel filed back into the room, their verdict decided in what seemed record time. Jess and Grace quickly returned to their seats and awaited the results. Jess fidgeted, nervous, but Grace sat with quiet dignity. She was obviously better at hiding things like that, because Jess knew she was anxious, too.

"My colleagues and I have come to a unanimous agreement." The adjudicator spoke formally. "We agree that Dr. Willoughby's research is scientifically valid and nothing said by the defendant serves to disprove that. We therefore ban sale of the Delta or any related pet food until such time as evidence can be provided that the carcinogenic elements of the product have been fully removed. This concludes this hearing."

Grace turned to Jess and their gazes locked in shared triumph.

At the earliest opportunity, they escaped the oppressive meeting room and the glares of the PetZone representatives. It was not until they were in the privacy of Jess's car that Grace finally let her excitement show.

"I have been trying to achieve this outcome for so long! It feels unreal that I finally did it!" She bounced up and down on the car seat and beamed.

Jess grinned. "We should celebrate. Can I take you to dinner?"

"No way."

Jess looked at her, crestfallen.

"Oh, no," she said hastily. "I'm not refusing. Dinner would be great and it would be especially great with you, so *I'm* going to take *you*. I want to thank you for everything. I just can't imagine what the last week would have been like without you." Her voice was solemn with gratitude.

Dinner would be especially great with me? "Then I accept your kind invitation. Thank you." She laughed at her own mock formality.

"Would your brother like to join us, do you think? He sounds great fun, I'd like to meet him." Grace asked.

Jess smirked. "Nick is always happy to accept a free meal," she joked with affection. "I know he would love to come. He's still badgering me for a full account of what happened at your place." Jess stopped then. "Um, I mean—we can make that subject off limits," she back-pedalled, silently reprimanding herself for her insensitivity. "I don't want to dredge up bad memories, after all."

"Don't worry." Grace placed her hand on Jess's leg reassuringly. "You won't make me feel bad. The other day was a pretty big thing for both of us and talking about it will probably help us—especially me—come to terms with it. I know you're still worried about whether there'll be any fallout from your self defence, but I honestly think no news is good news." She smiled confidently. "Do you think Nick'll bring his new girlfriend and even up numbers?" She asked brightly, moving the conversation on from the heavier topics.

Jess tried to ignore the pleasant warmth and weight of Grace's hand resting on her leg. "Marie? Well, I could certainly ask him. To be honest, I haven't spoken to him much since they got together. I suppose it's the honeymoon effect kicking in." She grinned at the memory of her brother's reaction when she had approached Marie at the re-enactment fair. "I think he really likes her," she said indulgently. "Hopefully, this time things will work out okay for him. He needs the love of a good woman," she said, her phrasing deliberately corny but the sentiment true. "He usually scares himself with the thought of commitment and runs away instead."

Grace laughed. "Perhaps I'm stereotyping, but I thought that was quite a common male trait."

"True," Jess admitted. "But they always seem to succumb eventually. I just hope Nick gets on with it. Otherwise we'll find ourselves in our seventies, a bachelor and his spinster sister, and he'll still expect me to cook him a Sunday roast!"

"Never," she said in disagreement. "I'll stick around and then we can be a bachelor and *two* spinsters."

Jess reached down and gave Grace's hand a squeeze, "I'd like that." Her response was spontaneous, and it surprised her with its authenticity. Nervously, she looked across to check Grace's reaction but she needn't have worried, because Grace was smiling warmly at her.

Chapter
Thirty

JESS STRUCK THE match then cupped it with her hand, holding the flame to the wick of the first candle. When it had taken hold, she shook the match out and put it on the hearth to cool. She used the first candle to light the remaining three then dotted them around the dining room for ambiance. I'm glad we're eating here, she thought, looking forward to a fun, informal meal. Nick had accepted the invitation although he said Marie wouldn't be able to make it. *Perhaps I can find out what that's all about tonight.* Still, Jess was looking forward to the chance to introduce Grace to him.

A light-hearted meal with Nick and Grace was just what she needed. When they had got back from the hearing she found the answerphone message from her boss. She was due to submit her final report but still, his request for an immediate meeting was unusual. She normally enjoyed autonomy in her role as Lewknor had enough confidence to give her free rein. The unexpected message was odd and had left her feeling rather apprehensive.

The chime of the doorbell was quickly followed by Grace's shout from the kitchen. "Are you there?"

"Yes," Jess called back, positioning the last of the candles. Returning the box of matches to their home on the mantelpiece, she then opened the front door.

"Hey, Jessie," Nick beamed at her before enveloping her in a bear hug. "Thanks for the invite. I feel like I haven't seen you properly in too long." He stepped back and eyed her with concern.

"Are you eating properly?" He asked, his voice tinged with worry.

Jess tried not to be irritated at his intrusion. "Of course," she replied dismissively. "It's Grace you need to thank for the invitation. It was her idea."

Nick dropped the subject, probably for the sake of peace. "Lead on, then. I can't wait to meet your new lady friend."

Jess turned on her heel and glared at him. "Nick, you can't say things like that. We're just friends, I told you. And I'm pretty sure she's straight and I don't want her to freak out."

"Okay, okay." He made a calming motion with his hands. "I thought she knew about you?"

"She does," Jess said, "but there's a big difference between sharing a house with someone who happens to be gay and a great big predatory lesbian."

Nick laughed and lightly pinched her cheek. "Aw, Jessie, you're about as predatory as Mary Poppins. Now come on and introduce me," he demanded, still grinning as he followed Jess to the kitchen.

Grace was bustling about the kitchen with evident enjoyment in spite of her vaguely dishevelled appearance. "Hello," she said as they entered the room. "Gosh, you can tell you two are siblings," she laughed, looking between the two of them. "I'm pleased to meet you Nick, Jess talks about you a lot."

"Hi, Grace." He planted a polite kiss on her cheek, surprising both her and Jess with his audacity.

"Let's go pick some wine," Jess suggested quickly, trying to usher him out of the kitchen. She managed to get him to turn but not before he gave Jess a beaming smile and two thumbs up. "Nick!" She exclaimed with exasperation before shoving him bodily through the doorway. A giggle from behind made her turn. Grace had her back to them stirring a saucepan but her shoulders were shaking.

"GRACE THIS IS fantastic. Thank you." Jess voiced her appreciation at the meal. They were sitting around the aged oak dining table, enjoying their food in the ambiance that Jess had worked to create. At first she had worried that lighting candles would give an inappropriately romantic feel to the meal but then she decided that lighting several and placing them in the various nooks and crannies of the room set an acceptable and relaxing tone.

"Mmm," Nick agreed, waving his fork in the air appreciatively.

Grace smiled, "I enjoyed cooking it. I've never had a range myself but I'm an Aga convertee."

"So come on," Nick began, "tell me all about the dramatic rescue." He looked between them expectantly.

Jess checked Grace's expression, reassured to see she looked relaxed. She proceeded to tell the story, glossing over her own actions as much as possible.

"I'll bet you're glad you had all those practice sessions with me." He stabbed the air with his fork in a mock display of swordsmanship.

Jess smiled and rolled her eyes at him. "Good thing I had something larger than a fork."

He stuck his tongue out at her and Grace laughed.

"I never expected to need to use them in earnest, but it gave me confidence, that those skills felt so familiar."

"Pretty gutsy," Nick said. "Quite a difference from the mild-mannered pen-pusher you pretend to be!" He teased her affectionately. He paused then asked in semi-seriousness, "But you would tell me if you were, say, Catwoman or something, wouldn't you?"

Jess almost choked on her food at the outlandish suggestion. "No, that's Grace." She kept her voice serious. "I'm Wonder Woman." She held a straight face as long as she could then burst out laughing as Nick's gaze whipped to Grace's face despite himself.

"I'd love to see you two give a demonstration sometime," Grace said, getting Nick off the hook. "I wasn't really in a fit state to see much but I find myself fascinated."

"Sure." Nick readily agreed.

"Okay," Jess agreed as well, though hesitantly. She had already noted her own reservations about picking up the sword again and knew that the best thing would be to just get on with it.

"So how do you like the Cotswolds, Grace?" Nick asked as he lifted another forkful of his meal.

"Stunning. I can see why so many people rave about it. I'm a country girl at heart and the space and the views are just fantastic."

Jess smiled at Grace's enthusiasm, reflecting on how nice it was that they appreciated the same things. She glanced down at her plate then back at Grace, and for a moment, Jess was struck again at how beautiful Grace was, especially when she smiled.

"I'm so glad and really grateful that Jess didn't mind me gate-crashing for a while," Grace continued, "although I suppose I ought to be making arrangements to return to the farmhouse now that the hearing is over." She looked at Jess, whose happiness evaporated in the face of this latest news. She had known that Grace was only staying temporarily, but she had fallen into such a nice routine with her that an unmistakeable sense of loss at Grace's imminent departure enveloped her. She busied herself with her food and tried to hide her feelings, glad that Nick was happily oblivious to the emotional undercurrents in the room.

"Yeah, I suppose you have to get back to work and everything," he said, thoughtful.

"I can't leave George looking after the chickens and keeping an eye on things for too long either." Grace took a sip of wine. "He's very willing, but I know it's an imposition."

"Is George your fella?" Nick asked with his trademark absence of tact.

Grace looked up, slightly startled by the question. "Oh, no," she replied, her eyes widened with surprise and then she looked away for a moment, then back. "I'm gay."

Jess's shoulders jerked in response to her admission and a strange mixture of hope and confusion swamped her. She avoided looking at Grace.

"George is my neighbour," Grace explained, her voice quiet.

"I get it," Nick responded. An awkward few moments of silence ensued until Nick broke it. "How many chickens have you got?"

In any other circumstance Jess would have laughed at his feeble attempt at changing the subject. On this occasion she continued to push the food around her plate, her actions symptomatic of her inner turmoil. She risked a quick look at Grace, who was watching her with what looked like concern.

"Eight," she answered, still looking at Jess.

"Do you have any other animals?" Nick asked.

Grace turned her attention to him. "No. I would love a dog, but my hours are too unpredictable with locum work. I often end up on emergency call-out and it just wouldn't be fair to leave a pet for that long. George and I have a good system. He takes care of the chickens whenever I can't and he uses my spare outbuildings for additional storage."

C'mon Jess, pull yourself together. She didn't lie, she just didn't volunteer information. She's not Rosalind. Jess stole another glance at Grace. The expression of concern on her face only made the situation worse. She needed to distract herself from the recent revelation. "So, Nick. What's the story with Marie?"

Nick cleared his throat and fidgeted. "Things just haven't worked out." He shrugged.

Irritated by his reticence when he had earlier bulldozed through her own personal life, Jess pressed the point. "What happened?"

Nick shrugged. "I guess she just wanted more than I did. It happens."

"Your old commitment phobia kicking in?" Jess asked,

frustrated at his predictability. She knew she shouldn't have said it but she was angry, she didn't want to think about why, and he was as good a target as any.

"What is this, the Spanish Inquisition?" Nick retorted, clearly peeved at her persistence.

"Nice double standards," Jess said sarcastically, oddly relieved that she now had a genuine point to argue. "You're quick enough to tell me what to do in *my* personal life but you can't stomach it yourself."

"Hey, that's not fair and you know it. I try to help you out because I want you to be happy. I thought you knew that." He glared at her.

"So why is it any different for me to tell you that Marie seems really nice and I think you're a fool to throw away the chance of a mature relationship just because she wants to know how you feel?" Jess glared right back at him, her food forgotten.

"In case you didn't notice, I'm a grown man, even if I am your little brother."

He was angry as well, and Jess heard it in his voice. If I push him, he'll go, she thought. A flash of anger blazed through her. *Go, then.* Jess could practically feel her barriers coming back up. *If everyone wants to go, it's best they just get on with it.*

"You don't know what the situation is with Marie and me," he continued, his tone hard. "You just make assumptions that I'm incompetent to run my own life."

"Maybe because you *are* incompetent? Look at you. You're twenty-five and you've done nothing since school. You're the most talented mechanic I know but you waste that gift because you don't have the commitment to getting out there and being all you can be." She was on a roll now and the words spilled out of her mouth. "Then there are the women in your life. You lead them on and then you dump them when you get scared."

Nick stared at her. "What the hell, Jess? How dare you criticise my life? *You're* the perfectionist who's never happy with your own achievements. *You're* the one who lets one bad relationship turn you into an emotional hermit. *You're* the one who can't even see you have a bloody eating disorder. Wake up to yourself Jess, before you start to criticise others." He pushed his plate away and stood up. "Grace, thank you for a lovely meal. Sorry things worked out this way." He looked over at Jess. "I'll see you around," he said, the hurt and anger in his voice unmistakable.

Chapter
Thirty-one

"GOOD MORNING," GRACE greeted Jess cheerily. "Would you like a coffee? The kettle just boiled."

"Thanks, I'll get it." Jess avoided making eye contact as she moved toward the mug cupboard.

Grace picked up another triangle of toast and spread it with butter. She studied Jess's hunched, tense form unhappily. Last night's supposedly celebratory dinner had ended prematurely with Nick's sudden departure and left a sullen, insular Jess. The two of them had struggled through the remainder of the meal with poor appetites and much uncomfortable silence. As soon as she could, Jess had made her excuses and gone to bed. Evidently, she appeared to be feeling little better this morning.

This version of Jess was a stranger and Grace wasn't sure what to do. She had broached the subject of her leaving last night because she didn't want to outstay her welcome. The subsequent argument and Jess's obvious distress made her want to stay longer and offer her support. *Any excuse.* She had already privately admitted that she didn't want to leave though she had not allowed herself to think too deeply as to why. "I guess you're probably looking forward to having your house back to yourself," Grace said, deliberately keeping her tone light.

"Yeah, I guess." Jess didn't look round.

Despite herself, Grace felt a pang of disappointment. She pushed it away impatiently. Jess had been very kind to share her home for so long. "I can make my way today, if you'd like."

"Sure." Jess stirred her coffee vigorously. "I have a meeting at lunchtime but I can drive you home after that."

"Don't worry," Grace said, thinking of the four-hour round trip. "Perhaps you could give me a lift to the station on the way to your meeting? You've been so kind, I'd really hate to impose on you any more."

Jess shrugged, still avoiding eye contact. "Okay."

A sense of desperation clutched at her chest, Grace didn't want this detached, stilted conversation to be the way they left things. "I've really enjoyed spending time with you, Jess, despite the unusual beginnings."

Jess turned to face her properly. She was pale and dark smudges lined her eyes. Grace wondered if she had slept at all. "I've liked having you here."

Grace tried to read her but failed. *Is that just the polite response?*

Does she want to stay friends? Does she want me to stay longer? "I'd love to keep in touch —"

"Yeah, we should." Jess interrupted. "I have to go and get ready for that meeting now." She moved quickly to the door.

Grace heard her footsteps on the stairs and what sounded like a sniff. Somehow, things seemed to have gone from bad to worse. She sighed, at a loss of how to repair the damage. *I suppose I had better go and pack, then.*

JESS STOOD OUTSIDE her boss's door and hesitated, trying to calm her nerves. Her tension about the meeting was persistent and she felt emotionally unbalanced by Grace's departure. *Deep breaths. Just focus on one thing at a time.* She knocked and waited, anxiety twisting in her stomach.

"Come in."

She pushed the door open and stepped forward.

"Ah, Jess, thank you for coming." Jeff stood in welcome and ushered her to the chair opposite him.

"Of course," Jess said, trying to keep her tone professional. "My Image Conscious report is almost complete so I will be free to start the next assignment imminently."

Jeff steepled his fingers in front of his face. "I won't beat around the bush, Jess. There is a problem." He smoothed his tie then looked at her with a serious expression. "I've heard some very discouraging things about the Image Conscious case," he said gravely.

Jess wasn't surprised it was about Image Conscious. Willis was a friend of Jeff's so they had probably been talking about Marcus's scam and the unfavourable police attention. She had reported the farmhouse incident so there was always a possibility he was unhappy with the way she had handled things. Still, she couldn't see how.

"Theodore Willis contacted me yesterday morning and was verging on inconsolable. It is his understanding that you are —" he paused, looking vaguely embarrassed, "of the *other* persuasion. Furthermore, he was advised that you wantonly pursued both Image Conscious employees and clients, leading to the resignation of the former and the loss of the latter."

Jess listened in stunned silence.

"As you can imagine," he continued, "this situation has caused me considerable embarrassment. Theodore is an old friend and he trusted my recommendation faithfully. If I had thought for a moment that something like this could happen, then I would have taken steps to prevent it."

Jess stared at him, astounded and humiliated by his words. The allegations were so unexpected that she floundered to defend herself.

He looked at her with a reconciliatory expression. "You know I have always been very happy with your work and that you would be sorely missed in the team. Can you reassure me that these are unfounded lies?"

She looked at him, unsure of how to respond. He had made it clear how high the stakes were and the temptation to say the whole thing was lies was immense. Knowing she only had one real choice, she opted for the truth. "I am gay and I did pursue a romantic involvement with an Image Conscious employee." She held herself with dignity despite how uncomfortable she felt discussing this. "The relationship existed between mutually consenting adults. The other accusations are lies, almost certainly created to discredit me."

His sharp intake of breath and look of revulsion communicated his reaction clearly. "I see." His expression turned stony. "As you know, our professionalism is key to our business success. I cannot allow the per—" he quickly substituted a different word, "peculiarities of individuals to undermine that." He followed the argument to its logical conclusion. "I'm afraid your position in this company is no longer tenable."

Jess stared at him in disbelief. She had always known he was a conservative man but his unwavering prejudice shocked her. *He probably thinks I molest children at the weekend.* It was evident that his mind was set and that further struggle would only reduce the dignity with which she left. "I can see that your decision is final."

"It is. Please take any personal belongings you may have here and leave immediately." His instructions sounded mechanical, as though he couldn't bear to speak to her. "I will arrange for two months' salary to be transferred to your bank account with immediate effect. That will cover your notice period and any outstanding holiday." He stood, indicating that her presence was no longer required.

Part of Jess wanted to stay and fight the injustice of the situation. However, she knew that Lewknor would not change his mind. If she stayed to fight today she may give him genuine reason to dismiss her. It was better she left quietly and reassessed the situation when she felt more emotionally stable. "Good day, Mr. Lewknor."

"Good bye."

JESS CRIED ON the way home. A mixture of anger, humiliation, and shame washed through her, and she vacillated between wanting to treat Lewknor to an impromptu vasectomy and the desire to curl up in bed and sob. In one ten-minute conversation, she had lost the career she had worked her life to achieve. For ten years she had kept her emotions locked away, passing up opportunities she wanted to accept, limiting her romantic inclinations to wistful thinking from afar. Rosalind had been the first temptation she couldn't resist and her capitulation had led to this. Now she had neither job nor relationship, and all because she had been foolish enough to ignore her instincts.

She gripped the steering wheel harder. She shouldn't have allowed herself to get involved with a client but the way it had been twisted was downright offensive. It was pretty obvious who had started such malicious rumours and she wished wholeheartedly that she had the evidence to bring Marcus to justice. It was hard to say who was worse, Marcus or Lewknor. Her ex-boss must have known he was acting unlawfully by sacking her for sexual orientation. *He must be blind with prejudice to do it anyway. Or maybe Marcus had created some evidence to back up his lies.* The thought was a chilling one and she pushed it away.

Her thoughts turned to Nick and the argument. She was trying to avoid it but his words haunted her. Deep down, she knew he had hit upon truth but she was not ready to accept that fact. The subject of Grace was little better. She had tried telling herself that Grace hadn't lied by not voicing her sexuality. Equally, she knew it was to be expected that Grace would be ready to leave after the hearing. *So why do I feel so discarded?* She had almost said something at the station but words eluded her. *How do you tell someone you've known for less than two weeks that their departure will mean so much to you?*

Jess turned the radio on to try and distract herself from her head full of worries. She felt as though she was on the edge of an abyss. She just needed to balance long enough to get home. When she rounded the last corner approaching her cottage she recognised the red convertible parked outside the house. With a defeated sigh, she parked, steeling herself for yet another confrontation.

Chapter
Thirty-two

JESS WIPED AT her face impatiently. If there was any time she would least like to see Rosalind, it was now, but she had little choice. "Hello," Jess said as she got out of her car, knowing her exhaustion sounded in her voice.

"Jess, what's the matter? Are you hurt?" Rosalind's voice sounded fearful and she reached a hand out in comfort.

Jess stepped back quickly. *Don't be nice. I can't hold it together if you are.* "I'm fine," she said brusquely. "What are you doing here?"

Rosalind seemed to accept the brush off. "I know you don't want to see me but I really need to tell you something. I promise I won't take much of your time."

Jess looked at her but felt too tired to argue. It wasn't as though things could get much worse. "Come in, then." She unlocked the door and waited for Rosalind to precede her inside. Jess motioned toward the kitchen. "Would you mind making some coffee while I change? I can't bear to be in this monkey suit any longer than I have to."

"Of course," Rosalind assented in a tone that sounded surprisingly gentle.

Within a few minutes, Jess returned to the living room, where Rosalind was waiting. "Take a seat," Jess motioned vaguely, accepting the mug Rosalind handed her before settling into the armchair. As she took her first sip of the drink, her throat tightened with emotion. Rosalind had made it just as she liked it. The small detail, synonymous with the understated but meaningful relationship she had wanted, proved to be her undoing. She placed the mug on the table and retrieved a tissue from the box on the windowsill before succumbing to the tears.

"Oh, Jess. What's happened?" Rosalind was at her side in an instant.

"Get back," Jess commanded as she desperately tried to regain her composure. "Don't you realise that fake comfort from you will only make matters worse?"

Rosalind visibly recoiled and returned to her seat. "I'm sorry," she said. "I'm so sorry. I didn't want to cause you any more upset. Honestly, I'll go right now if that's what you want."

Jess wiped her nose and eyes, wishing for silence and solitude so that she could piece together the scattered fragments of her life. At the same time, a part of her wanted to know the real Rosalind. Now that the work dynamic had been stripped away, this was the obvious chance. She shut her eyes for a few moments and indulged in several deep breaths, willing calm to settle over her. When she reopened her eyes, it seemed to have worked. "All right. Tell me what you came to say."

Rosalind hesitated, looking uncharacteristically subdued. "I wanted to tell you that I'm profoundly sorry and to ask your forgiveness and see if there was any chance we could try again. Starting from scratch." She held Jess's gaze.

In some ways Jess found it easier to see Rosalind without the power suit, without the executive persona. It almost made her believable. "Does Marcus know you're here?" Jess asked, knowing it was rude, but it was borne from Rosalind's betrayal.

"Marcus sacked me." Rosalind said it quietly, dropping her gaze to her mug. "He made me the scapegoat for what was both his responsibility and mine and sent me away in disgrace."

"Snap," Jess said with a short, humourless laugh. "I've just come back from being sacked myself. For unnatural perversions against you and the clients."

Rosalind's sharp intake of breath convinced Jess of her innocence. "Oh, God. I'm so sorry. I had no idea."

Jess shrugged and reached for another tissue. "Nor did I, but I should have expected it, dealing with someone like Marcus."

Both lapsed into silence. Jess picked up her mug now she was feeling a little calmer.

"I admit," Rosalind said, "that when I first met you I did have an agenda. I used you and I cannot tell you how ashamed of myself I am. The irony is that through spending time with you I realised that my feelings had depth and then one day, I realised that I'm in love with you."

If this was more scheming, Jess couldn't see the motivation behind it. Part of her wanted to run to Rosalind and seek mutual comfort, but she knew it wouldn't work. She couldn't be in a relationship that had started with such a fundamental betrayal. "I loved you, too," Jess confessed, "until I realised it was all an act. Then I knew that it wasn't you I was in love with. It was the character you had played. In actual fact, I have no idea who you really are." She regarded Rosalind, making no attempt to keep the sadness from her face or voice.

Rosalind nodded, seemingly unsurprised. "I understand."

"What will you do?" Jess asked after a brief silence.

Rosalind sighed. "I'm not sure yet. I was thinking about relocating to sunnier climes and starting afresh. Believe it or not, I was about to leave Image Conscious and Marcus's schemes." She smiled then, sad. "I had hoped you and I could go somewhere together." It was a simple statement, and one that conveyed truth.

"I believe you." It didn't change the situation but it provided some closure for Jess. She hoped Rosalind felt it, too.

"Anyway, I wanted to talk to you about Marcus," Rosalind said, as if she was trying to move beyond the past. "I was selfish enough to want to talk about *us* first, but I didn't seriously expect you to forget everything that happened." She looked at Jess, and her eyes were filled with sympathy. She cleared her throat and continued. "Have you submitted your report on Image Conscious yet?"

Jess shook her head. "I'm not sure it's appropriate now, given that I was dismissed with immediate effect."

"Ultimately, it's up to you, but I wanted to tell you something that may affect your decision."

Jess looked at her, waiting for her to continue.

"Do you remember a couple of home-based workers on the payroll with the names Fredericks and McGuire?"

Jess's brow furrowed. "Yes."

"They don't exist," Rosalind stated simply.

Jess stared at her. "What do you mean, they don't exist?"

Rosalind smiled slightly. "They're on the payroll, but they're dummy entries. The people don't exist. Marcus had the names set up, added to the payroll, and their salaries are paid into two secret bank accounts he keeps."

Jess was stunned. It was such a simple plan, but probably one of the most effective frauds that could be done. Getting to her feet she walked through to her office and retrieved a report from a stack of papers next to her laptop. "Here we are," she spoke aloud as she walked back through reviewing the payroll report. "McGuire and Fredericks started working at the company at the same time and their combined salaries match Marcus's." She let out a low whistle. "That slick bastard doubles his earnings with this little scheme, *and* pays reduced income tax."

Rosalind sat back into her chair looking vaguely smug.

"After all the complex things I've been looking for, how ironic that it was there in front of me the whole time." Jess smiled, her sanity validated as the final pieces of the puzzle fell neatly into place. "How long have you known?"

"I found out when he did it," Rosalind admitted, "but it was before I realised what a slippery slope I was on. He asked me to keep it quiet so I did. I only decided to tell you about it a few days ago."

"Thank you," Jess said, feeling significantly better now she had some information with which to balance the scales of justice.

"You're welcome," Rosalind said, smiling back. "It was the least I could do. So will you be updating your report and submitting it?"

"I think so. It's the only thing I *can* do in all good conscience." *I'm going to enjoy hitting that send button, too.*

"Good." Rosalind said before finishing her coffee. She set the mug on the coffee table. "I suppose I should be going now." She hesitated, perhaps loathe to go.

"Okay." Jess stood to walk her to the door.

"Good bye, Jess." A note of sadness marred her voice as she leaned in and placed a chaste kiss on Jess's cheek.

"Good bye." Jess squeezed Rosalind's hand then waited for her to settle into her car and begin to manoeuvre out of the driveway. "Rosalind?" She called suddenly. "Send me a postcard when you get to where you're going. I'd like to know you're well and happy."

Rosalind smiled in acknowledgement before driving away, waving briefly before the car disappeared from sight.

With a feeling of completion, Jess went inside to process the final update to her Image Conscious report.

Chapter
Thirty-three

GRACE WAS SUPPOSED to be washing up but instead she stood, her hands submerged in soapy water, gazing out her kitchen window but not really seeing anything. She had notified the agencies she was registered with that she did not wish to be offered any assignments for another two weeks. She was eating into her savings, but there had been and continued to be so much going on that she didn't feel confident in her ability to concentrate. It was against her personal ethical code to put herself in a position where she might fail to do anything but the best for an animal through any distraction on her part. Instead, she had attempted to give herself enough space to sort out the issues on her mind and move past what had happened to her.

The events of the last couple of weeks seemed unreal. She knew that PetZone had always resented her interference, but she had never suspected the level they would sink to in order to protect their profit margin. The verdict from the hearing had been thoroughly satisfying, and it allowed her a sense of closure on that part of her life. The attack was a different matter, though.

Usually a very practical person, Grace had been disappointed at the level of anxiety she experienced when she returned to the farmhouse. Logic dictated that the threat had passed and any additional attacks were highly unlikely, but that didn't stop her from hurrying past dark corners and jumping at odd sounds. At night she checked the doors and windows several times, ensuring they were securely locked before she could sleep. Once in bed, she spent many wakeful hours staring into the darkness, reassuring herself with the knowledge that she now slept with her mobile phone next to the bed.

Her one consolation was that her fretful mind was distracted by pleasant thoughts of Jess as easily as it was disturbed by her own fears. Thoughts of the time they had spent together invariably made her smile. That was until she relived the awkward dinner with Nick and her equally uncomfortable departure the following morning. With hindsight she wished she had mentioned to Jess earlier that she was also a lesbian. She had selfishly avoided it, not wanting to create tension in their new friendship. The alternative had been far worse. Jess had shut herself off and now she had no idea what Jess was thinking or even if she still wanted to be friends. It had been four days since she had left and Grace had left three messages on Jess's answerphone, all of which had been ignored. Even if Jess didn't want to keep in touch, she just wished she knew that she was all right. She hated the thought that Jess was out there unhappy because of her.

Her time alone had also given her the space to recognise how her feelings for Jess had developed beyond friendship and physical attraction. What had started out as gratitude and respect had blossomed when she began to get to know her better. When Grace realised how sensitive Jess was and how she could lack confidence in her own abilities, it made her actions at the farmhouse appear even more heroic. The time they had spent together, sharing interests and laughter, had left Grace missing Jess's companionship frequently, much to her surprise. Jess had an unusual outlook on life and a questioning mind, and she had often said things that hinted at a depth of character that left Grace wanting to discover more.

Many times during the long wakeful hours of the last few nights, Grace imagined returning to the little Cotswold cottage. In her ruminations, Jess had always responded positively to Grace's admission of her feelings, but that was what fantasies were all about. Grace knew that Jess had risked a lot when she trusted Rosalind and she also realised how thoroughly that trust had been abused. Every instinct in her body told her that Jess was not ready for another relationship. She needed a chance to rebuild her trust and to see that not everyone would act as Rosalind did.

Grace caught herself and continued washing the last of her crockery in the now cold water. Her decision was made and she felt much better for it. She would not give up on Jess that easily and through platonic consistency she would show her exactly what more she could be.

MARCUS RAMMED THE gear stick of his beloved Aston Martin roughly into third, growling a curse under his breath when the transmission ground in complaint at his rough treatment.

Checking his rearview mirror, he glanced at the suitcase on the back seat, so hastily stuffed with his belongings that a shirt sleeve was still protruding. With a sudden change of heart he slammed his foot against the break pedal and turned hard to the left into a nearby lay-by. The driver behind blared his horn as he swerved past. Marcus gave him the middle finger salute before he pressed the speed dial on his mobile phone.

"Good afternoon, Image Conscious."

"Hilary. I need an address."

"Mr. Gibson?" She sounded surprised. "I'm afraid I'm not supposed to talk to you."

"I don't care. I need an address for Jess Maddocks."

She sounded hesitant. "I don't know, I really don't think I'm supposed to —"

"C'mon baby," he forced his voice to sound intimate. "You've always looked after me so well. I'm going to need you as my right hand when I set up my new company. I just need this one small thing to get things moving."

There was a pause. "What do you need it for?" She sounded sceptical.

"Maddocks has offered to invest in the new company, I want to drop in some files I've been working on. I think Rosalind knows the address. Can you try her on her mobile and find out? You should probably avoid mentioning it's to do with the investment, she'd only get jealous she's not involved. Say something like Maddocks left her laptop cable and you need to post it to her."

"Okay." Hilary acquiesced. "It'll take a minute."

"Thank you. I knew I could rely on you." He used his most charming voice as he terminated the call.

Hilary called back with the address within a few minutes. Marcus scribbled it on a scrap of paper before hanging up on Hilary with unceremonious pleasure. *Right, bitch. Time for some payback.* He put the car into gear and accelerated toward his new destination.

Chapter
Thirty-four

JESS'S LETHARGY HAD worsened over the five days since she was sacked. By Tuesday evening she hadn't bothered to change out of her pyjamas other than to shower. The feeling of light-headedness from hunger had passed after the first day or so but the

self-destructive path she was on prevented her from eating
properly. Today she had allowed herself an aging apple and a
handful of dry cereal. Currently lying on the sofa, she was flicking
an elastic band between her fingers and half-heartedly listening to
the answerphone messages that had built up over the previous few
days.

Beep. "Jess? It's Grace. I just wanted to check and make sure
you're holding up okay after the other night. Everything is fine
here, it gets a bit eerie at night but I guess I'll get used to it. Give
me a call when you can."

Beep. "Ms Maddocks, this is P.C. Johnson. I just wanted to
confirm that any possible charges against you have been dropped.
Apologies for the delay in letting you know but please call me
should you wish to discuss it."

Jess was relieved at that message, but it seemed very distant,
as though she were observing her life through the wrong end of a
telescope.

Beep. "It's Grace again. I just spoke to P.C. Johnson and I
gather you're in the clear—congratulations! I'm sure you must be
very relieved. Call me when you get a chance, I'd love to hear from
you."

Beep. "Uh, Jessie? It's me. Nick. I um, well, Marie and I are on
again. She's pretty cool. Let's have a takeaway soon, okay?"

Beep. "Jess, it's Grace again. I'm not sure if you are ignoring all
your messages or just mine. Please call me back and let me know
you're okay, I'm pretty worried here."

Jess listened as the machine bleeped twice to indicate the end
of her messages. She knew that she should phone both Nick and
Grace but the lethargy that pulled her down prevented any
movement. She wasn't sure how this had crept up on her when only
a fortnight ago she had felt so happy. At first she had thought it
was the ups and downs of her relationship with Rosalind but she
had felt a natural sense of completion about the whole thing. Even
though it didn't work out, Rosalind was more like a trial run than a
failure.

The loss of her job was definitely a major factor, compounded
by the absence of the only two people she wanted to discuss it with.
For so long her career had defined her, given her the status and
reassurance of her own worth that she seemed to need so badly.
Now that it had been ripped away, she wasn't sure there was
anything worthwhile left over. Her current state served only to
reiterate that. Ordinarily, Nick would be a source of support,
guaranteed to get her smiling and seeing things from a different
perspective, but thinking about him just made her think about his
eating disorder allegation and she didn't want to talk to him and

have that come up again.

In some ways Jess found herself marvelling that Grace was someone she wished she could speak to. The gift of a connection that had become so important so quickly was one she treasured. However, Jess was paralysed with emotional confusion.

She glared at the ceiling for the thousandth time. She wasn't sure when, but her platonic feelings for Grace had begun to change. It was only when Grace had announced her intention to leave that Jess realised the extent of her own feelings. Now she felt frightened to open her heart to such a powerful force, especially in the midst of everything that was happening.

An unusual creaking in the house attracted Jess's attention and she focussed her hearing, searching for a repeat of the sound. After a few minutes stretched out with no duplicate noise, she decided it was her imagination and closed her eyes against the swirl of thoughts that plagued her. Once again her senses alerted her but this time when she opened her eyes, it was to the sinister form of Marcus towering over her.

"Bitch," he screamed at her, ramming his fist against her unprotected face with as much force as he could muster.

What the — ? Jess tried to evade the blow but her position on the sofa left her vulnerable with no room for manoeuvring. "No," she screamed, seeing his fist rise again, terrified at his intrusion into her home.

"I've lost everything because of you," he was unhinged, his face almost contorted beyond recognition with the rage that overwhelmed him. He struck her again.

Injured and panicked, Jess beat at him desperately but he had every advantage and her hunger-weakened state left her even more vulnerable.

Marcus responded to her struggles by pinning her on the sofa, straddling her with his legs but keeping his hands free for inflicting damage. "I've lost my job," he punched her in the stomach. "My wife threw me out," he smacked her face. "And I face jail." His last punch connected painfully with her ribs. He grabbed her wrists and pulled her arms up over her head, leaning in so his face was inches from hers. "You are going to pay," he spat the last words.

Jess gasped for breath after the blow to her stomach. A sharp pain shot through her side as she breathed. She could taste blood in her mouth. In vain she struggled against his superior weight and strength, but to no avail, even though her panic had given her extra energy. "Marcus, stop. Think about this," she rasped, hoping to talk some sense into him. "Whatever you face now will only be worse if you continue with this. Maybe you don't face prison at all but if you don't stop this now, you will."

He eyed her, perhaps sensing some truth in her argument but still overcome with his need for revenge. "I have a little girl," he said, not relinquishing his hold on Jess. "How do you think she'll feel knowing her father got sent to prison?"

"Terrible. She'll feel terrible. Stop this, Marcus. It's in your power to do so," Jess pleaded with him, and her voice was trembling with fear, much to her chagrin.

"Do you know what happens to men in prison?" he asked as though he hadn't heard her speak. "I've seen films. I know what happens. A man is not a man by the time they finish with him." A glazed expression crossed his eyes.

Jess tried to keep still, not wanting to attract his attention. She considered her options. The telephone was out of reach and no neighbours were close enough to hear her scream. If she could get away, she could head for the nearby pub where she knew the locals would rally to protect her. The problem was how to get out from under Marcus to make a run for it. Silently, she went through a mental inventory of the items that would be within her reach from her current location, trying to keep calm when none seemed to be of use.

"Looks like I best have some fun while I can, doesn't it?" The smirk on Marcus's face was demonic as he ripped open Jess's flimsy pyjama top.

The strength of desperation combined with the temporary shift of her attacker's weight gave Jess the opportunity she had been waiting for. She focused all her hatred of the man, all her fear and all her hope into the knee she rammed into his groin.

Marcus bellowed in pain and shifted involuntarily to cradle his crotch.

The movement was all Jess needed. Hauling her legs out from under him, she rolled off the sofa and scrambled to her feet. Fighting back an untimely bout of wooziness, she navigated her way around the furniture in a frantic flight toward the front door.

Marcus charged after her. His better physical condition gave him an advantage and he slammed into her just as her hand reached for the doorknob. He grabbed a fistful of her hair and viciously dragged her back to the sofa. Pushing her down, he landed a blow across the side of her face that left her vision blurred.

An odd detachment swept over her, and her spirit seemed to distance itself from her body. It was a protective thing, she supposed, somewhere in the back of her mind that was still cognizant of what was happening. There was nothing left that she could do to protect herself physically and all she could do was distance herself emotionally from the inevitable. She saw images of herself and Grace, laughing over some triviality. Nick's grinning face seemed to smile out at her from her memories.

"I'll make you pay for what you've done to me," Marcus snarled at her as he began to fumble with his belt.

Jess shut her eyes and hoped it would all be over soon.

"Get the hell away from my sister!" Nick's burly form hurtled toward Marcus. He had the advantage because Marcus had not heard anyone come in. There was a sickening crunch as the two connected and began to roll on the floor in a bid for supremacy.

Jess watched, still strangely detached, trying to sort through what was happening. *Is that Grace? What's she doing here?*

"Jess? Oh, God. Jess?" A small cry escaped Grace's lips. "Oh, honey. Oh, God. It's okay, love. We're here now. We won't let anyone hurt you. Here, take my hand."

Jess automatically gripped Grace's fingers, still trying to figure out what was happening.

"That's it," Grace said, tucking the tatters of her pyjama top together. "Come with me."

Jess let Grace lead her upstairs, away from the fight.

Grace took Jess into her bedroom and settled her into the comfortable familiarity of her own bed. "You just stay there for a minute. I'll be right back."

Jess nodded absently, confused but relieved. Grace disappeared for a few moments then returned with a moistened flannel, which she used to dab Jess's face gently. Jess winced but maintained her silence.

"Sweetie, can you speak to me?" Grace asked, worry lacing her tone.

Jess turned her gaze toward the voice. Everything was still blurry but there could be no mistaking the familiar voice. "Grace?" Was it really Grace? How strange everything seemed.

"Yes, it's me," Grace said, and relief was palpable in her voice. "Nick's downstairs and everything's going to be okay. Where does it hurt?"

Jess pondered the question. It was so hard to think, like trying to swim through mud. "Where doesn't it?" She concluded, laughing feebly at her own wit then wincing at the pain in her stomach and side. "I can't see properly."

Grace inhaled sharply. "Can you see my fingers?" she asked, holding three up in front of Jess's face.

"Yes." She confirmed.

"How many can you see?"

Jess peered at the pink blur she knew to be Grace's hand. "Um, two?" She smiled. "I'm glad you're here. I've missed you."

"Me too," Grace said softly, tenderly stroking Jess's cheek.

"Can I go to sleep now?" Jess asked hopefully.

"No, sweetie, you have to stay awake for me. You might have a concussion and you've got to stay awake a bit longer."

At that moment Nick charged into the room. "Jessie, are you okay?" He rushed to the bedside and took the seat on the side of the bed that Grace vacated.

"Hey, bro." Jess smiled at him gingerly. "Your turn to be a hero." She was having a hard time talking. *Why was that?* She puzzled over it, but dropped the thought because it was so good to see Nick.

"Yeah, well, that scumbag's out cold. We should call for police and ambulance." Nick flexed both fists, his face unusually grave.

"I'll do that," Grace volunteered before giving Nick a pointed look. "You two have a chat. No napping, Jess, or I'll have to wake you up and test your trivia."

Jess smiled weakly. It would be hard to stay awake, she was so tired suddenly.

She felt Nick's hand squeeze hers. "So where've you been hiding these last few days? I wanted to tell you about Marie."

"Just hanging." Jess's tongue felt heavy.

"Well, you'll be glad to know we talked, me and Marie. She's cool, you know."

"Mmm."

"C'mon Jessie, no sleeping. You heard what Grace said." Nick's voice sounded nervous. "Tell me what you did today."

Jess frowned, trying to remember. "I watched Sesame Street. They were learning the letter G and the number five."

Nick laughed. "Are Bert and Ernie still together?"

"Yeah." Jess smiled. Her eyelids were closing of their own accord. She tried to open them but each time it got harder.

"I'm sorry about the other day." Nick's voice was thick with emotion. "I never meant it to be like that. Maybe the four of us can have another stab at dinner when you're feeling better. And no arguing this time."

"Yeah, I'd like that." It was so hard to fight the sleepiness. *Maybe just a little rest?* "I'm so tired," she murmured.

"No, you don't," Grace was back, moving to the bed. "No sleeping for you, young lady. Come on, I brought you some water. Will you drink some for me?"

Jess would do anything that velvety voice asked. She mustered enough energy to sit up and with all her concentration managed to swallow some of the refreshing liquid.

"That's it," Grace's voice was encouraging. "Now how about you tell us what happened while I try and clean you up a bit more?"

Jess's brow furrowed as she tried to remember the events of the evening. It was as hard as searching her mind for her earliest childhood memory. "I was lying on the sofa, listening to my messages. I knew I should call you both, but I just felt so tired."

"Don't worry, Jessie, you can't get rid of us that easily." Nick smiled wanly at his sister, and his expression was worried.

"Good." Jess paused, trying to remember what happened next. "I thought I heard something but nothing happened. Then suddenly he was there. He was hitting me and shouting." Her words were coming faster now as she relieved her earlier fear. "He said I made him lose his job and family."

"Do you know what he meant?" Grace asked, evidently confused by who the man even was.

"Yeah," Jess confirmed quickly. "I nailed the bastard." She erupted into satisfied laughter before flinching and clutching at her damaged ribs.

"Who is he?" Grace asked.

"Marcus Gibson, the boss of Image Conscious."

"Ah, that makes sense," Grace said in comprehension.

"The baddies always have to have one last go," Nick observed wryly.

Jess smiled then stopped because it hurt her lip. "I should have remembered that. He caught me off guard." She paused, wondering what she could have done differently. "Hey, maybe I should have my sword permanently strapped on?"

"The ladies like it but it can get awfully inconvenient." Nick replied gravely.

"Seriously?" Grace asked, giggling, "I thought that was just me."

A flutter of excitement danced through Jess's chest but she couldn't make sense of it in her befuddled state. "I'm glad you're here," she said instead, addressing both her visitors simultaneously. "Hey," her brow furrowed again. "How did you know I needed you?"

Nick smiled at Grace before answering. "It's Grace you have to thank for that," he said proudly. "She was worried that you weren't answering your phone. I thought you just wanted some space but she kept on at me. As it turns out, I'm pretty relieved she did."

Grace returned his smile. "Glad to be of service. Besides, I needed your key." She downplayed her concern with practicalities. "Of course," she addressed Jess, "you know we'll keep turning up if you don't answer your messages from now on." She grinned at Jess even though there was a hint of seriousness to her comment.

"You're always welcome," Jess advised them. The sleepiness was overwhelming, pulling her toward a dark warm place where nothing hurt.

"Jess?" Grace said. "Jess!" Her voice was more insistent.

Jess could hear them calling her name but she was too deep to swim back up. With a sense of relief, she stopped fighting and gave herself willingly to the darkness.

"Jess!"

"Jessie."

Chapter
Thirty-five

UGH. JESS WOKE up feeling dreadful. She didn't want to open her eyes, hoping she might be able to go back to sleep again. Maybe it would feel better tomorrow. Gradually, unfamiliar sounds began to filter through. Lots of bleeping. Strange voices in the distance. The whirs of alien machines. She was lying down and someone was holding her hand, stroking it gently. It felt nice.

"How's she doing?" Nick's voice sounded worried.

"The same." Grace replied.

Jess cracked open one eye. "Hey," she croaked.

Simultaneously the faces of Nick and Grace appeared in her line of sight. "Jessie!" Nick beamed at her.

"Hey, Jess," Grace spoke softly but her eyes seemed to shine with happiness. "How are you feeling?"

Jess considered the question, trying to differentiate between levels of discomfort. "I feel pretty rough," she admitted. "And thirsty."

Grace reached over to a nearby pitcher and poured a glass of water. Nick helped Jess to sit up partially while Grace carefully tilted the glass to Jess's lips.

"Thanks." She flopped back against the pillows and looked around the unfamiliar room. "Where are we?"

"Hospital." Nick said. "Do you remember what happened?"

Jess tried to think back. She remembered being at home, hungry and lonely. Then Marcus and pain and the memory of her torn pyjama top. She sucked in a breath with panic. "Oh my God, he didn't—" she felt a blush of shame colour her face.

Grace reached out and grabbed her hands. "No," she said vehemently, "Nick stopped him in time. He used you as a punchbag but nothing else."

Jess looked into Grace's brown eyes, searching for honesty.

The steadiness of Grace's gaze reassured her. She reached out and squeezed Nick's hand with silent gratitude. "What's the prognosis?"

"Bruising mainly, to your face and ribs. You're going to feel pretty rough for a while, I'm afraid." Grace smiled sympathetically. "The doctors took some X-rays of your skull while you were unconscious. Things looked okay and it's great to have you with us again." She paused and looked at Nick. "Speaking of which, I'll go and find a nurse."

"How long have I been out?"

Nick checked his watch. "About fourteen hours. It's Wednesday morning now."

Jess studied the ceiling. *What if I hadn't woken up?*

Nick interrupted her morose thoughts. "The police took Gibson. He broke bail so now he's locked up. The police want a statement from you so that he can be charged."

The thought of police questioning was unappealing but Jess was glad to know Gibson would be brought to justice. "Thanks for being there for me."

"No problem." Nick smiled, "I'm just glad to see you awake again. You had us scared for a while there. Grace has been great. She wouldn't leave you and kept asking the doctors complicated questions. Animals get concussions, too. Did you know that?"

"No, I didn't." She grinned at him. "My life is complete now that I do know, though."

"Yeah, yeah, you love me really." Nick stuck his tongue out at her.

"Yeah, I do." She replied soberly, unable to suppress a smile when his ears turned pink and began to inspect his hands closely.

The arrival of the nurse interrupted them. "Right, if you two will give us some privacy, I just need to examine Ms. Maddocks." She eyed Nick and Grace with a no nonsense look.

"We'll be just outside." Grace said reassuringly.

Jess watched them go then gave her full attention to the nurse.

"ARE YOU SURE you're okay?" Nick asked for the fourth time.

Jess rolled her eyes at Grace. "Yes. I'm sore but perfectly capable of walking."

"All right. Grace will take you inside and I'll pay the taxi." He retrieved his wallet from his back pocket and opened it. A sheepish look crossed his face.

"Swap," Grace suggested. "You take Jess inside, I'll pay the taxi."

"I'm perfectly capable of getting into my own house." Jess took the sting out of her retort with a smile. She followed Nick down the short path and waited as he unlocked the front door.

"I'll put you some new bolts on all the doors and the downstairs windows first thing tomorrow," He advised her as he held the door open for her to pass through.

Jess nodded. "Thanks, Nick." She was pleased to be home. It felt like she had been away for a lot longer than twenty-four hours. Walking stiffly to the sofa, she eased herself gingerly down into a sitting position.

"All done," Grace called as she joined them. "How are you doing?"

"I might scream if someone asks me that again." Although she made a joke of it, Jess was exhausted from people prodding and questioning her. When the doctors had finally finished mauling her, they gave the police the go-ahead to question her regarding the attack.

Nick laughed. "Getting back to normal, then. I'm still staying over, though." He added with an expression that said it was non-negotiable.

"Me too," Grace agreed quickly.

"Good plan," Nick nodded. "I'll take the sofa, you can have the spare room."

"You're not sleeping on the sofa," Grace looked at him sternly. "You have the spare room and I'll bunk with Jess. I think I'm safe the state she's in."

Jess felt her insides flip with anticipation. *I'm not.*

"Is that okay, Jess?" Grace seemed worried by her silence.

"Sure." She nodded, not trusting herself to say anymore.

"Great." She smiled. "How about I get some hot chocolate going? It's been a long day and I think we could all do with an early night."

"Suits me," Nick agreed readily.

By ten, the conversation had dwindled and their mugs were drained. "I think we should get some sleep," Grace said, looking at Jess.

Jess nodded slowly, both dreading and excited about the prospect. *Get a grip. She just wants to keep an eye on you.* "All right," she conceded.

"C'mon," Nick said. "I'll give you a hand upstairs."

Jess allowed herself to be guided up the stairs and deposited in her bedroom.

"Do you need me to get you anything?" Nick asked, his eyebrows raised.

Jess shook her head. "I'll be fine, thanks. I'll see you in the morning."

Nick nodded. "'Night, Jessie." He padded out of the room, closing the door behind him.

Jess went to the en suite bathroom and cleaned her teeth, face and hands. She was brushing her hair in the wardrobe mirror when Grace knocked.

"Are you decent?"

"Yes," Jess replied. She hadn't changed yet because her inhibited range of movement meant her normal tasks were taking a lot longer.

"It's all clean downstairs," Grace advised her. "Are you sure you're okay with me sharing? I really don't mind the sofa if you'd be more comfortable."

"No," she replied shyly. "I'd like to have you here."

Grace's smile reached her eyes, creasing the skin around them. "I'm glad." She watched for a moment as Jess returned to her hair. "Would you like a hand?"

Jess caught Grace's eye in the mirror and flushed. "I'm a bit stiff." She admitted.

Grace crossed the room and took the brush from Jess. "Here." She was gentle with the brush, easing the tangles from Jess's hair with smooth strokes.

Jess watched her in the mirror, drawn by the expression on Grace's face. It seemed so nurturing, almost trance-like.

Grace looked up and caught Jess staring. She coloured slightly. "There you go. Are you all right to get changed?"

"I could probably use a hand with this outer stuff."

They worked together to gently ease Jess out of her jeans and rugby shirt. "Hey, how come I'm wearing this?"

"Nick and I changed you before the ambulance got here. Your pyjamas weren't really suitable for going out." Grace busied herself folding the rugby shirt with excessive precision.

Jess felt herself blush to the roots of her hair. She decided humour was the only option. "Who picked my underwear?"

Grace looked relieved. "I did."

"Well, you picked my favourite." She flicked the waistband of her gingham boxers.

They laughed together, relieving any residual tension in the awkward situation.

Jess winced as the movement pulled at her ribs.

"Here, no funny business, I promise." Grace said, retrieving the clean pyjama top. She unhooked Jess's bra and eased it away from her bruised skin. Gathering the soft cotton top she slid it gently over Jess's head and held out the sleeves for her arms.

Jess knew she had blushed again. She resisted the temptation to suggest Grace strip to even the score. Obediently she manoeuvred her arms into place. "Thanks. I can do the trousers while you're brushing your teeth, if you like. There's a spare toothbrush in the cabinet."

"Great, thanks."

"I'm afraid I've run out of pyjamas but help yourself to shorts and a T-shirt from that drawer." Jess pointed to the chest of drawers near the door into the bathroom.

When Grace had shut the door between them, Jess hastily changed, nearly overbalancing in the process. Pulling back the duvet on her preferred side, she slipped into the bed. Her body relaxed into the familiar mattress and despite her thoughts of Grace, Jess found her eyes determinedly closing.

Grace emerged from the bathroom a few minutes later. "Do you have everything you need?"

"Yes, thanks," Jess confirmed. *Well, I will in a few seconds.*

She got into bed then reached up and turned off the lamp. "Just wake me if you need anything," Grace said, her voice sounding comfortingly close in the darkness. "'Night, Jess."

"Good night."

Chapter
Thirty-six

JESS OPENED HER eyes to almost pitch darkness. She lay still, completely disorientated. It took her a few moments to realise she was in her own home. For a moment she had been trying to reconcile the dimensions of the room with her childhood bedroom. As her senses began to connect with her brain, the pain from her injuries pervaded her body but she also realised that there was someone in bed with her. Memories of the attack flooded her mind, explaining the pain she was experiencing. She remembered Marcus trying to force himself on her and panic seized her at the thought that the sleeping form might be him. Before rational thought could kick in, she managed to get into a sitting position in preparation to run.

"Jess?"

Desperate to make her escape before she became trapped again, Jess struggled against the hand reaching for her.

"Jess, it's me. It's Grace. Everything's okay."

Jess tried to reconcile the familiar, velvety voice with the face of her attacker and failed. "Grace?" The words had begun to filter through her sleepy confusion.

"Yes, it's me. Nick is in the other room. We're both here for you."

A sense of peace settled over Jess as her tired mind absorbed the information. "Good," she said as she lay back down and rested her aching head against the pillow. "I thought you were him."

"No, he's gone. The police took him away."

Jess groaned, shutting her eyes against the pain in her head.

"Do you need some more painkillers?" Grace asked, the mattress flexing under her weight as she moved.

"Yeah, that'd be good."

Grace turned the lamp on then got out of bed. She returned a few moments later with a tablet and a glass of water. "Here you go."

"Thanks." Jess took the pill and placed the glass on her bedside table. She watched as an appealingly sleep-tousled Grace got back into bed beside her. When she had turned the lamp off again, Jess rolled over to face her, and she placed her arm on the mattress between their pillows. "Hold my hand?"

Grace slipped her own hand into Jess's and gave it a reassuring squeeze. "Get some more sleep," she advised. "We still have a while before morning."

A deep contentment settled over Jess and she fell asleep, her hand still in Grace's.

GRACE SUPPRESSED A giggle when Nick appeared in the bedroom doorway.

"Jessie, how're you doing this morning?" He asked, with far too much energy for the early hour. "Oh, that shiner's really coming on. Can you see me okay?" He waved a hand at her speculatively.

"I can see you well enough to know you're standing in your underpants in front of my house guest." Jess arched her good eyebrow.

Nick turned an appealing shade of pink and rearranged his hands to protect his modesty. "I heard you guys talking on my way back from the bathroom. I didn't think about clothes." His admission was accompanied by a sheepish grin.

"It's okay," Grace said. "After all, she's the one wantonly lazing in bed with a gorgeous lesbian." She gave Jess a wicked grin, hoping that she wouldn't be embarrassed by the joke.

"One all," Nick quipped. "Thanks, Grace. I'll be right back. Clothes." He smiled and left.

"Think you're gorgeous, do you?" Jess's expression was playful.

"Maybe," Grace said coyly, ruining the effect by the grin that followed. "How about some breakfast? I'm ravenous." She didn't give Jess the opportunity to decline, instead heading determinedly toward the kitchen.

She had a pan of bacon, sausages, and eggs cooking when Nick joined her. The kettle had just boiled and she was preparing coffee for three.

"Can I do anything to help?" Nick enquired, sniffing at the contents of the frying pan.

"Sure. You can make the toast if you like. I thought we could all do with a hearty breakfast to start the day."

"A hearty breakfast is the best way to start *any* day, in my opinion." Nick pronounced, filling the toaster with bread.

Grace moved the food around in the pan, her stomach rumbling in hopeful anticipation. She was becoming quite fond of the Aga. It suited the traditional cottage perfectly, but she also loved its simplicity.

"Jessie seems good this morning," Nick commented, opening the fridge and pushing a box of eggs aside.

"Yes," Grace agreed happily. "She did wake up in the night, at about three. She was pretty disorientated but soon straightened things out. She didn't wake again till seven, pretty much when you heard us talking." She went to the cupboard and retrieved three plates. "Her face is in a bit of a state but I think it's superficial. She seems compus mentus and the painkillers should manage her ribs and headache. Now we just need to get her blood sugar up a bit."

Nick was pulling the vegetable trays out in the bottom of the fridge and peering inside. "She had me pretty worried for a while there," he admitted.

"Me too." Grace said quietly.

He paused his search to look at her speculatively. "You really like her, don't you?"

"Of course I like her," Grace responded quickly. "What's not to like?"

Nick smirked at her poor attempt at avoidance. "No, I mean you *really* like her."

Grace turned to face him and immediately saw only warmth and friendliness in his face. She hesitated. "Yes." She smiled. "I do *really* like her." It felt good to tell someone. It made it more real, somehow. "Now come on with that toast," she said, swiping his backside with the oven gloves, "or it'll be lunch time." She turned back to face the stove and began the process of serving the food.

Nick gave an exasperated sigh. "I can't find the—"

"Next to the toaster, in the blue butter dish." Grace answered without turning around, fully aware of the soppy smile still plastered on her face.

JESS PULLED HERSELF into a sitting position when she heard footsteps on the stairs.

"Ta-da!" Nick announced the arrival of the toast with a verbal fanfare. "Voila, Madame," he said with a questionable French accent. Stepping forward, he held out a plate containing two blackened lumps that had once been bread.

"Thanks," Jess said with a laugh. "They do say that charcoal is good for you."

Nick feigned offence and settled himself in the chair by the window. All three were eating in the bedroom to keep Jess company, as Grace had resolutely banned her from getting out of bed for anything other than visiting the bathroom.

"Jess?" Grace asked.

"Mmm?" Jess responded around a mouthful of food.

"Why were you ignoring your calls?" She continued to eat while waiting for an answer but her expression suggested the question had been bothering her.

Jess was quiet for a while, knowing she would have to admit the truth sooner or later. "I was feeling pretty low. I guess a few things just piled up on top of me. Rosalind came to see me, and things worked out okay with us but it felt a bit strange watching her drive away to start her life over somewhere new."

Nick and Grace remained silent, allowing her the chance to explain at her own pace.

"I got into a bit of a state," she continued. "I started thinking about how my life wasn't going anywhere. I kept reliving the argument with Nick and I suddenly felt really isolated. I thought of you two going back to your lives, not needing me or missing me. I stopped eating and just bummed around in my pyjamas watching television all day."

"How can you think those things?" Grace sounded incredulous. "Okay, so you guys had an argument but who doesn't? We both care about you evidently far more than you realise and as for your life going nowhere, I can only think of a handful of people who have been as successful in their chosen careers at such a young age as you."

"I got sacked." Jess said, her voice devoid of emotion.

Both Grace and Nick exclaimed simultaneously. "What for?"

"For being a lesbian." She slumped her shoulders, humiliated.

"They can't do that," Grace exclaimed. "It's against the law."

"Well, they did it anyway. Marcus told them a pack of lies

about how I forced myself on anything wearing a skirt." It hurt to voice the words, even though they were based on lies.

"Surely they didn't believe that?" Grace was indignant.

Jess shrugged. "To be honest, I don't know if they believe it or not. I just know that they have no tolerance for homosexuality. The merest hint of it and they run a mile. I let my guard down for the first time in ten years but it's obviously a case of one strike and you're out." The bitterness she'd been carrying around since her firing spilled into her words.

"But your work is good. Isn't it?" Nick asked.

Jess allowed herself a rare moment of immodesty. "Very good. I was one of the best performing business analysts in the group." She knew it was true from the internal awards she had won. "It was never about my work, though."

"You should take it to an industrial tribunal," Grace said flatly.

"Yeah, probably," Jess responded. "It *is* unfair but part of me just wants to move on and start afresh. I know I shouldn't, but I can't help feeling ashamed of myself."

Grace tightened her mouth with what Jess suspected to be disapproval. "What will you do?" she asked, evidently allowing the subject to rest for now.

Jess pushed her plate away and resettled herself gingerly against the pillows. "I don't know." She shook her head sadly. "I have no idea."

Chapter
Thirty-seven

JESS WAS IN her home study, sitting at her desk and distractedly watching the stars of her screensaver. It was the first time she had been alone in the house since Marcus's invasion almost a week ago but she was pleasantly surprised to find herself calm and relaxed. The police had telephoned to advise her that he had been charged with assault in addition to his existing charges and was now locked up until his trial. Nick had added the new bolts and locks anyway, which helped her feel more secure.

He had stayed with her for a few days but once he had assured himself of her continued recovery, he went back home to be closer to work. Jess smiled as she remembered the hushed conversation he had with Grace and her promises to call him night or day if he was needed.

Grace appeared to have settled back into the cottage easily. Jess had been secretly disappointed when she reclaimed the spare room once Nick had vacated it. Before that she had gone to bed early each night, privately relishing the chance to spend so much time close to Grace. Both of them had kept things platonic, despite the potentially intimate arrangement. The one concession was that they tended to go to sleep holding hands.

Much to Jess's surprise, she had not been irritated by Grace's constant surveillance. Jess knew that Grace just wanted to ensure she was recovering well and was attempting to minimise any stress. Jess would have found such attention stifling with anyone else, but with Grace she simply smiled indulgently. However, she had still taken the opportunity to encourage Grace to go out and do some shopping this afternoon. She wanted to check how she felt alone in the house and she also wanted to protect Grace from imminent cabin fever.

She had already turned to share a thought with Grace, surprised to remember she wasn't there. At one time Jess had thought that things wouldn't be the same between them after Grace left the first time. In a way she had been right. Things were now better. Grace had come back and they laughed and chatted together as if she'd not been away. She had looked after Jess, helping her with dressing and remembering medication as though they were a long-established couple. *Couple?* Jess caught her own thoughts. *Yeah, couple would be nice.* She smiled at her laptop screen.

Out of habit, Jess had settled herself in her study even though she had nothing to work on. She knew job-hunting would have to come soon but she had decided to take two weeks off. She wanted to make sure her bruising and stiffness had passed before she contemplated interviews. She stared at the screen, thinking about the last report she had submitted and felt a grim satisfaction. Marcus was being held accountable for all he had done. Curiosity overwhelmed her and she navigated to the Image Conscious Web site and looked at the personnel page. The familiar visage of Theodore Willis appeared in the "Chief Executive" place. It seemed appropriate that he would take up his old position while he worked to source a more suitable successor. She idly wondered if he would consider another family member or avoid them at all costs.

Her curiosity sated, she meandered around the Web, spending several minutes looking at various recruitment sites, trying to get a feel for the business opportunities currently available and the commensurate remuneration packages. It was a worthwhile exercise even though she found nothing to spark her interest. The thought occurred to her that now would be the ideal opportunity for a change in career direction should she wish it.

She sat for a moment thinking about that and then, steeling herself, she searched on and found a comprehensive eating disorder site. The topic frightened her immensely but she told herself that she was simply investigating and it didn't mean anything. Still, she couldn't escape the fact that Nick's comment had sparked a chain reaction in her mind that had been compounded by subsequent events. On more than one occasion over the last few days, Jess had wondered if she would have been able to fight Marcus off had she not been so weak from food deprivation. It was a sobering thought and one that made her consider her behaviour in a different light.

She knew she had always had a troubling relationship with food that dated back to her days at boarding school. Her school years in general hadn't been happy ones, filled with bullying about her tomboy appearance and slight chubbiness. It was such an insidious process, but she had begun to limit her eating in order to control her weight and attempt to make herself more acceptable to her peers. Of course, it had never worked but once the mental and emotional links were forged, it seemed impossible to break them. Since her school years she had struggled with varying degrees of self-loathing, locked in a bitter battle with her body, which resolutely refused to be what she so desperately wanted it to be. Her happiness always seemed to be dependent upon the elusive aim of becoming slim.

As with most people, Jess had heard of both anorexia and bulimia and knew herself lucky enough not to suffer with either condition. However, poking around the site, she was surprised to learn that there were many more issues that existed. She was soon engrossed in the information relating to compulsive overeating. Reading the testimonies of sufferers she could see the tragic effect it had on their lives and she readily identified with a surprising number of the feelings and responses they described. The binge-starve cycle Jess knew personally. She held a common belief that fat people didn't have eating disorders. They were just greedy or had no will power. Reading the information on the site, she saw that she had been wrong. A rush of emotion welled inside her at these startling new perspectives as well as the emergence of a tiny bud of hope that her personal demons were not so abnormal after all.

"Jess? I'm home." Grace's voice called out from the vicinity of the front door.

"Coming," Jess called back, shutting down the Web site but not before she had added it to her favourite places. Springing up with a sudden newfound lightness, she went to help Grace unload the car.

"I hope you don't mind," Grace began as they unloaded groceries companionably together, "but I picked up some colour charts for you from that shop in town. I know you mentioned it the other day and I thought I may as well pick up the charts while I was out and about."

Jess smiled at her. "Thanks. I suppose now is as good a time as any to redecorate. It makes sense to take advantage of my career sabbatical even if it didn't come about through choice."

Grace held out the freshly baked loaf she had just bought. "Smell this," she instructed.

Jess did as she was asked. "I think that has to be one of the best smells in the world," she responded, smiling appreciatively.

"I think so, too. Anyway, if you do want to paint I'm happy to give you a hand. It's one of those things that's always nicer with company and I don't have any placements at the moment."

"Thanks. I'd appreciate that." *Yeah, and I'd appreciate having you around longer.* "Perhaps you can give me your opinion on the colour choices as well. I find myself overwhelmed when it comes to this sort of thing."

"Of course. Which rooms were you wanting to do?"

Jess thought for a moment. "I quite like how the living room and kitchen are looking, so I suppose it's my bedroom and your room that I really wanted to concentrate on." She caught herself, realising what she'd just said. Hurriedly, she busied herself with her back to Grace. It was true, though. Jess did think of the guest room as Grace's, but then the whole thing was on such an informal basis. She reminded herself that it could be any day that Grace announced her imminent departure and it was something Jess dreaded. The memory of that dinner, when she thought her time with Grace had come to an end, still stung.

Grace looked at her with an unfathomable expression. "Come on," she said, her voice light. "Let's have a muffin and see if the paint brochures provide any inspiration."

Relieved that Grace might not have registered her gaffe, Jess grabbed the muffins and followed her into the living room.

Chapter
Thirty-eight

"DO YOU GUYS always have such dangerous things happening?" Marie asked when she had heard the stories of both the attacks on Grace and Jess.

Jess laughed. "I suppose it must look a little extreme," she admitted. "But it's all Grace's fault. Nothing like this ever happened to me before I met her."

Grace slapped Jess's arm in mock offence. "How can you possibly say that? There I was, peacefully going about my life, minding my own business, when you crash into it with your intrigue and disreputable associates." She grinned and fidgeted into a more comfortable position on the sofa.

"Well, that is quite enough excitement for a lifetime, if you ask me," Jess declared emphatically.

"Are you sure?" Nick asked plaintively. "I could develop a liking for heroics."

"You should try being on the receiving end," Jess pointed out wryly, the humour in her voice taking any sting out of her comment. The conversation reached a natural lull and she relaxed into the moment. The foursome had enjoyed a pleasant meal together and Jess had been pleased to find Marie just as friendly as she had the first time they had met. "Have you got any more tournaments coming up?" She asked Nick, feeling a little out of touch with their mutual hobby.

"Nope. You know it always goes quieter at this time of year," he replied ruefully.

"Hey," Grace interjected with excitement, "why don't you give us that demonstration you've been promising?"

Jess and Nick eyed each other, Jess weighing the merits of the suggestion. The meal was still sitting a little heavily in Jess's stomach but neither had indulged in any alcohol yet so it was a good a time as any. "You'll have to go easy on me, since my ribs are still a little stiff," Jess warned.

"No problem," Nick replied, clearly pleased that she had agreed so willingly.

Jess retrieved her kit and the party relocated to the back garden and its plentiful space. Nick was already prepared and Jess flicked the garden floodlights on against the growing darkness.

Jess readily fell into the familiar circling routine, allowing her senses to get accustomed to the environment before committing to action. Nick made the first move, a relatively gentle swing that Jess evaded. She did so with panache, skipping nimbly out of the way of the blade, not even bothering to raise her own. She grinned, pleased to find she was enjoying herself despite her earlier trepidation.

"You're on form, Jessie," Nick commented, low enough that only she could hear. "Performing for the audience, are you?" He smirked at her knowingly.

"Perhaps." Jess's response was coy and noncommittal but secretly she acknowledged the hypersensitivity she felt, knowing

Grace's dark eyes were watching her. She moved forward and swung her blade in an impressively complex series of moves with as much eloquence as she could muster.

"Nice," Nick complimented, parrying each blow smoothly, almost certainly appreciating the opportunity to show off to his own audience.

The demonstration continued for another ten minutes until both were out of breath and glistening with sweat. "Phew," Jess said, lowering her sword and wiping her brow. "I'll have to call it a night."

"Good thing, too," Nick said with a laugh as he attempted to recover his breath. "Great workout."

"I needed that," Jess said with satisfaction as they turned toward the house. She caught a fading glimpse of an expression on Grace's face that sent a jolt of desire through her own body. Making a mental note for future reference, she addressed her audience, "Well, was it what you expected?"

Grace blinked a couple of times. "Yes and no," she started, then paused. "It was much more intricate than I realised. I thought it would be like a fight but it was more like a choreographed dance."

Nick jumped in. "Partly that's because we're not trying to win in these bouts," he explained. "We duel to practice our moves and responses and to build up our stamina."

"I like it," Marie volunteered as she smiled at Nick, an unmistakably wanton note in her voice.

Jess shot Grace a look but managed to avoid outwardly smirking. Grace dropped her gaze and hid her own smile behind her hand.

"Well, I suppose we should be making a move," Nick said in the most laughably transparent attempt at nonchalance Jess had ever witnessed.

"Are you sure you don't want to stay for another drink or anything? It's still early." Jess addressed Nick, and grinned wickedly.

"Thanks, but no," Nick replied quickly. "I'm all wiped out after that." He stretched his arms and yawned pointedly.

"Okay," Jess said with as much solemnity as she could muster. "I'm glad you guys could make it. I had a great evening."

"Me too," said Marie. "Thanks for everything."

Jess and Grace waved them off from the front door, then returned to the living room where they flopped down side by side on the sofa.

"Well, that was an interesting and somewhat sudden end to the night," Grace commented.

"Something tells me Nick is going to be doing a lot of sword practice over the next few weeks," Jess said, a grin tugging at her lips. She thought about the look she had caught on Grace's face. "Mind you," she said seriously, "I think I could do with it too, to help me get back in shape and everything."

"Uh-huh." Grace responded noncommittally.

Jess looked at her, unsure of how to take the enigmatic response.

Grace merely smiled. "Well. I'll go clean up a bit," she said, patting Jess's thigh before she stood, her hand lingering for just a fraction longer than necessary.

Jess watched her walk into the kitchen, the heat inspired by Grace's touch surging through her body. She sighed and got up to go and help.

JESS AND GRACE were sitting in the garden enjoying the last of the warmth from the late afternoon sunlight. A farmer was combining a wheat field nearby and they could see the clouds of dust hovering in the air. It'll be autumn soon, Jess thought. *The summer seems to have flown by.*

"Do you realise," she started, addressing Grace, "that we have known each other for one month today?"

"Really?" Grace looked at her with surprise. "How odd. It feels like ages."

"The happiest days of your life, right?" Jess teased.

"Surprisingly, they have been pretty happy. Despite being almost scared to death on more than one occasion." Grace shifted into a more comfortable position in her deck chair.

Jess watched as the tractor trundled off with another full load. "Yeah. Bizarrely, I'd have to agree." The second tractor positioned itself under the arm of the combine and the procession continued. Jess watched it until her eyes closed with drowsiness.

"You know," Grace's voice broke the companionable silence, "I think I could sit in this spot for the rest of my life and still feel awed by the beauty of it all."

Jess sighed contentedly. "I know what you mean."

Grace glanced over at her Jess. "There's something I wanted to talk to you about."

Jess's eyes flicked open and she felt the familiar knot of worry settle in her stomach. For the first time in her life she was taking each day as it came, trying not to let herself lose the value of the present by worrying about the future. However, the great cloud she knew hovered overhead was that of Grace's departure. She had been caught unaware before and was determined not to leave herself open to such hurt again, even if it had been totally unintentional. "Okay," she said simply, subconsciously squaring her shoulders in anticipation of bad news.

"I've decided to sell the farmhouse," Grace said, gazing out across the surrounding countryside. "It doesn't feel like home anymore."

"I can understand that." Jess spoke quietly, the news not entirely unexpected given the way Grace had spoken of her house since the attack. "Where will you go?" *Please let it be close. Please.*

"The agency has offered me a placement quite near here, actually. The high proportion of farmland means there are a lot of veterinary practices in the area, so I thought I would accept the temporary work and see how things pan out. I suppose if I get on all right I could even look for a permanent placement."

"Would you be able to find a position where you could live-in?" Jess asked, unsure of whether that still happened in the industry.

"Perhaps, but I was thinking I might rent a place until I had a better idea of where I wanted to settle for the long-term. It is such a beautiful area. I could see myself being very happy here."

Jess remained silent. The thought that Grace would be local was fantastic, but the implication that she would soon move out still saddened her. "You know," she said, her heart thumping in her chest with anticipation, "you could always stay here. I know it's a bit small for two, but I think we get on well and...everything." The last few words came out in an awkward rush.

"I think so, too," Grace agreed quickly. "And it is a lovely cottage. I wouldn't want to impose, though. Perhaps you should take some time to think about it," she suggested.

"You don't have to if you would rather find a place of your own," Jess said, "but I don't need time to think about it. You are very welcome. For what it's worth, I can't think of anyone I would rather share with." *Please say yes.*

"Great," Grace said with obvious relief and happiness. "I would love to." She treated Jess to a beaming smile. "I can have a look around on the Internet to find out an appropriate rent. I would want to contribute my own fair share."

Jess didn't respond. She didn't want the income. She wanted the company and only Grace would do. "Okay," She agreed simply, resisting the urge to run an excited victory lap around the garden.

Grace sank back comfortably into her chair and tilted her face to look at Jess, a smile still on her lips.

"Something tells me this is going to be fun." Jess said, her tone playful.

Grace reached out and gave her hand a squeeze. "I think you're right."

Breaking Jaie
by S. Renee Bess

Jaie Baxter, an African-American Ph.D candidate at Philadelphia's Allerton University, is determined to win a prestigious writing grant. In order to win the Adamson Grant, Jaie initially plans to take advantage of one of the competition's judges, Jennifer Renfrew, who is also a University official. Jennifer has spent the past ten years alone following the murder of her lover, Patricia Adamson, in whose honor the grant is named. Jennifer is at first susceptible to Jaie's flirtation, but is later vengeful when she discovers the real reason for Jaie's sudden romantic interest in her. A lunch with an old cop friend reveals that Jaie may very well have ties to Adamson's death.

Jaie is confronted with painful memories as she prepares an autobiographical essay for the grant application. She recalls the emotional trauma of her older brother's death, the murder of a police detective, her dismissal from her "dream" high school, and her victimization at the hands of hateful homophobic students. She remembers her constant struggles with her mother's alcohol-fueled jealousies and physical abuse she had to endure. This wake-up call causes her to look at her life in new ways.

But Jaie is not the only student applying for the grant. Terez Overton, a wealthy Boston woman, is Jaie's chief competitor. Jaie is drawn to the New Englander immediately but is also unnerved by her. She has no clue that Terez is trying to decide whether she wants to accept an opportunity to write an investigative article about an unsolved murder. Writing that article could put her budding relationship with Jaie in jeopardy.

And just when the angst of old memories and the uncertainty of her future with Terez are complicating Jaie's life, her manipulative ex, Seneca Wilson, returns to Philadelphia to reclaim Jaie using emotional blackmail. Senecas actions serve to wound and break Jaie in many ways. Will Seneca drive the final wedge between Jaie and Terez? Who will win the Adamson grant? And what did Jaie have to do with the death of Patricia Adamson?

ISBN: 978-1-932300-84-0

My Life With Stella Kane
by Linda Morganstein

In 1948, Nina Weiss, a snobby college girl from Scarsdale, goes to Hollywood to work at her uncle's movie studio where she's assigned to help publicize a young actress named Stella Kane. Nina is immediately thrown into the maelstrom of the declining studio system and repressive fifties Hollywood. Adding to her difficulties is her growing attraction to Stella. When a gay actor at the studio is threatened by tabloid exposure, Nina invents a romance between Stella and the actor. The trio becomes hopelessly entangled when the invented romance succeeds beyond anyone's dreams. This is the "behind-the scenes" story of the trio's compromises and secrets that still has relevance for today.

ISBN: 978-1-935053-13-4

OTHER REGAL CREST TITLES

VISIT US ONLINE AT

www.regalcrest.biz

At the Regal Crest Website You'll Find

- The latest news about forthcoming titles and new releases

- Our complete backlist of romance, mystery, thriller and adventure titles

- Information about your favorite authors

- Current bestsellers

- Media tearsheets to print and take with you when you shop

Regal Crest titles are available from all progressive booksellers and online at StarCrossed Productions, (www.scp-inc.biz), or at www.amazon.com, www.bamm.com, www.barnesandnoble.com, and many others.

.

9 781935 053125